DINOSAUR RED

EDWARD J. MCFADDEN III

SEVERED PRESS
HOBART TASMANIA

DINOSAUR RED

Copyright © 2020 Edward J. McFadden III

WWW.SEVEREDPRESS.COM

ISBN: 978-1-922551-47-4

"Deep in the human unconscious is a pervasive need for a logical universe that makes sense.
But the real universe is always one step beyond logic."

- Frank Herbert, Dune

1

The Space Exploration Vehicle's harsh LED floodlights illuminated the desolate rock-strewn plain of Aeolis Palus. Rust colored sand stretched into the distance in every direction, the SEV's eight semi-spherical slotted wheels kicking-up fine dust, thick clouds lifting from the Martian surface like red smoke. To the east a blue dawn leaked over the dark horizon, the sun a single white headlight in the blackness. The rover's electric motor whined as NASA Mission Specialist Bruce 'Psycho' Lindey piloted the SEV across flat terrain, traversing boulders and rocks, windswept red dunes, and shallow valleys that were part of the Peace Vallis overflow channel system.

Deputy Commander Forest Judge rotated his head and cracked his neck. It felt good not to be wearing his spacesuit helmet, though he was uneasy. He reached beneath his seat and found the smooth, round helmet where it was stowed. Judge was reassured knowing that in a pinch he could slip it on, yet despite what he believed to be sound self-rationalization, a chill ran through him. The rover's heaters worked overtime, but the cabin was a nipple-chilling fifty-four degrees. Temperatures on Mars plunge at night, and in the frigid darkness the SEV wasn't continually recharging its twin seven hundred-volt batteries.

"Tisa, how we doing on power?" Judge said. Lieutenant Tisa Lamar, M.D., was a NASA Assistant Chief Medical Officer and Chief Technical Support Technician, as well as an excellent rover pilot.

Tisa snuggled herself against the cold, pushing deeper into the copilot's seat. She wore a dull blue NASA synthetic knit cap, and her dark skin shined in the bright cabin lighting. She tapped her control panel and said, "We're at twenty-seven percent power. Right where we should be." She swiped her screen several times until her data set appeared. "We'll arrive at the anomaly right on schedule." The team had departed Gale Base Alpha in the middle of the Martian night, so they'd arrive at the site early, leaving a minimum of ten solar hours of light to investigate.

NASA Astrogeologist Charlotte Ramsey sat across the thin aisle from Judge, and she leaned toward him, red curls falling across her forehead, piercing blue eyes finding his. "Anomaly? That's what we're calling it now?" she whispered.

Judge felt the heat between them, and his heart galloped. Then Brenda's face filled his mind and shame washed over him. He'd run all the way to Mars, but that wasn't far enough to forget her.

The rover's cabin resembled an airliner, with four seats behind the pilot and copilot, a thin aisle running down the center, and a small storage bay in the rear that contained a research lab that could be detached from the vehicle. The international team of six had been chosen from the thirty-two astronauts currently inhabiting both Mars bases. In addition to himself, Psycho, Tisa, and Charlotte, Commander Silas chose JAXA Astroengineer Yoo Lee Seok and ISRO Astrochemist, Arjun Kapoor. A good crew, though other than Charlotte and Psycho, Judge didn't know them well.

The SEV was a marvel of engineering and compromise. The original design called for a sleek, movie-prop-like vehicle with sharp edges and science fiction aesthetics. What was actually built resembled two connected boxes, each with four wheels. The exterior of the SEV was covered in silver solar skin that continually charged the rover's batteries while the sun was up. The SEV had dictated the size of the mission crew, and could support the astronauts indefinitely because it had its own water reclaimer. Air wasn't a problem either. Judge was no chemist, but he knew the oxygen scrubbers cleaned the crew's air and vented the excess carbon dioxide, and this allowed for continual life support if the system's filters were changed. They'd brought enough filters, food and supplies for ten sols, and though the rover's solar skin was perpetually being covered by the fine red Martian dust, that was corrected by a simple extravehicular activity (EVA).

Judge was more concerned about the team's mental states and failing body odors. Every astronaut was rigorously tested in a variety of ways both mental and physical, but every person on Mars was overworked and tired. Showers on Mars were few and far between, and spending hours on end trapped in a two hundred square foot box with five other people who smelled like rancid sweaty socks wasn't like being poked by the white coats. He rolled his shoulders. Why was he worrying? The mission should be a piece of cake and he'd be back on base tomorrow. His stomach gurgled from his lunch of reconstituted stew and recycled water, but it was his jumping nerves that made him ball his fists every few seconds, then wipe his palms on his legs.

Seok ripped a snore, and jerked his head to the side as he dreamed. Arjun didn't move or make a sound, his chin on his chest, his head gently lifting and falling as he breathed.

Eight sols ago they'd all been entrenched in their tasks of research, exploration, and survival, but that had changed when the doors were discovered on the northern side of Aeolis Mons, an odd mountain at the center of Gale crater. A drone investigating a landslide on the mountain's northern face sent back images that confirmed mankind's greatest discovery. It had been a normal Martian sol and he'd been reviewing the station's mission log when the eternal question, "Are we alone in the universe?" was answered.

The SEV creaked and moaned as Psycho piloted the rover down a steep slope. Dark rust-colored streaks cut across the surface like tiny sand waves, jagged gray rocks with stripes of red, yellow, and blue dotting the Martian landscape. It looked like a beach straight-out of a child's nightmare.

"Moving through the Murray Buttes gap," Psycho said.

Judge had been this way before and knew the area well. They were threading through the Peace Vallis and approaching Bradbury Landing, the site of the Curiosity rover monument. Without the work done by Curiosity, as well as its parents and children, settlements on Mars wouldn't have been possible.

"All systems green," Tisa said.

"Psycho, what's our exact position?" Judge said.

The rover pilot squirmed in his seat and glanced over his shoulder. "We're thirty-one kilometers from the anomaly. I'm going slow and being careful until the sun's fully up. There's so many rocks sticking from the sand," said Psycho. The ex-Navy NASA Mission Specialist was another Swiss Army knife; he was pilot, rover driver, research support staffer, handyman and general all-around sample collector. Judge thought he was one of Gale Base Alpha's most important crew members, which was why he'd refused to suspend him from duty, despite orders from mission control back in Houston. There was plenty of time to deal with that.

Tisa said, "The rover's top speed is seventeen kilometers per hour, if the terrain is perfect. Our average speed so far is approximately seven kilometers an hour, so we're still on schedule, assuming we don't run into any unknowns."

NASA's Curiosity rover thoroughly mapped and studied Gale crater prior to the arrival of the first manned Mars mission, and subsequent drone and astronaut investigations revealed several excellent base sites around the planet. Along with data from the Pathfinder, Opportunity, and Vikings missions, Gale crater was selected as the location for the first permanent Mars base.

Gale Base Alpha was one of two permanent settlements on Mars, and was situated within Quad 51, better known as Yellowknife. Gale crater was believed to be a dry lakebed, and that meant there was two billion years of geological history packed below its surface and layered in the mountain of wind torn sediment known as Aeolis Mons.

Five more permanent settlements were scheduled for all around Mars, and Gale Base Alpha, and its substation, Gale Base Beta, would serve as the staging areas for settlements that would be established in the caverns of Hebrus Valles, on Acidalia Planitia, in Jezero crater, and within the deep mysterious valley of Valles Marineris.

That was the future, and Judge had to worry about the present. He ran through the mission parameters again in his mind, looking for flaws, potential problems. Gale crater had a diameter of 154 kilometers, and the mission plan called for the rover to traverse 109 kilometers in fourteen solar hours to get to the doors. The crater floor was mostly flat, but extra time and light was needed to cross certain sections of terrain, and with nothing but the mountain and rolling rust-colored hills in the distance, making visual judgments was difficult.

NASA planned for every possible negative outcome to occur twice. Despite this, Judge knew Mars always had surprises up its sleeve, regardless of how much the bigheads back on Earth prepared. No plan ever survives implementation, and this nagging worry ate Judge like a cancer.

Giving orders eased his nerves. "Tisa, give Gale an update, please," Judge said. They weren't scheduled to check in for another half an hour, but as the team approached the end of their journey his nerves were running double-time.

The flat Martian terrain gave way to the west, the mountain rising into the sky like the hub of a giant wheel. The blue and white glow in the east had faded to yellow-orange, the sun a small glowing orb rising in the eastern sky.

"Coming up on the monument," Psycho said. The SEV's electric motor buzzed as the rover slowed.

Through the murky yellow-gray dusk, the mound of Martian rocks materialized out of the gloom.

"Give me the port camera on main screen, please," Judge said.

"You want me to stop?" Psycho said.

"Negative," Judge said.

"Camera on," Tisa said as the monitor below the forward viewport came to life.

Atop a ten-foot mound of carefully placed stones, a reproduction of the Curiosity rover looked down on the Martian surface like a parent examining its child. The replica's stainless-steel exterior was covered in a coating of red dust, and its black painted wheels were buried. A brass plaque was mounted on the largest of the foundation rocks, which listed the name of every principal scientist and astronaut who'd worked on the Curiosity mission.

The construction of the monument had been a big deal. Every action on Mars required planning and resources, and bringing a fifty-two pound statue to Mars, which had no practical purpose, and wasting fifty Martian man-hours building a display to man's ego, irked some scientists who felt the resources would have been better spent on more experiments, not to mention the complaints from members of earlier rover missions wanting honors for their work. Thankfully, saner heads had prevailed. Judge liked thinking about the monument being on Mars long after the human race had perished.

The SEV rolled on, its wheels squeaking and popping as the Martian morning blossomed, Aeolis Mons steadily growing in the forward viewport.

"ETA is twenty minutes," Tisa said.

Judge leaned forward and tapped Seok on the shoulder. "Time to wake up, sleepyhead," he said.

Seok jumped, opened his eyes, leaned back and stretched, then woke Arjun.

The SEV churned around a sand dune, and the grade of the mountain slope got steeper. A road-like trail led upward into the foothills, and mounds of sand striated in countless shades of brown filled the forward viewscreen.

"Wow," said Charlotte.

At five and a half kilometers Aeolis Mons was one of the tallest mountains on Mars, and up close it resembled a massive windblown sand dune. In many ways, that was what the mountain was. The bigheads thought that Mars' winds created the mound of sedimentary layers that had formed over two billion years, and striations of red, yellow, brown, and blue showed the years like tree rings. The likelihood of fossil deposits in the crater bed, and in Aeolis Mons, had been one of the primary reasons Gale Base Alpha was constructed within the crater.

Judge rubbed his eyes and pulled his helmet out from under his seat. Charlotte saw him and did the same. The crew sat silent, the Martian wind pelting the SEV with fine red sand. He sized up his crew, wondering if they worried as much about what lay beyond the doors as he did. Just because you can do a thing, doesn't mean you should.

The doors were on the face of Hematite ridge, an escarpment of sand and tumbled stones. A large pile of rust-colored sand blocked the rover's way, and Psycho steered around it, revealing the doors.

Whatever race had built the entranceway, their design aesthetics were boring and simple. Two metal doors stood side by side. There were no markings, handles, or controls of any kind, and though the landslide had cleared away most of the sand, there was no obvious way to open the doors. The bigheads on Earth had concluded that meant whoever built them didn't want the site disturbed.

Little did the builders of the doors know. Humans don't roll like that.

The SEV crunched up the last few kilometers and stopped before the doors.

"Bringing up main camera and shutting down engine," Tisa said.

The doors were big. Judge estimated two hundred meters high and a hundred across. He said, "The drone images don't really do it justice."

Seok said, "No they don't."

"They're huge. Hard to believe they were made here," Charlotte said.

"That's what we're here to investigate," Judge said. "Tisa, let base know we've arrived. The rest of you, get the gear ready for EVA."

2

Some people are born spacers. Judge wasn't one of them.

He didn't like EVAs because they brought him to the edge of claustrophobia. A mild fear of heights and confined spaces had dogged him his entire life, and it had taken every ounce of strength and cunning to hide these weaknesses from the white coats during the rigorous NASA testing. He'd always wanted to go to the stars, and fear of what might happen if he didn't get away from Brenda brought renewed focus to his dream of being an astronaut. The five-month trip to get to Mars was difficult, but eventually Judge came to believe he'd beaten his fears. On base he only had EVA to get to different habitats, and those were only thirty seconds in duration. This EVA would be hours, and sweat dripped down his back and his throat went dry at the thought of it.

He could stay behind. Safety protocol dictated that someone stay in the SEV and be available to communicate with base and act should there be an emergency. The EVA suits had intercoms, but their signal strength wasn't strong enough to reach Gale Base Alpha, so communication had to be routed through the SEV. This procedure was often discarded, and control was given to the rover's computer, but given the long list of unknowns, he thought the precaution a necessary one, at least initially.

Judge sighed and rolled his shoulders. He knew he couldn't be the one to stay behind. He pulled on his helmet and snapped the clasp closed. He was the mission leader, and he was needed on site. As he considered which astronaut to piss off, he pulled on his gloves. Who was the most valuable member of his crew? Psycho. No question. But he needed the NASA Mission Specialist by his side if things went sideways. That left the other rover pilot, Tisa.

Gloves on and fully suited up, Judge activated his intercom, and linked it with the rover. "Tisa, you're going to have to hang back."

"Figured," she said. "Always happy to be a team player." She turned her attention back to her display monitors, so the rest of the crew didn't see her sulk.

"Don't be upset. If everything looks OK and we don't have any issues, you can join us. OK?" Judge said.

Tisa said nothing.

Judge checked the status report on the heads-up display on the inside of his helmet. All systems were green. The EVA suits were specially designed for the Mars mission and were more advanced than the Extravehicular Mobility Unit (EMU) spacefarers had used since the birth of the space program. The new suits were much lighter, had a sleeker life support backpack, and could provide air into perpetuity via advanced oxygen scrubbers similar to the device used to provide air to the rover. The new EVA suits were powered by a top-secret high-tech battery locked into the life support backpack so it couldn't be examined, and there were rumors it had been designed and manufactured by Tesla Industries.

Psycho snapped out of his harness and pulled his helmet free. The long scar on his right cheek was deep red, his graying hair barely visible due to his tight crew cut. Hair on Mars was a chore, so the less you had, the easier your life was. Another genetic and societal screw you to women. As Psycho pulled on his gloves, he said, "Anyone need help?"

Judge said, "Can you assure me with 100% surety this thin fabric won't rip?" He knew the answer and was trying to lighten the situation. The tension in the SEV was thick. It was time to put up or shut up, but the huge doors that filled the forward viewscreen made his nerves pulse every time he looked at them. Now that he was here, thoughts of what lay beyond the entryway made his hands shake.

"100%? This is NASA." He chuckled. "Your suit has built-in alarms that will notify you if something isn't right. You know that," Psycho said.

Judge did, but it was still good to hear, and it eased his nerves, which were doing summersaults.

Tisa sighed. "You baby. Your EVA suit constantly monitors your body functions, and modulates the temperature and air flow based on your vitals and conditions inside your suit."

"I know," Judge said. "I just worry. There's a ton of jagged rocks out there. If I rip my suit—"

"You'll be fine," Psycho said. "Aside from all the assistance you'll get from us." He paused and swept his arm expansively, indicating the group of astronauts.

Judge frowned, and said nothing.

Psycho put his hands behind his back as if lecturing. He cleared his throat. "In the event of a breach the EVA suit will adjust the oxygen and nitrogen mix to compensate while you patch the hole. As long as your filters are relatively clean—"

"Which yours are," said Tisa.

"The oxygenator in your suit uses a simple chemical absorption process to remove oxygen so it can be rerouted back to you, while filtering out the carbon dioxide. You can live in your suit for hours… theoretically days, before you run out of air."

"No shit, Mr. Wizard," Judge said.

"Seemed like you'd forgotten some basic stuff," Psycho said.

Judge straightened, sweat dripping down his back, the tips of his fingers and toes chilled. For his own benefit as well as his crew's, he said, "Time to get serious. Remember your training out there. Don't panic. If you get flustered, or don't feel right, notify me immediately." Back on Earth Judge bitched about the amount of rescue and safety training they'd been put through, but now that he was about to leave the safety of the rover, 109 kilometers from base, he didn't think he'd had enough. On base he was the duct tape that kept things running. Out on the surface, he was a plebe compared to his crewmates.

Psycho said, "Don't forget you've got your breach kit if you need it, but be sure to call for help before you attempt a repair on your own." Every EVA suit was equipped with a breach kit, which was strapped on the side of the suit's helmet. It was nothing more than a funnel with a valve on the thin end and glue on the wide end. In the event of an EVA breach, the astronaut placed the wide end over the hole with the valve open. With the valve open air escapes and doesn't interfere with the glue on the wide end, getting a good seal. Then the valve is closed, and the integrity of the suit is restored.

Judge took in a deep breath and surveyed his crew.

Seok was ready, his dark eyes peering out from inside his helmet. Charlotte struggled to get on her left glove—wasn't that always a bitch? Even if Judge put on the left glove first, pulling on the right always brought frustration. The redhead's blue eyes were bloodshot, and she grunted as she yanked and pulled on the glove. Arjun stood silently, waiting by the airlock door. The guy made Judge nervous. He was so quiet and polite, Judge often felt uncomfortable joking with Psycho and the others for fear of offending him.

With everything ready, Judge said, "Tisa, check-in with Gale, please."

Tisa opened a channel and informed Commander Salis that the team was starting its first EVA. The mission plan called for an evaluation of the site and an investigation of the doors. Then Deputy Commander Judge was to report back to the base commander for further orders.

With the safety checklist completed, and the integrity of each suit verified, Tisa slipped on her helmet and pressurized her suit as she prepared to unlock the rover's door. The SEV was equipped with a portable airlock—nothing more than a neoprene tent—and in an emergency it could be used to allow astronauts to leave the rover without decompressing the SEV. Since there was no emergency, the team would exit via the main door and when they were gone Tisa would re-pressurize the cabin and restore normal life support.

"Everyone ready?" Judge asked.

Nods. Grunts. Seok gave a thumbs up and said, "Camera on. Everything, including audio, on the permanent record starting now." A live transmission wasn't possible for a variety of reasons, and after the EVA the footage would be pumped to Gale Station and Commander Salis would decide what got sent back to Earth.

Judge lifted the safety on the door and undogged the latch. The SEV's door popped open and the inrush of Martian air was louder than an elephant fart.

Wind could gust up to 250 kilometers per hour on Mars, but on this day, there was nothing more than a gentle breeze pushing around the red Martian dust that found its way into every gap and crack. The sun was overhead, and the northern face of Aeolis Mons stood before Judge as he stepped out onto the Martian surface. Like a clown car, the crew exited one by one, and when the five astronauts were all standing on sand, the SEV's door slid closed.

"Arjun." Judge's voice crackled over the comm.

"Sir?"

"Judge." He knew everyone called him Jughead behind his back because of the knit cap he wore all the time while on base and his affinity for old Archie comics. With his dark hair and wild bowl cut, he looked like the original Jughead. He hated the nickname. "Arjun, can you and Charlotte clean off the rover before you join us up by the doors?" Martian dust and sand covered the vehicle, hampering its ability to recharge its batteries.

"10-4. On it," Arjun said.

"No problem," said Charlotte.

Mars was known as the red planet because of the iron oxide in its soil. Most of the planet was desert-like, and because the sand had been baking under the sun for so long it was literally rusting, leaving a distinctive reddish hue that was visible from Earth even without the aid of a telescope. Judge looked back the way they'd come, the SEV's thick tracks trailing away from the doors. Mounds of striated soil rose from the slope all around the rover, but through it all a path led to the giant doors. Rocks protruded from the sand at odd angles, sunlight glinting off the mineral deposits that dotted the rocks like freckles.

Judge checked his suit and adjusted his oxygen percentage. On Earth, people breathed about twenty-one percent oxygen, and he adjusted his suit to supply excess oxygen so he wouldn't get so easily winded. Oxygen in its pure state is toxic and corrosive, but he only nudged his percentage up ten percent. If his body levels skewed too far out of whack the EVA suit would sound an alarm and make adjustments. Easy peasy.

Psycho and Seok took the lead, trudging up the sand and stone that had slid down the side of the mountain, Judge trailing after. It was exhausting work, and the EVA suit made it that much harder. He thought about how things might have gone if he hadn't increased his oxygen supply. He'd probably already be face down in the sand. He tried to crack his neck, his nerves dancing on a wire. No crack, so he balled his fists, breathing in through his nose and out through his mouth as he steadied himself.

"Are you OK?" Seok asked.

He wagged his head. Despite having his fellow crewmates around him, the silence, being jammed into the EVA suit, and his stomach campaigning for food all made him uneasy and wary. He chuckled to himself as he climbed. Wary. That was some funny shit. He was more than sixty-five million kilometers from home, in a harsh environment that could kill him in a hundred ways. Wary was a constant state of mind, or you died.

Judge joined his crew as they stood before the tall doors. "They are something," he said.

Nobody spoke as they awaited orders. Sand pelted his face shield and his bladder started to bitch about having to be drained. He could urinate in his suit, which was equipped for such things, but he held it. "Spread out and do what you do."

The two metal doors were set in a frame of red stone, but closer inspection revealed that they were in fact part of a much larger metal object. Seok and Psycho cleared sand from the base of the doors and found there was metal beneath, and Judge concluded the doors were part of a large structure.

Psycho said, "Sure was easy to get up here. Almost like there was a road or landing strip here at one time."

"Agreed," said Seok.

"Look how the doors are encased entirely within that deep brown ring. That must have been the surface at the time of the door's construction," Charlotte said.

"Or placement," Judge said.

"I'll get some samples, but my guess, based on prior testing at that strata, is that this layer is from roughly sixty-seven million years ago."

Arjun and Charlotte joined them, and a static-filled whistle buzzed over the comm.

"Doesn't look like the metal detector is going to be much use," Charlotte said.

"Why's that?" Judge asked.

"If the doors lead to a larger metal structure that's all we'll pick up." Charlotte sniffled and coughed.

"Will the ground penetrating radar work?" Judge said.

Charlotte's helmet rotated side to side as she shook her head. "It doesn't like metal, but I should be able to get you an image by combining my data from all my instruments."

"Give it a go. You know that's what the commander will want," Judge said.

"That's a 10-4, boss."

Judge sat on a stone, watching his crew run their tests, take samples, and reconnoiter the area. He studied every inch of the doors, focusing on the thin black gap that ran around the edges and down their center. If he could get a wedge in there, he'd… what? And where the hell would he get a wedge big enough out in the middle of nowhere? He was stumped, and if the team didn't figure it out by sol's end, they'd most likely be ordered back to the station for more evaluation and planning. Is that what he wanted?

As he looked up at the giant metal doors, he feared the answer.

3

"Sir, come take a look at this," Seok said.

"Call me that again and you'll be relieving Tisa. Savvy?" Judge said. Most of the crew on Mars thought he didn't like the moniker because it made him feel every one of his forty-eight years. That was only partly true.

"Sorry, s... Yes, Judge. Got it."

Judge hauled himself off his comfortable stone and went to the base of the doors where Psycho and Seok knelt, Charlotte gazing over their shoulders. Psycho dug at the red Martian sand with a foldable shovel, heaving red silt aside like a child on the beach.

"It appears the door's upper and side edges were mostly cleared by the landslide, but there's still quite a bit of sand and dust at the base," Psycho said. He didn't look up from his work, and his labored breaths echoed over the comm between words.

"How deep do you—"

The ring of metal on metal froze the explorers like pirates that had found their treasure chest. "Not bad," Psycho said. He rotated his head and examined the base of the doors. "Give me two helpers and we'll have this dug out in a couple of hours."

"Then what?" Charlotte said.

That was the zillion dollar question. With Arjun's camera rolling, Judge said, "We figure out how to get these bitches open. Charlotte, get that data we spoke about. Anything you can get on the composition of the doors, what's holding them in place—hinges, locks, and what's beyond. Arjun, film the entire location and remember the bigheads will be zooming in on every frame. There is no image that's not important. Seok and I will help Psycho, and we'll meet back at the rover for an update and debrief."

Seok and Charlotte went to get tools and gear, but Arjun stood watching Judge, his brown eyes wide.

Judge knew the protocol. EVAs weren't to be conducted solo unless it was an emergency or within twenty clicks of a base. Out here, Judge considered the SEV the base, but technically Arjun was supposed to have a partner. He could have Tisa join Arjun. Either way he was taking a risk, but not being able to communicate with base was the bigger one. "It's OK, Arjun. Just contact me if you have any problems and don't go further than thirty meters."

The ISRO Astrochemist watched Judge for several seconds, the camera lens on Arjun's shoulder zooming out. Then he turned away and started a grid pattern, so he'd cover the entire area.

"I forgot one thing," Judge said, addressing the team via suit comm. "I'm going to need theories and practical ideas fast or we're going to lose our chance at this thing."

Static, then, "Tisa here. Feel free to send data my way. I can have it organized and Q'd for you when you come home."

Charlotte said, "Thanks, Tisa. You're not missing anything out here. It's quiet and kinda unnerving. Over."

"We'll see."

Seok returned with a second shovel and an empty sample container. "We'll have to take turns using this," he said, holding up a one-gallon container.

The fan in Judge's EVA suit whirred as it balanced temperature and pressure. With the sun at its zenith, Judge sweat from the exertion of digging despite the twelve-degree Celsius surface temperature in the shade on the northern side of Aeolis Mons. His stomach gurgled as he sucked air, and his arms cramped despite breathing the rich oxygen mix. Judge was in good shape, but every ounce of food and water was rationed on Mars, and he was as lean as he'd ever been. Despite this, his lack of daily physical activity and skipping exercise due to overwork had left him with what spacers called 'ship fat' around his waist. Brenda would call them love handles.

Two hours slipped away as Judge lost himself in the work. He'd always been intrigued by archeology, and enjoyed watching scientists brush dirt off stones and divers vacuum sand off underwater statues, revealing the past. He was helping clear away sand that would change the course of the human race forever.

Arjun came over a dune at the western edge of the doors, slipping and sliding in the thick sand. He dug himself free like he was trudging through a meter of snow, and worked his way along the doors, his head moving up and down as he documented every inch.

"You all good?" Judge said, using Arjun's arrival as an excuse to stop digging.

"Once I'm done with the doors, I think I'm good. Then I'll head back and pump the video to Gale."

Judge's stomach tingled. "No. Hold off. Nothing goes off site until I review it."

"Judge, the more—"

"That's an order, Arjun. Thank you."

Arjun's eyes grew wide, and he said, "Yes, sir."

That 'sir' was the first time Arjun's veil of politeness slipped and it reminded Judge where he was. No humans had ever been so alone. He gazed east, the horizon dotted with round sand dunes striated in every shade of red and brown. Out here, thirty-five million miles away… fifty-six million kilometers—he still preferred miles, but there came a time when it made more sense to join the crowd than stand on your own. Plus, NASA. On Mars, so far from Earth, he missed everything he'd taken for granted. He missed crowds. He missed the guy in the coffee line that waited fifteen minutes then didn't know what he wanted when it was his turn. He missed paying bills. Watching TV. And below it all Brenda's voice soothed and beckoned, his brother's trusting face over her shoulder.

When most of the sand and dust had been removed, Psycho went to work with the vacuum, revealing a fine groove at the base of the doors. "Looks like they might slide like pocket doors, and not swing in or out," Psycho said.

"Makes sense. Sand build-up on the exterior of the doors was inevitable, even if the builders hadn't anticipated a full burial," Judge said.

"Means they probably require power to open," Seok said.

"Power?" Judge said. There were many ways to generate power on Mars, but up until that moment Judge hadn't thought of what lay beyond as modern. Despite the metal doors, his mind had painted pictures of ancient stone and strange hieroglyphs. The idea that whatever lay beyond the doors might have power as he understood it added another layer to his unease and worry.

With the doors fully cleared and the site documented, Psycho and crew started back to the SEV, and Judge hung back with Charlotte, who was finishing taking readings. Judge collected rock and soil samples as she finished. "Have you seen anything out of the ordinary so far?" Judge asked the NASA geologist.

"Nothing. If it hadn't been for the landslide, we might never have come to this site," Charlotte said. "Nothing special here geologically speaking, but let's see what the computer shows. Initial readings on the doors and what lay beyond looks promising, but I need to see the data plotted."

Judge helped her stow her equipment and carried the samples back to the rover, where he placed them in the sample bin below the main fuselage of the SEV.

Back in the re-pressurized cabin of the rover, the team ate in silence. Judge was frustrated. Unless Charlotte's data showed something, he had nothing, and Commander Salis was sure to order them back to Gale Base Alpha. There the samples and other data would be pored over by the bigheads back on Earth, and a plan developed. That could take months. His hesitancy and fear of what lay behind the doors had faded, and curiosity and competition had taken over. He wanted in. His thoughts strayed to Neil Armstrong, the first astronaut to walk on the Moon. What Judge and his team did and said now would be remembered forever.

Charlotte returned from the bathroom, her lips a flat line, eyes downturned. It was always fun when everyone in the room knew you just took a dump. Bodily functions were handled in a special compartment in the rear of the research lab, and the closet-like room made an airliner bathroom seem like a marble loo with cloth towels at The Ritz.

Between bites of reconstituted chicken, Judge said, "Before we get started, I want to make something clear. Once we report back to Gale, if we don't have a solid plan, we're going to get called back. Anyone want that?"

Sipping, chewing and the rustle of food packets filled the cabin, the sound of Martian sand pelting the SEV like a million tiny bubbles popping.

"Good. Charlotte, you're our scientist of the hour, so I'll turn things over to you," Judge said.

Tisa ceded the copilot seat to Charlotte so she could work the forward viewscreen. She tapped the monitor before her and brought up a compiled color enhanced image of the doors and surrounding area.

"You may have heard of the 'Radar Imager for Mars' Subsurface Experiment', known as RIMFAX?" Seok and Judge nodded, the others stared at Charlotte and made no sign. "The device used radar waves to probe the ground beneath several of the first Mars robotic rovers. What I use is similar to that, but more powerful and greatly enhanced."

"Yay, RIMFAX. So what does the map show?" Psycho said as he pointed at the radar image.

"I've combined all my data onto one map. The blue represents the doors and whatever it's connected to. The grayish speckled mass is the surrounding sand and stone. This regolith contains a variety of minerals, all of which are showing up on the metal detector. That's why the area is gray. I believe the thin white area represents a one-hundred-meter-long void beyond the doors that leads to the much larger cavity here." She pointed, looking at each of her crewmates in turn. "See how the blue curves away in all directions? I think Psycho's guess might be right. This entire thing could be one piece."

"You mean like a ship?" Tisa said.

"Possibly, but I doubt it. The size of this thing… it would be a very big ship," Charlotte said.

"What about the doors?" Judge said. Right now, finding a plan to get them open was all he cared about.

"The doors are still a mystery. They're made of about 70% known iron alloys, but the rest…"

"What?" Judge said.

"My instruments can't identify many of the substances, and you could say my metal detector is the best in the known universe," Charlotte said.

"So the doors and whatever they're connected to is definitely alien in origin?" Seok said.

"Affirmative." Charlotte's eyes grew wide, as if she didn't believe what she'd just said.

"Or it's from our future," Psycho said.

"What?" Tisa said.

"Maybe humans in the future built whatever the hell this thing is and sent it back."

Nobody spoke.

"It's clear the doors lead to a large structure. Perhaps it was on the surface at one time long ago," Arjun said.

"That would solve the mystery of Aeolis Mons creation. If whatever this thing is was put in the crater, then buried over the eons," Charlotte said.

"Question is, how the hell do we open the doors?" Psycho said.

"They're a foot thick, and I scanned every inch, and there doesn't appear to be a lock of any kind, but I did pick up magnetic activity. Also…" She paused and stared at her screen, and Judge knew she was avoiding eye contact. "Also, there appears to be another door of some kind directly behind the outer doors."

Sand pelted the rover and Tisa coughed softly.

Judge said, "You mean like an airlock?"

"Possibly," Charlotte said.

"What would a security lock made by an advanced culture look like?" Psycho asked. "I mean, would we even recognize it?"

Judge rubbed his chin, his mind spinning. Then he remembered the security system at NASA headquarters in Houston. Every door had a magnetic lock that required a card to gain access. "Is it possible the lock is magnetic?" he said.

"If it is, whoever built the doors most likely has a code of some type to open them. Without the code, I don't know what we can do?" Seok said.

Psycho said, "There's only a few ways to demagnetize a magnet. I assume that's what you're thinking, right? A culture advanced enough to build all this would have a pretty solid security code I'd think."

"Psycho is right," Seok said. "A magnet produces an invisible magnetic field. This field is responsible for the force that pulls on other ferromagnetic materials, such as iron, and attracts or repels other magnets. A permanent magnet is magnetized and creates its own persistent magnetic field. An everyday example is a refrigerator magnet used to hold notes and shopping lists."

Arjun jumped in like the two were co-lecturing. "There are only a few ways to demagnetize a magnet. Heat it past its Curie temperature so the molecular motion destroys the alignment of the magnetic domains and removes all magnetization. Or, place the magnet in an alternating magnetic field with intensity above the material's coercivity. Demagnetization progressively occurs if the magnet is subjected to cyclic fields, or when in doubt, hit it with a hammer."

Judge said, "You're joking?"

"No, he isn't," Seok said. "Hammering or jarring the magnet creates a mechanical disturbance that can randomize the magnetic domains and reduce magnetization."

"Well, since we don't have enough power, and can't heat it, or create an alternating field of sufficient strength, that leaves the sledgehammer," Psycho said.

"There's no way we're hammering through anything, even if the doors are magnetically controlled," Tisa said. "So, what now?"

Judge laughed, the answer so obvious he worried it couldn't be so simple. "We pull the fire alarm."

4

"OK, I'll bite," Psycho said.

Judge ignored him and said, "Charlotte, did you see anything indicating a power supply? Something that might feed a lock, if in fact there is one?"

The redhead's eyes narrowed as she stared at the forward view screen, her middle finger tracing the edge of the radar image. "Nothing that would indicate traditional wiring as we would think of it, but there does appear to be power at the base of the doors as well as at their tops and mid-sections."

"An electrical field?" Seok said.

"That provides power?" Tisa said.

"Tesla lit a series of light poles without wires and that was over a hundred years ago," Seok said.

"If we disturb the energy flow the lock might disengage?" Charlotte said.

"Like the mag locks at NASA during fire drills," Psycho said.

"One problem," Arjun said. "How do we cut the power?"

"We drill," Judge said. "We've got the core sample drill with a host of bits. We'll drill the thing open like old school safe crackers. Might take a while, but the core drill was designed to penetrate the hardest of metals."

"We've got enough power to do this?" Seok asked.

"We'll see. Don't know until we start, but I think we'll be OK," Tisa said.

"Based on the data, this metal is hard, but it was shaped, so heat and friction should work... eventually," Charlotte said.

"OK. Everyone get their part together while I contact Salis. I want the process underway when I call. Tisa, any reasonable way to delay my transmission to Gale?"

Tisa and Seok stared at Judge open mouthed. Judge knew if their plan was already underway, and Judge had a solid excuse for giving the order without consulting the commander—like lack of communication—it would be harder for Salis to pull them back.

"There's some solar disturbance at the moment. I can give you an hour," Tisa said.

"You notified them when we returned from EVA?" Judge said.

She nodded.

"So they'll be expecting our report soon. I do need that hour, Tisa. Thank you."

Seok said, "Si... Judge, is that wise? This is a major discovery, and—"

"And it's ours. I thought we were all in agreement?" Judge said.

Seok looked at the deck, but said nothing.

An hour slipped away while the crew prepared and started their second EVA. Judge called Salis, who seemed pleased with the progress and wasn't upset that Judge had taken the initiative. He told Judge to report back as soon as he knew something.

Psycho and Tisa unloaded the drill and its stand from its case beneath the research portion of the SEV, and set it up at the base of the doors. Psycho burned through drill bits like they were made of butter, but as the drill whined and spat, Judge saw progress was being made. Two boreholes had been completed, and Charlotte's readings were showing a disturbance in the door's electrical field.

The ground trembled and Psycho turned off the drill. "Did you feel that?" he said.

"Keep going," Judge said.

The entire crew huddled behind Psycho, peering over his shoulder as he worked. Nobody wanted to miss the momentous event, and the entire team was present, nobody backing the crew up in the rover. Judge had heard Michael Collins speak when he was a boy. He was the astronaut who stayed in the command module while Armstrong and Aldrin walked on the Moon. Judge couldn't do that to any of his crew, so he patched their comm through the rover because the risk was negligible.

Psycho fired up the drill and it shrieked, and had it not been for the thin Martian air, Judge was sure sparks would be flying. Instead the drill ground to a stop, white smoke lifting from the tool. "Well, I guess that's tha—"

The door shuddered and began to slide, pulling the drill, its stand, and Psycho along with it. It took the NASA Mission Specialist a few moments to realize what was happening before he let go of the drill's frame as it was dragged through the sand as the doors opened.

Metal ripped and tore as the drill's platform was crunched and flattened. A piece got stuck in the door's bottom groove, and the sound of metal raking over metal echoed across the desolate Martian surface.

The doors came to a stop with a thud, revealing a round doorway with silver holes around its edges just inside the opening. The door didn't look like a door at all, but more like a sealed anus. Pink and white skin-like tubes stuck from its center like hair, a series of lines like folds in skin spiraling away from center.

"Looks like you were right, Judge. It appears to be an airlock coupling," Charlotte said.

Before anyone could respond, Judge reached out and poked the flesh-like door with the tip of his gloved hand. There was a loud beeping sound, and the door irised open like folding skin, and beyond a tunnel led to another sealed door at the opposite end. Lights blinked on overhead, and red dust moots floated in the air. Silver lines, like rope, crisscrossed the tunnel's ceiling, and they glinted under the harsh light.

Judge stepped into the airlock as he turned on his helmet headlamp. "Arjun, you getting all this?"

"Yes," Arjun said.

The team eased into the tunnel, its dimensions the same as the exterior doors. Mice ran up Judge's back, and he said, "Psycho. Take someone with you and get the emergency supply chest."

"10-4. Tisa, you're with me," Psycho said. The pair moved off and the remaining members of the party waited, the oppressive silence in the airlock unnerving.

"Should we report back to Gale?" Seok asked.

Judge was getting tired of the man's constant suggestions, which in his mind amounted to second guessing. "Not yet. Let's see where this goes." Judge turned his head and shined his headlamp on the door at the far end of the airlock.

Several tense minutes slipped away before Psycho and Tisa returned carrying the supply chest between them.

As the crew eased down the tunnel, Arjun said, "The airlock door we came through looks like it was designed to mate with a ship."

"Agreed," Judge said. Thoughts on what lay beyond the far door danced in his head like the anticipation of birthday presents.

The team was twenty meters into the tunnel when the airlock door they'd come through closed with a hiss and that brought the team to a halt.

"Umm," said Charlotte.

Judge backtracked and poked the door the way he had prior. Nothing. It was then the loss of the drill hit him like a hammer. He kicked the airlock door several times in frustration. Nothing.

Transfixed with what might lay beyond the airlock, Psycho, Tisa and Arjun worked their way forward.

"Hold up," Judge said as he joined his crewmates at the opposite end of the tunnel. "Tisa, can you reach the SEV?"

Tisa tried to contact the SEV. "Nothing," she said.

"Should we head back?" Judge said, but even as he spoke, he knew the answer.

"How? You got a way of opening that door I don't know about?" Psycho said.

"No, but that doesn't mean we should blindly go forward. What if there's a—"

A mighty inrush of air stopped Judge midsentence as the airlock door before them hissed open, revealing a slice of green jungle beyond. A roar echoed down the tunnel, and the Martian ground trembled. A massive shadow passed before the open door as Judge and crew stood rooted like trees, a cacophony of birds braying and insects buzzing filling the tunnel.

Psycho and Seok stepped forward, enthralled. Charlotte and Arjun stepped back, their natural defense mechanisms taking over and sounding an alarm. Judge, Tisa and Arjun didn't move.

Judge couldn't believe what he was seeing. It wasn't possible. Couldn't be.

Another roar thundered down the tunnel. "Hey, Psycho. Better break out those guns."

Psycho tore his attention away from the open door and said, "Yeah. I think you're right." He and Tisa put down the metal trunk, and Tisa had it open a second after it hit the ground. The emergency supply chest had minimal food rations, scientific equipment, safety items relating to the EVA suits, some personals, water, and three guns.

"Commander Salis was a Marine in his former life," Judge said as he accepted a pistol from Psycho. The gun was a black Beretta M9 with a full clip of twenty rounds. Judge hefted the weapon. He didn't like guns, but holding it eased his jumping nerves.

"Yup. I was happy when he insisted we take weapons from the base's meager armory," Psycho said. "Extreme caution, he said. Doesn't seem so extreme now."

"Gale Base has an armory?" Seok said.

"Like I said, Salis was a Marine. He's got a locker in the back of his office with knives, guns, and extra rounds just in case," Judge said. He glanced at Psycho, and the NASA Mission Specialist averted his eyes.

Psycho pulled a second M9 from the trunk and held it out to the group. None of them accepted the weapon, so Psycho looked at Judge and lifted an eyebrow.

"Charlotte, you know how to shoot, right?" Judge said. He knew she'd won marksmanship awards when she was in the Air Force, but that was a long time ago.

The redhead reached out and accepted the weapon like it was covered in disease. Once the gun was in her hand, Judge could almost see her confidence rise. She gripped the weapon and racked the slide. "I'm good."

"Cool," Psycho said as he lifted a black plastic box with silver latches from the trunk. "Now, the only official NASA approved weapon." He snapped open the case revealing an XK Laser Assault rifle. He lifted the sleek, science fiction-like weapon and displayed it for the crew. "It's got a battery with enough juice for twenty bursts."

"Where the hell did that thing come from and why is it on Mars?" Arjun asked.

"Need to know and all that," Judge said. "But I can tell you it was here for testing. If there's a—"

Another roar made Judge jump, and all helmets rotated toward the open airlock. Green vegetation rustled beyond the door and shadows danced as something pushed through the trees.

The rest of the party received NASA survival knives. The M-6 was an updated version of the M-1 from W.R. Case & Sons Cutlery Co. used by the Gemini and Apollo missions. Fitted with a lightweight polypropylene handle, a 17″ blade, and saw teeth along its spine, the knife provided utility for astronauts who found themselves in situations not dreamed-up by the bigheads.

Judge wasn't really a military man. He'd never led a combat mission—he'd never been in combat—so he did what good leaders do. He put the most experienced soldier on point. "OK," he said, breathing deep as he tried to ease the nervous tingle that ran through him like an electrical shock. "We've come this far. Let's proceed carefully. Psycho, take us in. Tisa, watch our backs. The rest of you, stay close together."

The team of explorers eased down the tunnel, the metal walls reflecting the light of their headlamps, creating dancing shadows on the smooth walls. A bird shrieked in the trees beyond the door, and the scent of earth and flowers pushed through the airlock.

Psycho panned the laser rifle back and forth, scanning the jungle before him. He reached the end of the tunnel and stepped through the airlock. A bird cawed and Psycho paused, holding up a closed fist as he dropped into a crouch.

Judge stared out the airlock door like he was looking through a window onto another world—and wasn't that exactly what he was doing? Seok and Arjun moved past him, gazing like children at a world that shouldn't be. Bright white light filled the sky, but Judge didn't see its source. It was as if the entire cavity had a giant LED light on its ceiling.

Tisa and Charlotte joined Judge. "This is… impossible," Tisa said.

"And yet there it is," Charlotte said.

The ground beyond the airlock was brown hardpan, and looked like Earth dirt. The six astronauts stood gazing at the jungle in disbelief.

The trees ahead rustled and a giant lizard-like head poked through the tree canopy. Dark baseball-sized eyes searched the area, a jagged red stripe running between the beast's eyes and down its back. The creature was at least ten meters tall, and as it pushed through the trees, Seok gasped.

"Is that what I think it is?" Judge said.

"Not possible," Arjun muttered.

The massive T-rex stepped from the trees, red stripes running the length of the beast's body to the tip of its twenty-foot tail. It threw back its head and roared, then it clawed at the ground as if spoiling to run.

Psycho brought the stock of the laser rifle to his shoulder.

The T-rex growled and gurgled, slime dripping between its foot-long teeth. Short arms dangled from the creature's torso and its muscular legs stomped the ground, dust clouds obscuring the beast from view.

A gentle breeze pushed through the trees and everything went still for a heartbeat. A roar thundered through the subterranean chamber, and the Martian ground trembled as the beast pushed through the dust clouds.

"We need to get out of here. Now," Arjun said. "We should never have come in here."

"I think you're right," Judge said.

As the six explorers headed for the airlock, the door irised closed with a hiss of air, and the team was trapped.

5

The T-rex lowered its head and growled as its mouth slid open, long teeth glinting under the harsh overhead lighting. The beast came forward, its footfalls shaking the hardpan. Red stripes ran the length of the dinosaur, and amidst the chaos and fear, Judge laughed to himself. He shook his head, refocusing his eyes, but the creature was still there, coming on like a freight train from the past. A living, breathing dinosaur. He was still trying to wrap his noodle around what he was seeing when Psycho took control.

"Everyone scatter," Psycho yelled as he dropped to a knee and brought the laser rifle to his shoulder.

Judge said nothing. Curiosity had been replaced with fear, and Psycho was better equipped to lead the team through the current crisis. "Psycho is in charge until further notice," Judge yelled. Even when under attack—especially when under attack—it was of prime importance to have a clear chain of command.

"Find cover!" Psycho yelled.

The fierceness of Psycho's tone jerked Judge into motion. He ran for the tree line, a tall metal wall that disappeared into the white light above on his left, the charging beast on his right. The jungle ahead was a tangle of vines, trees and underbrush, and though his EVA suit wasn't as bulky and cumbersome as the older models, it wasn't a sweatsuit. Every branch and pricker tore at him as he pushed into the vegetation.

The zap of the laser rifle, and the ensuing screech of pain from the T-rex, spun Judge around.

The beast stopped, a black burn mark on its lower torso. The creature shrieked and clicked, its eyes rolling side-to-side. Psycho fired again and the burst grazed the dinosaur's leg.

That was enough for the T-rex. It inched backward into the line of trees, the ground shaking, and lumbered away into the cover of the forest.

Judge rejoined his crew, dropping to the ground, landing on his butt and letting his helmet-covered head fall into his gloved hands. Everything had gone wrong so fast, and the rabbit hole they'd fallen into looked stranger than Wonderland. He sucked in deep breaths as the dust settled and his crewmates emerged from their hiding places. Sweat dripped down his face and back, and his stomach burned.

"Well done, Psycho," Arjun said.

"Eighteen bolts left," he said.

"Everyone alright?" Tisa asked.

"As alright as I can be. What the h—"

A shriek echoed through the jungle, the call of a beast in great pain or really pissed.

"We need to get out of here," Seok said. He strode forward and poked the airlock door. Nothing. He searched around the door's edges, looking for a control panel. He found nothing.

"That alien code would be real useful right about now," Psycho said.

"Or at least the drill," Tisa said.

Charlotte held out a hand to help Judge to his feet. "How you doin', cowboy?"

"I need a drink," Judge said.

"A double," she said.

Judge dusted himself off and checked his suit readings. Everything was still green. "Everyone, run a system check on your EVA suit."

The jungle symphony resumed, show over, and insects trilled, birds chirped, and an uncountable number of growls, clicks, barks, and groans filled the forest. The sheet of white light above filled every empty space, and perpetual dusk ruled beneath the thick forest canopy. The wall had no markings, no grooves or rivets or screws. It was as if the metal had been poured in place. The hardpan ran right up to the wall, and paths big and small ran away from the clearing before the door.

"What the hell is this place?" Tisa asked.

"I think that might be a question for another sol. Right now, we need to get settled, take inventory of what we have—because we might be here awhile—and figure out a plan of action," Judge said.

"Plan of action?" Tisa said. "The plan of action is to get the hell out of here ASAP. No?"

"Maybe, but even if we didn't want to explore, we still need to find a way out. We have no way to open the airlock door, so we'll have to find another way," Judge said.

"What's that all about? This the roach motel? You can check in, but you can't get out?" Psycho said.

"I'm thinking they didn't want... the specimens to get out," Seok said.

"Specimens?" Judge said. "Is that what you think this place is? A research habitat?"

"No, but until we do know, we have to assume from what we've already seen that it's a biosphere of some kind," Seok said.

"Shouldn't we take this conversation under cover?" Psycho said.

"Good point. Lead on," Judge said. He rolled his shoulders, and they followed the metal wall east.

As the team walked, Judge noticed the equipment trunk was gone. "Psycho, where's the supply trunk?"

The NASA Mission Specialist's helmet rocked back as Psycho's eyes grew wide. "Shit," he said. "We put it down in the airlock."

Anger and frustration built in Judge, and he pointed his M9 at the sky and fired. The loud snap of the gunpowder expanding echoed over the jungle and everything went still for a heartbeat. A brief bolt of static ran across the sheet of white light above. Judge's anger dissipated when he saw Arjun watching him, the lens on his camera zooming in and out. "You can stop recording for now," Judge said.

"But don't we want to—"

"I said shut it down, now!" Judge yelled. He stuffed the gun back in his belt.

Arjun's eyes grew wide behind his face shield, and he said, "Got it, boss."

"I'm sorry," said Judge. His gloved hand went to his face, but was blocked by his helmet. "I don't want our personal conversations recorded right now. What we do here is going to be analyzed and reanalyzed for the next hundred years. I don't want us on record saying something stupid before we know anything."

"If we ever get out of here," Charlotte said.

A bird shrieked, a lizard bleated, and a roar reminded the party of the bigger beasts roaming the forest.

A thin path ran along the base of the wall and prints of various types and sizes marked the loose dirt. Judge spotted a large conifer tree, its lower branches full and wide. He ducked and pushed through the branches, the tiny green spike-like leaves scratching his spacesuit.

Once the team was beneath the tree's boughs, Judge sat and put his back to the trunk. His mates joined him, sitting in a rough circle like a kindergarten class.

"I don't know about you all, but I need some water," Charlotte said. She sucked on a tube and drank from her suit's water supply.

Judge's stomach gurgled, and suddenly NASA's freeze-dried food didn't sound so bad. Judge sighed, a crackle of static running through the suit comms. "With the trunk gone, our first task is to find water, food and shelter. Tisa, have you tried to contact the SEV and Gale Base Alpha?"

"Not yet. All I've got is my suit comm. The good radio and its booster are in the supply trunk," she said.

"Great, so we're on our own," Charlotte said.

"For now," Judge said.

A lizard the size of a bunny bolted through the jungle on its hind legs and hissed at them as it tore past. Insects hummed and buzzed, and a shadow fell over the jungle as a huge creature with tent wings glided in circles over their position, shrieking and cawing. Rodents and small dog-like animals crawled from the forest, and several ostrich beasts with dark gray leathery skin inched tentatively out of the underbrush, heads bobbing as they stared at the newcomers as they hid beneath the conifer.

Judge let his hand fall to his M9 where it was stuck in his utility belt. Pain stomped down his back, a tingle of worry and fear running through him. Every creature for twenty clicks had heard the airlock door open and close.

"We're trapped, and we need to start making provisions for our survival," Judge said.

"There are plenty of living beasts, so unless this is Westworld, there should be water," Seok said. "But until we find a supply, I'd conserve what water you have in your suit reservoir."

"What about the air? Can we take these suits off?" Psycho asked.

"Not yet. We can't make any assumptions," Judge said. "While I do agree with Seok, we can't trust our eyes. Even though these creatures look familiar to us, that doesn't mean they're what they appear to be."

"Agreed," Arjun said. The man hadn't spoken in so long, Judge had forgotten he was there. "Food seems to be the bigger issue."

Seok nodded agreement. "Perhaps we can hunt, but without fire I'd be concerned about pathogens."

Tisa said, "If this is a closed environment, like we think, there's no way to know what diseases are lurking. Something basic and simple could take us down because our immune systems aren't equipped to deal with it."

"The irony there is epic," Arjun said.

"How so?" asked Tisa.

"We might die because we have a space program, but the dinosaurs went extinct because they didn't have a space program," Arjun said.

Seok and Judge chuckled. The others made no sign.

"Didn't Larry Niven say that?" Seok asked.

"Something like that," Arjun said.

"Focus. Focus," needled Judge. "Tisa, you're the MD here, what do you recommend? We can live in our suits, but eating would be a problem," Judge said.

"If we find food," Charlotte said.

"We'll find food. Like Seok said, unless these beasts are robots, they've got to eat and drink," Psycho said.

"That leaves security," Judge said. "I think we need to assume we're spending the night, so we'll need a better shelter than this." He motioned around the conifer tree they hid beneath.

"There appears to be a lot of.... wildlife, so I recommend we get off the ground. Build a platform in the trees," Psycho said.

Judge nodded. Back on Earth, Psycho was a hunter, yet another store of knowledge that made the Mission Specialist so valuable.

Charlotte said, "That will make things much harder."

"Doesn't need to be high. Off the ground five meters? That should do it, right?" Psycho glanced around, but nobody spoke.

"OK," Judge said, more to himself than the group. "Psycho and I will go look for water and food. Seok, I want you and Charlotte to take a look around also. Food, water, but I'd like a general report on the area. We need to attempt to identify our... boundaries?"

Seok chuckled. "Yes. We need to know how big this place is so we can figure out the best way to search."

Nods and grunts of agreement.

"So, the suits," Judge said.

A bellow echoed through the jungle, like a cow dying. The mournful call was answered by another, and soon the forest was filled with a great braying and yipping and shrieking.

The ground trembled.

Judge put a finger to his face shield as he pushed his head through the tree boughs. The tiny green leaves scraped on the suit's helmet, and to Judge it sounded like an alarm.

The ground shook, a roar silenced the trilling insects, and a momentary calm fell over the forest.

Judge's hand fell to the M9 and he said, "Our suits can't really measure external environmental conditions very accurately. The suit's main processor uses all available data to make predictions—which are usually very accurate, but without a data stream from Gale, estimates might be off by a magnitude of two or three. That said, my suit is showing the air to be breathable based on available data."

A chorus of affirmation.

Seok said, "There are several ways using our suit data to calculate—"

Two loud clicks as metal hasps were undone, the sigh of air, and the scrape of metal on plastic as Psycho removed his helmet.

"What the hell are you doing?" Judge said.

The Mission Specialist put up a hand, cheeks turning red as he held his breath. Psycho's crew cut was damp with sweat, and beads of perspiration slid down his face. He looked up, exhaled, and took a shallow breath.

Two heartbeats passed as the jungle chorus reached a crescendo.

Psycho exhaled, smiled, and took another breath. "Seems OK. Air's a bit thin, but we'll be alright."

Nobody spoke or moved. Seok's eyebrows knitted, and the rest of the party looked at their feet.

"We don't know exactly what the air composition was when dinosaurs roamed, but it's very possible the oxygen content was different," Seok said.

"If what we saw was really a dinosaur," Arjun said.

Judge's head jerked back, and he frowned. "You saw that thing. If it wasn't a T-rex I don't know what it was."

Psycho took several deep breaths and exhaled, yet still none of the other team members took off their helmets. Psycho shrugged and started stripping off his suit.

Judge looked at Charlotte, who shrugged.

When Psycho stood in his blue NASA jumpsuit, his bulky suit boots on his feet, life support backpack resting atop his folded, dirty white spacesuit, Judge figured it was time to set an example.

With a trembling hand he broke the seal on his helmet and lifted it off. Judge's nerves stomped on his spine, pain running to the tips of his fingers and toes as he pulled off his gloves. He took several deep breaths, and Psycho was right. It felt like breathing in Denver, a mile above sea level.

Judge took off his suit and the rest of the crew followed. "Be careful," Judge said. "We're going to need these suits to get back to the SEV. If anything happens to them, we're screwed."

An angry roar pierced the calm.

"I think we're screwed already," Psycho said.

6

Judge grabbed his M9 from atop his folded suit. He racked the slide, chambering a bullet, and put a finger to his lips, but this time the ground didn't tremble, and trees didn't shake. A low growl echoed through the jungle and got louder when it bounced off the metal wall. Screeches and howls filled the jungle, a great braying and buzzing and roaring. Stray beams of light leaked through the conifer's dense boughs, and he watched an ant trek over the root-torn hardpan. He looked each team member in the eye.

Every instinct he had told Judge to hide, wait it out, don't take any risks. This was the NASA way. Despite astronauts being the greatest adventurers and explorers in history, they were trained to be automatons. There was a procedure to make a request to ask to develop a procedure. When there was no air, no food, and you were sixty-five million kilometers from home, safety was paramount.

Psycho's knee bounced up and down as he stared at Judge with his 'what are we waiting for' face. No question where he stood.

Tisa was a blank slate, Seok looked to be containing his worry and fear just below the surface, and Arjun and Charlotte looked terrified. Guilt ran through him as the old fears resurfaced, and suddenly the space beneath the conifer felt small. Sweat dripped down his back, and a chill ran through him. He had to get it together. "Change of plan," he said. "Psycho and I will take a look around before we do anything. Get us some information before we trudge off into the jungle with no clue what we're dealing with."

Psycho stood and disappeared into the tree branches without a word.

"Always such an understanding guy," Charlotte said as she sent daggers at Psycho's back with her eyes.

"Not now, Char, really," Judge said. This was what he was good at. "That goes for everyone. Whatever bullshit you all carried in here, bury it. Questions? Good."

Judge got to his feet and put the M9 in the pocket of his jumpsuit.

"May I make a suggestion?" Seok said. "Sir." When it came to vocal tone sarcasm, Seok was unrivaled.

A pain ran down Judge's back as his chest tightened when he suppressed a sigh. He said, "Yes. What? You have to go to the bathroom? Find a bush."

Seok stared at Judge wide-eyed.

"What is it?" Judge said. His patience was naturally thin and getting thinner by the instant.

"If you brought one of the suit helmets, we could have communication," Seok said.

"Tisa, do the intercoms work without the life-support backpack?" Judge said.

"No. Power supply is in there."

"We could bring a pack, but is communication that necessary? We're not going far, and my guess is if you hear gunshots you can assume it was us." Judge parted the boughs of the conifer and started through, then stopped. He needed to be a team player if that's what he wanted from his crew. "Seok, that was a good idea though. See if there's a way you can make us radios without damaging the suit. If we can…"

Seok was shaking his head no.

"What?"

"I can't access the EVA suit's battery without cracking the housing, which would damage the battery and make it inoperable," Seok said.

"As long as Tesla's copyright is protected," Judge said. "Good idea about the suit comms, though. Keep thinking. I need all the ideas you can give me."

Seok nodded and a slight smile spread across his face. "I can do this," he said. Seok knelt and drew his knife.

Judge's eyes grew wide and he looked at Charlotte.

Seok carefully cut the water bladder from the lining of his spacesuit and handed it to Judge. "The suit will still work fine."

"Thanks," Judge said. "If we're not back in…" What to say? Nothing needed to be said. He pushed through the evergreen's boughs like the kids who entered Narnia through their uncle's wardrobe, tiny needle-like green leaves pulling and scraping his jumpsuit.

"What's going on in there?" Psycho said.

Judge shrugged. "They're just trying to help and my team building skills are a bit rusty."

Psycho chuckled. "I think that's why we get along so well."

To their left, the metal wall disappeared into the solid white glow above, thick jungle and underbrush filling every empty space. Around them, tall trees with round tops and oblong leaves towered over palms and tropical plants with elephant ear-sized green and yellow leaves. The ground was covered in thick loam, and here and there bugs of various sizes and shapes trundled about their business, hoping to go unnoticed.

"Should we keep our backs to the wall?" Judge said.

Psycho considered the question, eyes squinting, lips a thin red line.

A bleating cow-like moan rose above the cacophony of insects and birds.

Psycho's eyes shifted to the jungle, and he said, "That's the safest course of action. Sure. But if we want some real information, we're going to have to go in there," he said as he pointed at the thick jungle.

Judge nodded. "We'll work our way along the wall. Let's call that east, for reference purposes." He faced the wall and was pointing to his right. "That way could be north for all we know, and from what I've seen there isn't going to be a sunset tonight for us to get our bearings. Once we've gone a ways along the wall, we can head inland and see if we can make a half circle back to the wall in the west. Make sense?"

"Yes and no," Psycho said. "We could get lost in the thick underbrush, and not be able to find our way back to the others. I'm more—"

"We can mark the wall, rocks, trees, leave other markers. Didn't you ever see Land of the Lost?"

Psycho squinted and shook his head no. "What I was going to say before I was rudely interrupted, was I'm more concerned with being able to keep any type of reasonable course with all the thick underbrush. With no machetes how are we going to trailblaze? If we get lost, sure, we can backtrack, but..."

"We have to take some risks. Let's go."

Psycho clapped Judge on the back, and said, "That's the spirit. Less talking and more doing." The Mission Specialist's eyes shifted to the hardpan.

Judge shook his head as he made his way along the metal wall. "Poor choice of words. You need to pay attention to... the little things. Like what you say. Especially in here with two women."

"Do they know about me?" Psycho asked.

"I don't know what people know."

"Are you going to tell them?"

"No," Judge said. The ordeal that led to Mission Control ordering Commander Salis and Judge to suspend Psycho and confine him to his bunk except for work supervised by the Commander's designee, wasn't the highlight of Judge's career. Earth had been adamant; sexual harassment complaints were to be taken seriously, and Psycho was to be sent back to Earth on the next transport to face a military tribunal. Problem was, the next transport ship wasn't due to arrive for eighteen months, and the allegation made against Psycho was the first reported crime on Mars. Ever.

It didn't help that his nickname was Psycho because he'd do just about anything. Things were further complicated by the Commander's initial investigation and report. Judge confirmed the investigation, and the report concluded that the facts didn't fully support the accusation. It was a he said, she said, situation, and the complainant and Psycho had a consensual relationship that everyone at Mars Base Alpha was aware of. He hadn't hit her, there were no marks. He'd grabbed her arm during a fight. The only facts that were in dispute were: did Psycho mean harm and had the complainant done the same in the past as Psycho claimed? The situation was far from resolved, but given neither Salis or Judge thought there'd been intent to harm, nor was there currently, they'd postponed the inquiry and related punishment to a more opportune time. Judge knew that decision might cost him his career, if he ever went back to Earth. Judge didn't intend to ever go back.

"Thank you," Psycho said. "I overreacted. I shouldn't have grabbed her arm, but do you know how many times she did the same to me? Norms had been established."

"You don't think people will understand? Think she's the bad one here? Were you breaking up? What was the fight about?"

Psycho said nothing.

Judge looked over at his friend and saw his cheeks were red. "What? Spit it out."

"She found out that…" He shook his head. "She'll kill me if I say."

Judge stopped walking and crossed his arms over his chest and stuck out his chin.

"She found out I'd slept with… someone else."

Judge bent under a branch and pushed through a thick line of ferns with deep green leaves that encroached on the base of the wall.

"Ah. Were you exclusive?"

"We're on Mars, dude. Normal rules don't apply."

"She should have punched you."

"See. Double standard. Was I a shit? Yup. Did I sexually harass her? That's just grade A bullshit right there. Though I shouldn't have grabbed her arm. 100% wrong there. Just don't think I should lose my life because she's pissed I betrayed her on a personal level."

A path led away from the wall and disappeared into the tangled jungle. Birds sprayed from the trees, fluttering and squawking.

"That's why you're here. If I'm ever questioned, I'm going to say you were on duty, and I'm the Commander's supervisory designee."

"Pretty thin shit."

"Maybe. You're worth it."

"Awww, you want to hug?" Psycho held out his arms. "Seriously, though, thank you for standing up for me. I know this is a thorn in your ass that might never go away. Might even get infected."

"Look at these." Judge knelt.

There was a dip in the trail and the hardpan was wet, a thin coating of mud covering the hardpacked dirt. Tracks led down the path, heading deeper into the jungle and away from the wall. The prints had been made by a beast walking on two legs, and two up-side-down teardrops and a third small slash made up the footprint.

"Looks like the creature's feet have two regular claws with another hanging just off the ground. Normally that third claw is to tear into and kill struggling prey," Judge said.

"Looks like giant chicken prints," Psycho said.

"Do chickens have four-inch retractable claws?"

"Question is, should we follow them? Judging by the size of the prints, this thing is big. Not as big as our T-rex at the gate, but big."

"You know what I haven't seen? Or smelled. Scat," Judge said.

"One of the many mysterious questions that stand before us, like how does it rain?" Psycho said. The Mission Specialist looked up into the solid sheet of white that stretched horizon to horizon in all directions, the harsh LED-like light reflecting off the metal wall like a mirror.

Vines snaked through the underbrush on both sides of the path, and thick roots covered the hardpan like a spider's web. Judge caught the glint of metal and stopped.

Psycho kept walking, the laser rifle cycling back and forth as he searched the path ahead.

Judge whistled.

Psycho spun on his heel and pinned the stock of the rifle to his shoulder. When he saw Judge gazing into the forest, he lowered his weapon and joined him. "What you got, boss?"

"Look on the ground there. Where the roots and vines have ripped through the hardpan."

Psycho stared, confusion spreading over his face.

Judge pointed. "Where the vines have upheaved the ground. Don't you see the black pipe?"

Psycho laughed. "Pipe. What the hell are you talking about? I don't—" Psycho's head jerked back. "Got it. Definitely not natural."

"Not surprising, right? There has to be an industrial underbelly to this place. The power, water generation and dispersal. I don't see how it all stays in balance."

"Perhaps the greatest mystery of all," Psycho said.

Gurgling and clicking sounds echoed through the forest.

Judge drew his M9 and dropped into a crouch, scanning the path in both directions. Nothing moved.

"I don't—" Judge said.

"Ssssh," Psycho whispered. He pointed into the jungle in the direction they'd been looking.

Judge saw the pipe, the tangle of vines and roots. Rodents and ants scuttled across the jungle floor between the ferns, weeds, and bushes with two-inch stiletto-like prickers covering their branches. A faint layer of mist hung in the jungle just above the underbrush, thin white streams reaching for the treetops like ghostly fingers.

"I don't see—" Judge's words caught in his throat.

Two dark, glassy, tennis ball-sized eyes stared out from the foliage, black pupils sinking into red irises. The beast's eyes narrowed as it pushed through yellow fern leaves, and when it honed in on the duo it threw back its head and roared, muscles rippling under dark leathery skin covered in red stripes of various earthly hues.

A loud clicking sound broke the stillness, then the faint *womp womp* like an approaching helicopter pulsed through the forest. A stiff breeze wafted through the jungle, bringing the scent of flowers, earth, and something Judge couldn't quite identify.

The creature cried again, its head shifting like a bird's, but as Judge strained to find the beast in the underbrush, dread crept through him. He was in this thing's territory. On its turf. Judge's confidence fled as the sound of breaking branches and stomping feet echoed through the forest.

7

The underbrush rustled and swayed as the creature pushed through the vegetation. Judge brought up his M9, panning it back and forth the way he'd seen Psycho do it. He hadn't fired a weapon since Officer Candidates School, and the gun didn't feel comfortable in his hand. Grunts and wheezes rose above the buzz of insects, the sounds of snapping branches and growling filling the forest.

The creature burst from the foliage twenty meters from Judge. It paused on the path, lowering its head to the ground, its mouth sliding open revealing sharp white teeth. The beast clicked and sighed as if bored, then cawed as it stepped forward, head bobbing and jerking.

Psycho and Judge aimed at the creature.

The dinosaur launched into the jungle and was gone.

Judge fell in behind Psycho and the two men stood back to back scanning the forest.

"That was a... a raptor. A raptor with red stripes," Judge said. He couldn't believe what he was saying.

"That's sure as hell what they looked like in Jurassic Park, minus the red stripes." Psycho's eyes grew wide. "Do they really hunt in threes?"

"No idea. I think I heard that was bullshit, but given the situation we should assume there are more of them lurking."

"Great. I don't—" Psycho started.

"Shiiiiiiiiittttttt," Judge screamed as a raptor burst from the tree break, slamming into him, and knocking him to the ground. He rolled to avoid the beast's snapping jaws, slime dripping onto his face. The raptor bit and pecked at him as Judge dodged.

The laser rifle chirped, and the beast wailed. Breaking branches, howls of raw pain, then bright white light.

Judge rubbed his eyes as he rolled onto his stomach and crawled toward Psycho, who scanned the jungle, panning the laser rifle.

"You alright?" Psycho said.

"I think so." Judge felt his body for wounds and breaks.

Psycho spared him a glance and lifted an eyebrow.

"I'm fine. You get it?"

Psycho said nothing.

"I thought you knew how to shoot? Two misses?"

Psycho rolled his shoulders. "I've never fired this thing before. It isn't like a real gun. No recoil. No vibration. It's like I'm holding a battery."

"Wait..." Judge got to his feet, scanning the jungle. "It gone?"

"For now, I think."

They worked their way down the animal path, the forest chorus returning to full volume.

"So, back to this two misses thing," Judge said. No way he was letting that go after all the bragging Psycho had done the last two years. "I thought you said you could shoot any gun accurately?"

"I never said that." The Mission Specialist smirked, the apprehension draining from his face for a moment.

"No? I could hit an apple from a hundred yards out with a musket, you said. Hit a quarter on end with your M9 from fifty paces, you said. Pick off a fly from a handrailing ten stories up, you said."

Psycho kept his eyes on the path and said nothing.

"Hold up here a minute," Judge said.

The path was thinning. Judge pulled his knife and carved an X into a thick tree branch that hung over the animal path. As he worked, he said, "What do you make of this vegetation? The evergreens look kind of familiar. Some of the tropicals, though, couldn't say what they are."

"No Mark Watney with us on this trip, unfortunately," Psycho said.

"Who the hell is Mark Watney?"

"The guy from The Martian. Who got stranded on Mars alone?"

"Ah. Yes. Potato boy."

They laughed, and it was a welcome sound to Judge, but the squeal and roar of the creatures of the forest drained his positivity like mosquitos sucked blood. Bugs were an essential part of any ecosystem, and he'd already seen several species within the biosphere, but no blood suckers. He gazed up at the sheet of white light, trying to get his brain around the complexities of building the habitat. Every time he thought of a way to solve a problem, he stumbled on the issue of balance. How was everything kept in balance?

"I think Seok knows a little about plants. Had a garden, at least," Psycho said.

"The vegetation looks like what I'd expect from a dinosaur habitat, but who knows? We'll have to watch the animals. See what plants they avoid, what they eat."

They came to a large clearing, walls of green surrounding the open area like an arena. Footprints of every size and shape crisscrossed the area, birds sprayed from the thick forest canopy, and clouds of insects hovered just above the hardpan. At the center of the clearing, a metal trapdoor set in stone glistened like a soda can in the desert.

Judge stepped forward and Psycho threw out an arm to stop him.

"Looks clear," Judge said.

"That's what I'm afraid of."

"A trap? But who—"

Psycho put a finger to his lips and inched forward into the clearing, rifle stock at his shoulder. Nothing popped up from underground. No dinosaurs attacked. When he reached the trapdoor, he examined it closely before calling Judge over.

"Definitely an entry point of some kind," Psycho said. "But where does it lead?"

"Assuming we could get it open, which I doubt we could. There are no hinges, no handles. No lock or latch that I can see. If it's magnetic like the main door outside, then maybe we could beat it with a rock? But that sounds nuts. Plus, are we prepared for what's down there?"

Judge didn't answer. The rabbit hole could be their way out, but going into the backroom of the biosphere without more information, planning, and support, wasn't smart.

"You just marked a tree, so we'll be able to find it again if we want," Psycho said.

"Why do I have a feeling there's more of them?"

The team of two headed what they'd agreed to call east, and started circling back to the wall. For the most part, the beasts of the jungle fled before them, but several times Judge and Psycho had to hide beneath conifer boughs, or within bushes to avoid the larger beasts. It was hot, but not oppressively so, and the occasional push of wind was always preceded by the *thump thump* of what sounded like a huge fan.

"Our first lucky break," Psycho said.

"What? A burger hut?"

"No, that." Psycho pointed through the trees to a flock of birds covering a tree like ants on a candy bar.

"Berries? Nuts?"

"That's what I'm thinking." Psycho pushed through the underbrush with the laser rifle, not making noise, but not being silent either. When he got to the foot of the tree, thick roots crawling over the hardpan, he kicked the trunk three times.

"That hurt?" Judge said.

"A little."

Psycho's kick and the ensuing dull thud hadn't disturbed the birds, and they continued to sing and squawk as they pulled black fruit from thin branches with oval green leaves.

"Looks like a wild berry tree. There was one by my house when I was a kid, or one like it," Judge said.

Psycho knelt and picked up a broken tree branch and threw it up at the birds. The flying rats didn't even look in his direction. "Ok, you want to play?" He lifted the laser rifle and sighted the tree canopy.

"Hold up," Judge said. "We don't want to worry Seok and the others more than we probably already have."

"How then? There's no goddamn stones."

Judge thrust his chin forward and squinted. "Yeah. I haven't seen a single rock. Maybe—"

Psycho fired, and birds sprayed from the tree as the bolt sliced through branches, across the sky, and into the white light above. Dark lines spread across the sky like lightning, and the light dimmed, before returning to full strength.

Judge sighed, but said nothing as he pulled berries from the tree and stuffed them in his mouth.

The two NASA astronauts ate in silence for a time, stuffing in berries like children ate popcorn. Their hands were purple, and berry juice dripped from their mouths. Above, a giant beast circled over their position, its sail-like wings still as it glided. There was no sign the creature had seen them beneath the thick tree canopy, but Judge felt uneasy, like the animal sensed them.

"We've got to bring some back for the others, but what can we carry them in? I don't want to damage the water bladder," Judge said.

"I saw some elephant ear leaves a ways back. We can bundle some berries in those if we fold them. We'll have to be careful."

Judge picked while Psycho went to get the leaves. He made a neat pile, and when his teammate returned, they carefully packed up six large leaves with berries.

"I think we should start back for the wall," Judge said.

"We haven't gone very far east. We could still be west of their position, and we might not know which way to go when we hit the wall."

"Good point. Let's backtrack. Follow our footprints," Judge said.

Psycho pushed under the boughs of the fruit tree and threaded through the thick underbrush, Judge in tow.

"So what's the deal with you and Charlotte?" Psycho said.

"What do you mean?"

Psycho's forehead scrunched. "Everyone knows you guys were... close friends."

"Really?" Judge couldn't get people to complete their mission reports. The documentation of mankind's greatest exploration, but there was always time for gossip. He sighed. "My situation is complicated, and I didn't... don't, want to hurt her. It was my fault. We never should have..."

Psycho turned his hard stare on Judge, the one that made people do things without him saying a word. Even Judge wasn't fully immune.

"For another time," Judge said. "Look, I can see the wall."

An animal path cut through the jungle and they followed it, the forest and its creatures paying them no mind. A ten-foot snake with black and yellow stripes slid onto the path ahead, paused and turned its dark eyes on them, flicked out its tongue, and slithered into the jungle. Small animals scurried in the underbrush, the rustle of their movements constant background static.

They reached the metal wall and Psycho gave Judge the last of his water, folded the plastic bladder, and put it in a pocket to be refilled. Though they hadn't found water, he knew there had to be some, they just needed to find it.

Psycho placed a rock at the base of the wall with an arrow on it pointing right. That would take them back to the team. The pair walked along the wall in silence, Judge combing through the events since they'd been trapped. He was good at judging time—though still had to remind himself to adjust his estimates a hair to convert them to sols—and he figured five hours had passed since the airlock doors had hissed closed, but it felt like five sols.

"Here we go," Psycho said. Two sets of footprints trailed away into the jungle, and two sets continued along the wall.

"Home sweet home," said Judge.

Judge and Psycho were almost back to their crewmates when a loud beep silenced the jungle noise, then it started to rain. Fat drops that smacked the large leaves, the thick forest canopy like a tin roof. Judge yelled, "Seok? Charlotte? Guys? Come on out."

Judge knelt and cupped a large fanleaf in his hand, directing the drips of water covering the leaf into his mouth. There wasn't much, and he licked the leaf and moved on.

The drizzle turned to a downpour, droplets hitting leaves like thunder. A beast roared in the distance, a 'get off my lawn' scream. Charlotte and the others joined them, and the six astronauts made their way through the forest to the wall.

The jungle rain had eased, but with the path running along the wall, there were no trees there to stop the rain.

Judge and crew put their backs to the wall and threw back their heads, taking in the falling rain. Seok moved away, and sat next to a stunted tree with wide leaves. He used the leaf as a funnel, and unlike Judge's attempt under the dense canopy, Seok's try yielded a steady stream of water. Judge joined him, and soon all six astronauts were drinking from leaves like infants sucked on bottles.

When they'd drunk their fill, the crew broke out the berries. Judge and Psycho watched with pride, the companions eating as the rain fell. For a moment, Judge felt at ease, and he and his crew were kids eating berries in a sun shower on a lazy summer afternoon.

Beep.

The rain stopped like a spigot had been closed.

8

The six crewmates from Gale Base Alpha stood dripping wet, the sky above a solid white sheet of harsh artificial light. Creatures crawled from their holes, insects took flight, and the grunt and sigh of larger beasts echoed off the metal wall. Judge wiped his face with his hands, rubbing his eyes as he rolled his shoulders. It was all too unreal.

"What's with the beeping? It happened when the rain started also," Charlotte said.

"My guess would be they're for training and control, like in a laboratory setting," Arjun said.

"Pavlov's dog?" Judge said.

"Yeah. You said it before, Judge. How does all this stay in balance? Maybe the creatures that live here are given cues to mark various times of the day. Keeps their body rhythms humming," Seok said.

"Do you think it will get dark?" Tisa asked.

"Most certainly," Arjun said. "Circadian rhythms play a large part in most lifeform's bodily functions and wellbeing."

Judge looked up at the endless field of white. "When it does get dark, we better be ready," he said.

"What does that mean?" Charlotte said.

"Let's get back under cover. We have no idea what point we're at in the habitat's daily cycle. It could get dark at any time," Judge said.

The group followed the now beaten trail to the conifer they'd been calling home. Psycho held back branches like he was holding open the door at the Waldorf as Judge and the others entered their fort.

When everyone was seated on the cushy pine needle strewn ground, Judge said, "So, I got nothing. Literally, beyond what you all know. Let's put aside the possible reasons for the existence of this place, and who built it. Right now I'd like to concentrate on what we should do. Split up? Explore? Try and get the airlock door open? Or the trapdoor we found?"

Nobody spoke.

"Floor's open," Judge said. "Speak freely."

"A strong argument could be made that we should stay by the main door. Focus all our efforts on getting it open," Arjun said.

"How? I mean, I'm not being a wise-ass," Judge said. "Well, maybe I am, but my point stands."

"The wise-ass does have a point. We've got no tools. No information. There's got to be a control room someplace. It's not possible that a place like this could exist and function without a brain, and we need to find it," Seok said.

"Do we try and do both?" Tisa said.

The jungle symphony rose in a crescendo then fell still when a roar pierced the day, and the ground trembled as something massive trundled through the jungle. Above, the flying beast still circled, its cawing and screeching rising above the forest static.

When the ground stopped trembling, Judge sighed and shook his head. "Unless we can find a cave, but since we haven't seen a single rock that's not likely to happen, is it safe to stay in one place? I don't like the idea of splitting up. In fact, I'm making that call right now. We stay together no matter what."

"To death do us part?" Psycho said.

"Yeah," Judge said, and he held out his hand.

Psycho put his hand on top of Judge's and soon the entire team had a hand on the pile. "To death do us part. At least until we get out of here," Judge said, and everyone laughed.

"To your question. Building defenses in one spot does make sense. Roaming around increases the danger exponentially," Tisa said.

"But given we have very little chance of getting the doors open, at least without more information, staying here doesn't seem to make much sense," Judge said.

"Maybe this will help," Charlotte said. She pulled a thinly rolled piece of white paper with writing on it from the breast pocket of her blue NASA jumpsuit.

"That what I think it is?" Judge said.

"A Pin'er? Where the hell did you get that?" Psycho said.

Charlotte put the thin joint in her mouth. "They grow a bit of medicine in the greenhouse. Very hard to get. Cost me three days' rations. Don't pretend you don't know."

Psycho blushed.

"I'm more impressed with the paper," Seok said.

"From a book," Charlotte said.

Seok's eyes went wide with disapproval. Print books were a rare commodity on Mars.

"I know, I know. One mustn't destroy literature," Charlotte said.

"Don't see how we'd light it even if we wanted to," Arjun said. He definitely sounded like he wanted to.

Psycho held up his laser rifle, raised his eyebrows, and smiled.

"That joint is thinner than a pin, Psycho, but we need to be clear headed," Judge said. He knew his team needed to blow off steam. Relax for a few minutes and try and get their minds off the fact that they were trapped in a biosphere on Mars that contained prehistoric beasts, so they could think strategically.

"Another time?" Charlotte said as she slipped the joint back into the breast pocket of her jumpsuit.

Judge hadn't smoked in a long time, but he said, "Count on it."

Judge bunched his space suit up into a pillow and propped it against the tree. He leaned back, his old body screaming with pain, his stomach yelling for food.

"Be careful with that suit," Seok said.

Judge nodded. He didn't know what to do next, and thankfully Psycho saved him.

"We need to get a sense of how big this place is," Psycho said.

"Is there a caboose on that train of thought?" said Judge.

"We could climb this tree? See what's what. But we need light, so if that's what we're going to do, someone better start climbing," Psycho said.

"Or we could follow the wall all the way around?" Tisa said.

"No idea how long that would take," Seok said.

"I'm thinking logic as we know it might be out the window," Judge said.

"Could that space cloud from a few years have twisted something up?" Tisa said.

"Like what?" Arjun said.

"If it did, there's no evidence that I've ever heard of," Seok said.

"Let's not reach for shit. I think Psycho's right," Judge said. "I'm going to climb this tree and see what's to be seen." Charlotte started to speak, and he put up a hand. "I think we'll have plenty of time to argue the larger questions. Maybe the biosphere was created by unknown builders intent on studying the Age of Reptiles? Preserving its creatures. Who knows, maybe we'll find out. Right now, I think we need to focus on finding the habitat's brain like Seok said."

Nods and general agreement.

"Why are you climbing? You want me to?" Psycho said.

Judge was the leader, and based on protocol that meant he should stay out of harm's way. That said, he wanted to see for himself whatever there was to be seen. He had to make the decisions for the group. Yes, he asked for advice and considered it, but ultimately, their little team wasn't a democracy and he wanted to see for himself what they were dealing with if he was going to have to make decisions involving life and death. Then there was the fact that Psycho, Seok, and maybe Tisa and Arjun might be better leaders than him. They were more experienced in the field. He was far from essential, and that decided it.

"I got it," Judge said after a long pause. "I need you to keep an eye on things down here in case one of our dinosaur friends sticks its snout into our fort here."

Psycho nodded, but pain cut across his face. "I think I should come. You shouldn't go alone."

Judge nodded his ascent. Not because he needed Psycho, or because it was justified, but because he felt a ton of stress seep from his body when Psycho made the suggestion.

Climbing was awkward wearing the spacesuit boots, but the conifer branches were strong and evenly spaced, and Judge easily pulled himself from one limb to another, checking his footing each time. He'd climbed the thick hundred-and-fifty-foot pines next to his house when he was a boy, and as he climbed, he heard his mother's voice screaming for him not to fall. "You'll hit your head on every branch," she'd said. He tried not to look down. He wasn't afraid of heights, but he wasn't comfortable up high, either.

His nerves danced on a high wire as he inched up the tree. If he fell, he was screwed. Everything on Mars was more complicated, and any injury—even of the mild variety—could become infected and he and his team had no supplies. He supposed in a pinch they could boil water if they could find it, but that was about it.

Psycho grunted as he pushed through a thick branch that blocked their way. The forest was so tightly packed, branches from surrounding trees were encroaching on the conifer's territory. "Wish we had some rope for safety line. We'd be able to go faster."

Judge chuckled. Faster? He couldn't go any faster, safety line or not. "We're going fast enough."

"What if we lose our light?" Psycho said.

That was Judge's main worry at the moment, and he instinctively reached for his jumpsuit pocket to touch his worry doll, then remembered he'd left it with his personals back on base. He usually carried the tiny handmade Mexican doll wherever he went. Brenda had given it to him, and legends said the doll could help its holder solve any problem a human could possibly worry about. That would sure be a help. Judge shrugged and tried to crack his neck. No luck. He stopped to rest, watching Psycho disappear into the thick tree canopy.

He waited as he caught his breath, trying to see through the conifer's dense branches. The scent of pine and dirt brought him back to Earth, to the trees and the parks, things he'd never really cared about before, but now missed. He even missed Gale Base Alpha, and there was nothing special there. The only person on Mars he really cared about was Charlotte, and she was with him. That thought made pain scamper down his spine. If Charlotte got killed because of him he'd never be able to forgive himself. Nerves under control, he took another deep breath and climbed.

As the conifer's trunk tapered down, Judge's anxiety continued to rise. Psycho had paused above, and the tree swayed slightly as he positioned himself. Then the now familiar *womp womp* of a giant fan starting echoed through the habitat. A gust of wind pushed through the forest and the conifer swayed and shifted.

"I think we've gone up high enough," Judge said as he joined Psycho. His hands were sticky with sap, and every time he took his hand off a branch it made a squishing sound.

The branch the Mission Specialist stood on bent under his weight, the tree swaying slightly because it was top-heavy. "Look at this place," Psycho said, sweat dripping down his forehead.

It was much hotter a hundred and fifty meters from the ground under the sheet of white, and sweat dripped into Judge's eyes as he was baked. He slipped beneath a thick branch covered in green needle-like leaves, shielding himself. As he braced his feet, Judge clung to the conifer's trunk, which was down to less than half a meter in diameter.

The harsh light reflecting off the metal walls made it difficult to see the edges of the biosphere, but Judge figured the habitat was no more than ten kilometers from side to side. The habitat was hexagonal, and on the far end a waterfall caught Judge's attention. Water poured from the white light, shining as it fell into the tree canopy, the fall's faint rumble adding to the jungle static. The waterfall was far off, but at least now he knew they had water.

Animal paths large and small crisscrossed the biosphere like a maze, a dark clearing in the jungle's center like the pupal of a giant green eye. Something glistened at the clearing's center, but Judge couldn't make out what it was.

"Wish I had a pair of binoculars," Psycho said.

Beasts of all shapes and sizes walked the animal paths and flying creatures with wide wings soared above the tree canopy, shrieking and squawking.

"Is that a river I see?" Judge said.

"Sure looks like it. Supplied by the waterfall, probably."

"And it just recycles? By pump?"

Psycho laughed. "Sounds good to me."

Another gust of wind pushed through the habitat, and Judge and Psycho held on as their tree swayed. Judge scanned the horizon, trying to memorize as much as he could, but taller trees impeded his view. It was hard to see much detail from his current height, and the blinding light wasn't helping.

A group of huge beasts led by two massive dinosaurs with long necks and tails trundled across the habitat. Their thick legs shuffled along, serpentine necks swaying, long tails curling toward the sky. "Those look like... like..."

"A thunder lizard," Psycho said.

"What now?"

"Brontosaurus. They're probably what's making the ground shake."

The largest Brontosaurus tore leaves off trees as it walked, throwing its head back as it sucked down the greenery. The beasts bellowed and moaned, but ceased when a roar telling all creatures to quiet down tore across the habitat.

"Looks like that clearing in the middle might be promising," Psycho said. "There's something glinting there. I wonder—"

A loud beep echoed through the biosphere, the overhead light flashed three times, then went out.

Impenetrable darkness filled the biosphere.

Judge and Psycho stood frozen, clinging to the conifer's trunk as it swayed and shifted. There were no stars. No light of any kind, and Judge couldn't see Psycho's feet above him.

Another loud beep.

A pillar of light rose from the center of the habitat like a flashlight beam, and a dull corpse light seeped over the jungle. Creatures brayed and roared as the artificial moonlight filled the biosphere, casting everything in flickering black and white. Shadows danced on the metal walls, and as the darkness pressed in around him, all Judge's worries and fears came at him like a bullet.

"At least now we know which way to go," Psycho said.

Judge nodded in the darkness.

9

Thin daggers of light pierced the tree canopy, tiny spots speckling the brown leaf-covered hardpan. The gray gloom that leaked beneath the conifer's boughs was the opposite of an early morning dusk that brought the promise of a new day, or the gentle release into darkness as the sun went down. This was sorrow light, death light, a light that illuminated nothing.

Judge's galloping heart hit the homestretch and slowed as he got closer to the ground. Hiking into the Grand Canyon was easier than hiking out, and thankfully climbing down trees was easier than going up. His body was drained, his energy reserve blown. He needed food, water, and he was thankful for gravity as he slowly worked his way limb to limb, his tension easing as the thickness of the tree's trunk grew in diameter.

Back down on the ground, surrounded by his crewmates, as he sat beneath the thick boughs of the evergreen, Judge felt the familiar tremor run through him as claustrophobia tried to take control. He rolled his shoulders, cracked his knuckles, and smiled at his crew, all of whom were looking to him for a debrief of what he'd seen.

Psycho bounced like a puppy who saw a bone within reach, but wasn't permitted to take it until given the command by its master.

Judge was bone weary, and he was still having trouble processing what he'd seen, so he nodded at Psycho, giving the Mission Specialist permission to brief the crew. As he listened to Psycho describe the waterfall, the various beasts, the paths, the river, it all felt like a dream. He watched his crewmates, their eyes flicking from Psycho to Judge, looking for assurances that Psycho was telling the truth and wasn't exaggerating. When Psycho got to the pillar of light, the group erupted with questions.

"What kind of light?" Tisa said.

"How far to this light?" asked Seok.

"How big? Ten kilometers by ten kilometers is pretty big," Arjun said. "So much for it being a one-piece structure. I think we sh—"

"Enough!" Judge hadn't meant to yell, but there it was. "I'm sorry." He took a deep breath and cracked his knuckles. "I'm sorry for yelling. I realize there are a million questions, and we'll work through them. One at a time."

Nobody spoke. Charlotte sniffled and wiped her eyes.

Judge sighed. "No idea what kind of light. It's sort of pale, like moonlight, and it's definitely focused on the center of the habitat where we saw... something."

"Something?" Tisa said.

"It was hard to see from that high with the bright light. Whatever it was glistened like metal or glass," Psycho said.

"Could it be making the pillar of light? Like a spotlight?" Charlotte asked. Judge was happy she was talking. He was worried for her.

"Sure," Psycho said. "And if the habitat is roughly ten kilometers across, that means we're about five kilometers from the center of the biosphere."

"It's going to be a tough five kilometers," Judge said. "The jungle is a tangle, the underbrush thick and unyielding, and the animal paths won't be safe to travel because of... because of the animals."

Seok nodded. "At least now we have a guidepost, and we've got enough to get us going in the right direction in the morning."

"And if we get lost, we can wait until dark to get reacclimated," Arjun said.

That certainty, that schedule, appeared to put his team at ease. Charlotte let out a long breath and leaned back against the conifer's trunk, nestling into her EVA suit as if it were a blanket. Seok and Tisa stretched out on the ground. There were no berries left, and no water, and that would be the first task of the new sol... day... Judge harrumphed.

Psycho leaned the laser rifle against the tree trunk as Arjun got up and stretched.

"I can make a fire," Arjun said.

The other five astronauts stared at him with varying degrees of amazement painted on their faces.

"And how, may I ask, do you plan to do that?" Judge asked.

The ISRO Astrochemist pointed at the pile of wood shavings he'd whittled with his knife. Next to the pile of wood curls was a stack of dried palm leaves and dead branches.

"Ya, and where are you going to get a spark?" Psycho said.

"I can use bark and a stick to make a bow."

"You mean like bow and arrows?" Judge said. He was no outdoorsman, and he couldn't see how a bow could make a fire.

"Yes, like that," Arjun said. "You wrap the bowstring around a thick branch. Then you place the end of the branch on a piece of dry wood, and pull the bow back and forth, spinning the stick. You mound some wood shavings and dried palm leaves around the end of the spinning stick, and the friction will create enough heat to ignite the dry shavings and leaves."

"I've seen that done. It's really hard," Psycho said.

"I've done it," Arjun said.

It would take a lot of work and energy to start a fire, and for what purpose? Comfort? They had nothing to cook. No water to boil, and the smoke might bring unwelcome guests. It was a no brainer. "Not tonight," Judge said. "Good to know you can do it, though, and we're going to need you to as soon as we find something to cook. I don't want to waste any of the laser rifle's bolts." Judge had no idea how he was going to boil the water without a pot, but that was a problem for another sol... day.

Judge leaned back, rolled up his suit, and used it as a pillow. Ants and other insects crawled and buzzed, the constant clicking, braying, chuffing, whining, and roaring like the buzz of a large crowd, ever-present and stifling. Dust drifted in and out of the spidery legs of light that penetrated the conifer's thick canopy. He struggled to see through the branches, to find anything familiar, but there was nothing except the gray corpse light that grated on his nerves like a strobe light.

He closed his eyes, and the last thing he heard before sleep took him was Brenda calling his name. Asking why he'd left, and when he was coming home.

Never.

**

Judge woke once during the night when a sharp beep pierced the darkness and it rained, thin rivulets leaking beneath the thick boughs of the conifer. At first, he thought he was waking from a dream, and the doors, the trip across Aeolis Palus, and the biosphere were nothing but figments of his imagination. A roar, followed by a sharp hiss, reminded him he was living no dream. He rubbed his eyes and rolled on his side, but there'd be no more sleeping on this night.

The rain ended before he could get out from under cover to drink, so he lay still, waiting for the beep that would bring the light of day. Psycho had also woken, but he could sleep on a bucking bronco and had no trouble getting back to dreamland. Judge listened to the faint pop and wheeze of Psycho's breaths. The others had stirred when the beep rang over the forest, but if they'd woken, they'd had no issues getting back to sleep. Leaves rustled, and the whish of fabric as his companions adjusted their positions, and their puffing and sighing and muttering was like a chorus.

The habitat flooded with light as the morning wake-up call sounded over the jungle. With no food or water, no camp to breakdown, and no supplies to pack, the company was ready to trek into the forest moments after being roused from sleep. They all had stomach pains, and Seok's insides screamed so loudly it sounded like something was trying to fight its way out of his chest.

"What about the suits?" Tisa asked.

Judge hadn't thought much about them. The helmets were awkward to carry, and they had no bags or other means to transport the spacesuits, but he worried about leaving them behind. If they lost the suits, they'd have no way to get back to the SEV.

Psycho said, "Fold them up as tight as you can. I'm going to get some branches and make a small platform in the tree above us, then cover everything with leaves."

Judge nodded. "That's the best we can hope to do, I think. Tisa, can you give him a hand?"

Tisa nodded, and she followed Psycho as he pushed through the conifer's thick branches and disappeared. Judge folded his suit, then helped Charlotte. "You OK?" he asked.

Arjun and Seok looked up from their work, but said nothing.

"Yeah, starving and my mouth is dry as paper, but other than that."

"It'll be OK," Judge said. He was starting to doubt that, but reassuring her was the only thing he could do to help her.

Several minutes passed before Psycho and Tisa returned with several branches. Judge climbed the tree and found two strong support beams, and like a manufacturing line, Psycho handed branches to Tisa, who handed them on to Seok, and so on, until Judge had a two-meter by two-meter platform constructed across two limbs. Then they handed up the spacesuits, and before long all the suits were stacked, covered in green leaves and branches, and Judge was back on the ground. "I can hardly see the platform up there and I know where to look," he said.

The party left the relative comfort of their makeshift shelter beneath the broad canopy of the conifer, and Judge's stomach sank as he lost sight of the tree as it blended into the forest.

It was tough going. The underbrush was a tangle of vines, pricker bushes, stunted saw palmetto, giant ferns, and huge spiked green plants with sail like elephant ear leaves. Judge and Psycho tied their knives to the tips of sticks using bark rope Seok made, and they used them like machetes as they sliced and cut their way toward the center of the habitat, but the blades were small and dulled quickly.

"Staying on course is impossible," Psycho said as he led the party through the vegetation, brushing off bugs and swatting gnats the size of dragonflies.

"I know. Do your best. When it gets dark, we'll see where we're at," Judge said.

"How long you figure it will take us to get there?" Charlotte said.

"Normally five meters would take what, a couple of hours? Tops? But with all this undergrowth I'm thinking at least a day. Especially if we stop to hunt and gather," Judge said.

"Yeah, keep your eyes out for fruit trees. Anything we can eat," Psycho said.

"I've seen a few hairy little rat things running around," Arjun said.

"And one of those evil bunny things was watching us a ways back," Tisa said.

Judge nodded. "I know, but there's nothing to these things. I'll blow them to nothing… and waste ammo."

"We need something bigger," Psycho said.

"We'll make camp and go hunting when we find a good spot," Judge said.

"Do you hear that?" Arjun said. He stopped and put out a hand and the party halted.

"What? I don't… wait," Tisa said.

"I hear it," Charlotte said.

Judge focused, tuning out the buzz of insects and the rumble of beasts going about the business of survival. "I don't—" Then he heard it. The relaxing sound of tiny waves breaking.

"It's this way," Seok said, and without another word he turned right and plunged into the forest alone.

"Seok, wait. I—"

The promise of water ruled, and Arjun followed, and before Judge could stop them, everyone had followed Seok into the greenery.

Judge's pulse raced. Running off half-cocked was exactly the kind of impulsive action that could get them all killed. The surrounding jungle seemed familiar, Earth-like, but Judge needed to remind his mates this wasn't Earth, and though they might not see them, dangers lurked around every tree trunk. "Wait. Slow up," he yelled, but even Psycho had disappeared into the dense vegetation.

He found his companions standing around a pond, nothing more than a puddle really, its water slightly cloudy. Footprints of various sizes and shapes marked the mud around the waterhole, and a wide path trailed away to the east.

Seok dropped to a knee and cupped water in his hand.

"Wait. Shouldn't we—"

Seok slurped water into his mouth and swallowed.

An animal cawed, and another beast responded with a growl. Breaking branches and pounding feet made Judge pull his eyes away from Seok and stare down the path. Dust rose from the hardpan as something came at them. The ground shook, and the jungle symphony went still.

Seok's eyes grew wide as he smiled, and he cupped water into his mouth as the others joined him. The astronauts slurped and sloshed, Judge's eyes straying from the pond to the path as he drank.

A bark that was half wail, half growl echoed through the forest, and the dust clouds swirled and were pushed aside as a massive animal with black armored skin thundered down the path. Three horns protruded from the beast's head, red stripes ran its length like gashes, and its long tail ended in an oblong club. The beast chuffed and boomed as it came on, the pounding of its footfalls like bombs exploding.

10

Judge bounced to his feet and plunged into the jungle, dirty water dripping down his face, muscles screaming. Branches whipped his arms as he fought through the vegetation with his knife-spear, insects divebombing his face. A spider the size of a pancake dropped onto his shoulder, and he screamed, brushing the arachnid away.

Seok, Tisa, Charlotte, and Arjun struggled through the underbrush behind him, but not Psycho. The Mission Specialist had dropped to one knee with the stock of the laser rifle pinned to his shoulder. He was cursing and ranting about how the weapon's sight sucked, but Judge's number one was rock steady.

The beast rumbled toward Psycho, the path opening up as it approached the pond. Plumes of dust rose into the air, the beast's black glassy eyes focused. A large horn curved up from between the animal's eyes, and two smaller horns stuck vertically from the sides of the creature's head like a second pair of ears. Armor covered the beast's head and back, and its tail swung back and forth just above the path. The creature threw back its head, and reared back, as if coiling, and surged forward and closed the last fifty meters.

The laser rifle zapped, and the dinosaur took the blast in its torso.

The beast wailed as it was knocked backward, a black burn mark dripping with blood and gristle marring the creature's chest. The dinosaur heaved and bucked on the path, flipping and screaming as its flesh burned. It rolled back onto its feet, and threw back its head, long white teeth glistening under the harsh light. The beast roared, reared back, then came on, blood dripping from its wound, dark eyes locked on Psycho.

Another laser bolt. Then another.

The creature crumbled to the ground, wheezing and choking. Half the dinosaur's head was gone, and white skull, fat, brain, blood, and bone splattered the ground. The beast let out a great sigh as its lungs emptied, and the scent of scat wafted over the pond as the animal's bowels released. The beast spasmed, bucked one last time, then fell still with a sigh, its body sagging in on itself like a deflating balloon.

"Holy shit," Judge said.

"Nothing holy about it," Tisa said.

The group joined Psycho, who stood bent over the creature's corpse. "Any idea what it is? Specifically?"

"I do," Arjun said.

Nobody spoke.

"Sure looks like an ankylosaur. The way its head is armored, the three horns, the club tail," Arjun said.

"Can we eat it?" Psycho asked.

The group burst out laughing, their stress draining away for a moment in a collective cleansing that only humor can provide. Judge said, "As funny as it sounds, it's a good question."

Psycho pulled his knife and sliced a piece of charred meat off the dead dinosaur. He held it up for the group to see. It looked like a bloody piece of blackened skirt steak. He missed steak so much Judge's mouth watered at the thought of it.

"Barbecued dinosaur. Another first for us here on Mars," Psycho said.

"Are there chemicals in the laser beam?" Charlotte asked as she scrunched her nose. "No, there isn't, but what about pathogens in the meat?" Charlotte smiled having answered her own question with a question.

"Could there be something in the air?" Tisa said.

"Possible, but we've seen no evidence of anything odd on that front," Seok said.

"The hell with it." Psycho tore off a piece of meat with his teeth and sucked it into his mouth. He looked around as he chewed, smiling. "A little tough."

The group watched him like he was a lab rat they'd just shot with a needle.

"Tastes like venison," Psycho said. He swallowed and took another bite.

Tisa pulled her knife and went to slice off a piece, but Judge stayed her hand. "No. Psycho is our test subject. Let's give it a few hours and make sure he doesn't keel over."

Seok wagged his head. "Yes, we can cut some unburned meat and wrap it in leaves to cook properly later."

The team spent the next half hour collecting leaves, cutting strips of meat, and wrapping their food using roots as butcher's twine.

"Not much meat on this thing for its size," Arjun said.

"All muscle," Psycho said. "But the backstrap should be OK," he said as he made a long cut along the dinosaur's spine. He whistled as he flayed meat off the dead beast, handing the strips off for packing.

The party rested for a time, drank some water, then continued on. Slicing through the underbrush was hard work, so the party had taken to slipping under branches, around vines, and adjusting course when particularly thorny or thick patches of vegetation blocked their way.

Without the sun moving across the sky, judging time was difficult. If the schedule was the same every day, which it probably wasn't, they had about two hours of light left when the afternoon rain came. He needed to have a campsite picked by then, and since they had meat, he didn't need to focus on finding a good hunting spot. The opposite. The more hidden and secluded the better. They could start a small fire, cook their food, maybe smoke the joint and regroup. They'd know for sure how far they'd come when the pillar of light rose into the sky.

"Judge, look at this," called Seok.

Judge held up a fist and the party halted.

Seok was behind Arjun, and he knelt, staring at the ground as if he'd found a diamond. There was a dip in the land, like water had streamed through the area at one time, and Seok was clearing away dirt, revealing metal.

"Another trapdoor?" Tisa said.

"No," Seok said. "It's a drain of some kind."

Judge pushed through the undergrowth and joined Seok.

Black steel grating with fine grooves was set into the hardpan. "Find the edges," Judge said.

Seok cleared away more dirt, revealing a two-meter square grate. There were no screws, latches, hinges, or handles. It had no lip, no crack to pry under. Nothing. The JAXA astroengineer said, "Looks to me like it was made to be covered in dirt. It's not for air, but water."

"Like a soaker hose?" Judge said.

"Except in reverse," Seok said.

Judge leaned in close, trying to see through the fine grating, but he saw nothing but blackness. "OK, we've been marking trees. We can find it again if we need to."

Psycho trekked on, the other five astronauts following like dwarves, the forest chorus going full tilt, the beasts of the biosphere huffing, cawing and sputtering as they fought, hunted, and foraged.

Judge called a halt when the party reached a small patch of dead trees and underbrush. The cause of the die off appeared to be a tree covered in slimy webs and clear goo.

Seok picked up a stick covered in the wet netting-like material. "Some type of natural fungus."

"It appears to have stopped dead in its tracks. I just walked it off and the spread area has a diameter of ten meters."

"Been thinking 'bout how the insect population and disease control are maintained," Arjun said.

"Me also. There must be a method to curtail and control contagions of various types," Seok said.

"Makes me question yet again what the hell we're breathing in here," Tisa said.

Aside from being a bit winded, Judge felt fine.

Arjun fell in beside Judge as they picked their way through the jungle. "Want me to take a turn carrying the meat?"

Though they weren't trailblazing in the traditional sense, finding a way through the tangle of vines, branches and weeds was hard work. "That's OK," he said. "I'm fine."

The forest gave way to a thin animal path that ran haphazardly through the jungle. It was big enough for the larger creatures, and it ran southeast away from the habitat's center, so the companions crossed it and plunged back into the jungle.

Judge noticed Arjun wore a red rubber bracelet on his right wrist. The remnants of white lettering ran around the bracelet's edge, but whatever it had once said had been rubbed clean by time. Judge had worn a similar pink band for years, a symbol of his sister's fight with cancer. Every ailment and cause had its own fundraising color, and he didn't know who had claimed red.

"Who's the bracelet for?" Judge asked. He stepped over a vine that ran across the hardpan like rope, his awkward spacesuit boot catching and almost toppling him over. He caught himself and braced against a tree trunk, catching his breath and taking a shallow drink of water. His bladder was already half empty, or half full. He still hadn't decided which type of person he was. Maybe when he turned fifty. If…

Arjun held up his hand, displaying the red band. "I wear it for my sister. She died of a rare blood cancer. It got her fast and left four kids without a mother."

"Damn. I'm sorry, Arjun. What happened to the children?" Judge looked away when he realized he may have insulted the ISRO Astrochemist. He might as well have asked "Why didn't you take the kids?"

Arjun smiled as he sensed Judge's unease. The man was good at that, his calm demeanor soothing. "They left India with their father who married a Canadian woman. Harriett. Wonderful lady."

"Why'd they leave India?" As soon as the words left his mouth, Judge wished he could have them back.

"India isn't the most understanding when it comes to things like second marriages. Especially when one is American and doesn't practice Hinduism."

Judge figured it was time to shut up, so he nodded and pushed his way through huge, yellow elephant ear leaves.

"Phew. What's that smell?" Judge said. Psycho was on point, and he couldn't see him through the thick underbrush. The scent of shit and rot pervaded the air, and Judge covered his nose with his hand.

"Damn. I've changed some diapers in my time, but that's some paint peeling shit right there," Psycho said from within the greenery.

The group stared at the hill of dinosaur scat like it was a pile of gold. Sticks stuck from the mound, red streaks of blood running through the brown waste like fudge through ice-cream, and leaves, nut shells, and balls of yellow and green grass topped the scat like fixings on a horrific sundae.

"Now that's a pile of shit," Psycho said.

"Must you always be so crude?" Seok said.

Psycho didn't answer. He was staring into the forest like a child who'd seen a unicorn. Judge followed his gaze but couldn't tell what his friend was staring at.

"Is that a palm tree?" Psycho said.

Judge shifted his gaze up, but didn't see a palm. He'd seen saw palmetto, and other palm-like trees, but no coconut trees.

"Yes!" Psycho wailed as he surged forward, traversing the pile of scat and slipping into the jungle. The party followed, and within minutes Psycho had his legs wrapped around a light brown tree trunk, and was inching his way up toward a cluster of green coconuts.

Judge and the others surrounded the tree, gazing up at Psycho as he pulled and jerked his way up the trunk. A roar pierced the day and Psycho paused, rotating his head as he searched the jungle for the source of the noise. The ground didn't shake, and Psycho continued his ascent.

When he reached the top, he pulled his knife and sliced free all the coconuts. There was eight of them, and Judge caught the first one. One by one they fell. Charlotte fumbled hers, and Arjun missed his altogether, but that didn't matter. The tough green exterior of the nuts was impossible to break open using brute force, but using the twelve-inch stainless steel blades to cut grooves into the coconuts, they could be opened in a way that allowed for the preservation of some of the nut's precious juice.

The party sat at ease for a time, cutting away the dense white coconut flesh, eating like they hadn't seen food in weeks. The berries they'd had the prior day were a distant memory, and Judge couldn't get the idea of bloody steak from his head. He leaned against the palm tree, thought of Brenda, how he used to fantasize about going to the Caribbean with her, sitting under a palm tree in a hammock, swimming in the crystal-clear water. Then he remembered the picture of Brenda and his brother on the mantle above their fireplace, and sickness and guilt washed over him, and he lost his appetite.

11

The trek through the jungle was more difficult than Judge had anticipated, and his toes and thighs tightened and cramped with each step. The afternoon rain had brought some relief, and he'd enjoyed standing in the downpour, sucking in water like a kid trying to catch a snowflake on the end of his tongue. The peace had been short-lived, and his feet hurt as they chafed in the wet EVA boots, and his jumpsuit wasn't drying beneath the shade of the tree canopy. He surveyed his troops, and only Psycho looked like he wasn't ready to fall on his face, so he called a halt for the day.

"Psycho, can you go find us a spot to sleep for the night? Take Arjun so he can get started making the fire as soon as possible. We'll hold here," Judge said.

"Will do," Psycho said.

When Psycho and Arjun were gone, Charlotte said, "Thank you. For stopping." She rubbed her neck.

"I'd really love to try and dry out my clothes. Put them in the sun... the light for a bit," Judge said.

"How's that going to work?" Tisa said.

The beautiful young M.D. had a point. "No clue," Judge said. He felt the faint twinge of arousal as he thought of Charlotte and Tisa walking around the jungle in their underwear. He rolled his shoulders and cracked his neck. OK, maybe a little more than a twinge.

Seok sat on a twisted vine that hung from a thick tree with white bark and small oval green leaves with yellow veins. His shoulders slumped, then he jumped, a thick black snake curling around the vine, tongue lashing out, dark obsidian eyes glassy and alert. "This place..." Seok folded his arms over his chest.

The four astronauts stood in silence as the minutes slipped away. Insects buzzed, birds chirped and sang, beasts brayed and shrieked, and an uncountable number of yelps, moos, clicks, growls, caws, and grumbles echoed through the habitat like crashing waves.

Waves. Judge shifted his position, putting his face in a beam of light that leaked through the tree canopy. The warmth felt good. He closed his eyes, trying to remember the ocean, the smell of the sea. Thoughts of the beach always led back to Brenda, and the time they'd spent walking the long shoreline by her house. He could almost hear the faint rumble of an outboard, the splash of jumping fish, and the crackle of seaweed tumbleweeds rolling across the sand.

"Judge. Judge, you in there?" It was Charlotte.

Psycho was back.

"I've got us a good spot about half a click from here. There's a little stream and the water looks much better than that last stink hole," Psycho said. "The vines are so thick in spots that if we do a little rearranging we should be able to create a decent roof. Arjun is already working on the fire."

Judge shook his head and clenched his fists. He tried to speak but his mouth was so dry he squeaked. He put up a finger and drained his water bladder. No need to conserve if they had a fresh supply. "Great," he said, his lips still dry. "Let's follow Psycho. Pick up dried twigs and sticks as you see them."

The companions trailed through the forest, picking up firewood as they went. There wasn't much, and that surprised Judge. With all the plants he thought there'd be more dead debris. He bent and picked up two huge, dried palm leaves with thick wooden spines. They would burn great—that thought made his head jerk back. What if there was an out-of-control fire in the habitat? They'd have to be extra careful. One small spark could destroy the entire biosphere. Something about that wasn't right. He shook his head. Not much about this place was.

Psycho was right, the campsite was perfect. Kudzu-like vines covered the lower boughs of a conifer, and when the astronauts were done cutting, pulling and readjusting vines, their shelter had walls and a double roof of vines and live evergreen branches.

Arjun had dug a small hole, and he pulled his handmade bow back and forth as he held a twisting stick in place. He stopped when the team arrived, sweat dripping down his forehead. Judge knelt next to the ISRO Astrochemist. Arjun's brown forehead crinkled, and he frowned.

"No luck?" Psycho said.

"My arms are rubber bands. You got anything left?" Arjun said.

Psycho harrumphed and took control of the bow. "Arjun, hold the stick."

Arjun did so, leaning over Psycho as he jerked the bow back and forth. Psycho slipped into second gear and pumped the bow so hard Arjun's body shook.

A thin tendril of smoke rose from a split branch covered in wood shavings and crushed palm leaves.

"Let's go, Psycho. Take it up a notch. Now. Do it!" Judge screamed. He knew this type of football motivational tactic was exactly what his friend loved.

Psycho skipped third and dropped the hammer, bracing his feet and pulling on the bow so fast Judge worried the bark twine might snap.

Smoke poured off the dried leaves and Seok rushed forward, putting dead leaves into the growing cloud of smoke.

"Don't smother it!" Arjun yelled, as he hung onto the stick, his arms shaking, head bouncing.

Flames licked the white smoke and Psycho stopped pulling the bow.

Arjun dropped to his knees, blowing on the flames. Smoke swirled and filled the shelter, but Arjun kept puffing like he was blowing up a balloon.

Fire rose from the pile of leaves and Arjun and Psycho stacked thick palm leaf stems in a tepee, and they high-fived as the small fire took root.

The smoke smelled good—like home, but that idea brought concern and worry. Would the smoke draw animals? "Psycho, help me. Take your spear and cut a hole in the roof above the fire." Judge used his knife-on-a-pole to start the process. With a garbage pail lid-sized hole in the roof the smoke was sucked and funneled upward like a chimney.

"Good thinking, mate," Tisa said.

With the fire popping and hissing, Charlotte and Seok speared the dinosaur meat with skewers they'd made from the veins of giant fan leaves. Each member of the party sat hunched around the tiny flame, holding out their stick of meat.

"Like an old hotdog roast," Tisa said.

Judge chuckled. "Any of you actually ever cooked a hotdog on a stick over an open fire?" Judge didn't experiment with food, wasn't well traveled—despite Mars—and he wasn't big on 'events', but he knew he had everyone beat on this one. When nobody answered, he continued, "I have. On the beach on Cape Cod. We used the same sticks to toast marshmallows."

"You live up that way as a boy?" Seok asked.

"No..." Judge paused and looked at the ground, and he felt Charlotte and Psycho's eyes boring into him. "No, my brother and his family."

Beep.

The lights went out with a suddenness that surprised Judge, even though he'd experienced the same thing the prior day. It was strange living indoors... but outdoors. Despite the thick vine walls, pale light surged through the shelter, the grayness finding every crack and crevasse. It was much brighter than the prior night.

"Let's go take a look," Judge said. He pushed through a curtain of vines and stood gazing toward the source of the light.

To the northeast a column of light rose from the tree canopy, its coldness radiating outward like a shard of ice.

"Not bad. We came much further than halfway," Seok said.

Judge nodded. "Psycho, I'm assuming you feel fine?"

"Tip-top."

"Then let's go eat and get some rest."

The companions shuffled back into their shelter, and Arjun fed the fire as the astronauts held their meat over the flame. Psycho was the first to eat his, and when he stabbed a second strip, nobody said anything. He was the workhorse.

Dinner done, the fire nothing but embers, Judge was whittling a thin piece of wood to use as a match to light the joint, when a loud scuffling and clicking brought the party's chatter to a halt.

Judge and Tisa pulled their M9s, and Psycho grabbed his gun as he slipped through the vines, keeping low, the stock of the laser rifle pinned to his shoulder. The clicking was replaced with a low growl that was on the verge of a roar, like a dog holding back a bark.

A branch snapped and Judge peered through the vines, trying to see in the gray corpse light. Two red eyes stared at him through the vegetation, and light glinted off a row of teeth.

"We got trou—" was all Judge got out before the beast rushed forward, pushing through the vines, jaws snapping.

Judge dodged and rolled, bringing up the M9 as the beast flew past him. He held his fire, his crewmates in his peripheral vision. A simple gunshot wound, even a graze, could be deadly given their current situation.

The beast surged forward on two thick legs, forcing its long snout through the vines.

Seok lashed out with his knife, but just missed slashing the creature as it disappeared into the vegetation.

"Looks like our friend from before," Judge said.

"A raptor," Charlotte said.

In the half-light shadows danced, and the vines that had been their shelter swayed and shifted like broken playground swings.

Tisa got low, panning her M9 around. Judge and the others stood back-to-back. Hoots and snarls, yawps and clicks, then a mighty roar silenced it all for one heartbeat.

That second lasted longer for Judge, his ears ringing, eyes squinting.

Screeeeeeecccchhhhhhh.

A raptor tore through the vines, using its snout to toss the thick creepers aside. Its head jerked like a bird's, its golf ball-sized eyes finding Charlotte, who was closest to the beast.

Tisa fired, and the bullet tore through the dinosaur and it screamed, blood spurting from the wound. The beast staggered as it lumbered through the vines, but didn't go down. Tisa fired again, but missed, and she screamed with rage as she chased after the creature.

"Nooooooooo," Seok yelled. He leapt to his feet and started after Tisa, then thought better of it and pulled up short, his eyes falling on Judge's Beretta M9.

The four remaining astronauts huddled together at the center of what was left of the shelter, Judge pulling for air though he'd done nothing to get winded.

A branch snapped, followed by growling and yipping as two creatures fought in the darkness.

The zap of the laser rifle made Judge smile, and Charlotte squeaked.

A dark nose nudged through the creepers, a snout, a long mouth sliding open, sharp white teeth. The creature lowered its head as it attacked, pushing through the vines as Judge swung the M9.

Charlotte screamed as the beast launched at her, but she brought up her knife and slashed the raptor across the face.

A second raptor with a deep red stripe between its eyes sliced through the creepers, bounding into Judge and knocking him from his feet. The M9 discharged, the bullet zipping through the tree canopy.

Seok moved in with his knife, and as Judge rolled, the JAXA astroengineer plunged his knife into the dinosaur's leg. It wailed and spasmed, but managed to fall through the underbrush and out of view.

Arjun kicked at the beast attacking Charlotte, screaming as he charged, knife held before him, rage filling his eyes.

Time slowed.

Judge brought up the Berretta, but Arjun was in his way. The man slashed and stabbed frantically with his knife, the creature's head bobbing, avoiding each strike. The beast bit at Arjun, its jaws snapping closed, just missing. The astrochemist danced and swayed, his eyes locked on the raptor's. They stared each other down in the small space, Charlotte and Seok putting their backs to what was left of the vine walls.

Judge took two fast steps to get a clear shot, aiming the M9 at the dinosaur's head, but his movement distracted Arjun and the man's eyes flicked toward Judge.

The raptor's head darted forward like a pigeon pecking a seed.

Arjun brought up his knife to defend himself, and for the briefest of instants, Judge thought the ISRO Astrochemist would fend off the beast.

The raptor was faster, and its head weaved like a snake, avoiding Arjun's thrust and clamping its jaws on his arm.

Arjun screamed and dropped his knife.

Another raptor tore through the shelter and Judge aimed the M9 and fired. The creature was knocked backward, and Judge fired again, and again, peppering the fallen beast with bullets until it lay still.

Arjun wailed as his arm was torn from his torso, blood spurting from the stump, gristle, fat, and muscle hanging like frayed meat. The beast threw its head back, tossing the arm deeper into its mouth. The sound of tearing flesh and cracking bone made Judge throw up the meat he'd eaten.

The raptor took hold of one of Arjun's legs and dragged him screaming from the shelter.

Judge dove after his crewmate, but it was too late. He looked at Charlotte and Seok, then at the ground.

Arjun's final wail made Judge's stomach burn with shame, anger, and fear.

12

Everything went still, all the beasts of the habitat together in that instant of danger. Shadows gyrated and fought in the pale dusk, the scent of scat and dirt filling Judge's nostrils. Heart thumping, he blinked rapidly, his neck aching, his stomach twisting and moaning. A trail of Arjun's blood led away through the dangling vines, a chunk of flesh and fat hanging from a broken tree branch. He turned to Charlotte and Seok, who stood rooted like trees, eyes wide as they stared at the thick strip of dark blood.

Judge rolled onto his back, drool running down his chin, and rubbed his eyes. Everything had just gotten very real. He'd lost a crew member. A first for him, and his stomach burned at the thought of telling the man's wife, if he ever got the opportunity.

"Are you alright?" Charlotte squeaked.

Judge nodded. "You two?"

Seok nodded.

Charlotte said, "Did that just happen?"

"Afraid so. We need to start being—"

"Judge! Judge!" It was Psycho.

Judge pushed to his feet, then hesitated. He wasn't prepared for what he was going to find. He was an astronaut, an ex-military man, but that all seemed long ago. He was a space bureaucrat now, an admin, and he had blood on his hands.

"Wait here," Judge said.

"I'm coming," said Seok.

"It's dangerous. I need to see what's happening. Hang here while I check things out."

Seok folded his arms over his chest and locked his dark eyes on Judge.

"Fine. Charlotte, you'll need to come also, I'm not leaving you here alone."

The three astronauts inched from their hiding place and didn't have to go far before they found Psycho and Tisa standing over what was left of Arjun's corpse.

In the pale pseudo moonlight the puddle of blood looked black, and Arjun's open eyes glistened. Both his arms were gone; a leg, and large pieces of his torso were missing. The area stank of death and rot.

The *womp womp* of the giant fan starting, then a gust of wind pushed through the jungle, rattling leaves. Oddly, no beasts stirred, and the insects and creatures of the night stayed silent.

A low drone reverberated over the forest, like millions of tiny servos sliding and pumping. A loud screeching and clicking filled the jungle, like roaches scuttling over the entire habitat. The tapping and scraping got louder, until it was the only sound. Leaves fell and tree branches snapped as something worked its way through the forest toward their position.

"I think we should take cover," Psycho said.

"I think you're right," Judge said.

The team backtracked the way they'd come, but they'd only gone ten paces when the scurrying and clicking got so loud Judge thought they were being overrun. He spun on his heel and brought up the M9, but held his fire.

Psycho stood before him, laser rifle trained on the empty forest. The others ran on, snapping tree branches and crunching leaves, marking their passage.

In the harsh white light Judge could hardly see the remains of Arjun's body splattered on the hardpan. The underbrush around the corpse gyrated and swayed, conifer branches snapping and bending.

Tiny metal half-spheres with many legs on the flat end scuttled from the jungle like a colony of ants. The things swarmed over Arjun's corpse as they shined in the half-light, their squeaking and clicking echoing through the jungle. Judge and Psycho watched transfixed as the tiny robots—there was no doubt that's what they were—covered Arjun's remains and the blood stain that marred the ground. The bots beeped and buzzed as they worked, scouring the hardpan and devouring what remained of the corpse.

"WTF?" Charlotte said. She and Seok had stopped running and backtracked.

The pace of the bots increased, and the buzz became a whine as the miniature robots cleaned the area. When no sign of Arjun's corpse remained, the bots froze, a red light appearing on the top of each device. A low hum spread over the habitat, and then the bots burst into motion like a swarm controlled by one brain, disappearing into the jungle as fast as they'd appeared. The rumble of their retreat faded as the robots tore through the forest, and one by one the instruments of the night symphony came back online and the biosphere filled with braying and yelping and buzzing.

"Arjun's remains were a foreign contaminant," said Seok.

Judge looked up into the dense tree canopy, then turned his gaze back on the spot where Arjun's body had been. The soil was a bit darker where the blood puddle had soaked the hardpan, but other than that, there was no sign the corpse had ever been there.

"Makes sense, doesn't it?" Psycho said.

Judge nodded and rubbed his palms together. His nerves jumped like he'd been hit with an electric shock, his brain struggling to process the fact that he'd never see Arjun again. Sorrow seeped through him, and he felt the urge to cry. Just drop to the ground on his ass and weep like a child, but his crewmates were holding themselves together, so he could too.

Seok said, "We've been trying to piece together how this biosphere could function, keep the ecosystem in balance over a long period of time. The bots adjust here and there, balancing the population, restricting and providing food and water. Removing unforeseen foreign contaminants."

Judge blurted, "That solves the fire problem. If a fire ever got too big or out of control, the sweeper bots would come and take care of it. We'll need to be careful."

"Sweeper bots?" Charlotte said. "I was thinking scrubble-bubbles."

"Whatever the hell the things were, they paid us no mind," Tisa said. Her tears had left streaks of dirt down her brown face, and her eyes were red and puffy.

"That is odd," Seok said.

"How so?" Psycho asked.

"It's just..." Seok paused as he searched for the words, his eyes flicking to where Arjun's corpse had been. "Like I said before. This place must have a brain. Something that controls the sweeper bots, water flow, etc..."

"So why's it ignoring us?" Charlotte said.

Seok nodded.

"Maybe we haven't knocked things out of balance enough yet?" Judge said. That was hard to believe. They'd drilled through the front door for shit's sake. But had that affected the habitat? Not that he could tell.

"They didn't come after the dead raptor in the shelter," Seok said.

"Things must die in here all the time. Their bodies go back to the land and all that," Judge said.

"But not humans," Tisa said, her voice a low whisper.

With a dead raptor bleeding out in the remains of their shelter, the party had no place to go.

"Every hungry animal in here is gonna be here when the scent of blood gets around," Psycho said.

"Let's go find a place to hide for the night," Judge said.

Psycho led, and the party threaded through the dark forest, the pale evening night light unsettling. They didn't find a comfortable sheltered conifer, but Psycho did find a depression in the land with a thick patch of pricker bushes. The crewmates cut their way in, being careful to replace the vines as they passed.

Once in the center of the large bush, the team used their knives to carve out a space to sleep.

"I'll take first watch," Judge said. There was no way he'd be able to sleep with his nerves doing summersaults.

Psycho eyed him, but his friend knew him well and didn't protest. Psycho lay flat with his head on his hands, and was asleep in moments. For the rest of the crew, sleep didn't come, and Judge watched his companions shift and fidget until the beep of morning light.

The LED-like light wasn't the sun, but it was better than the death-dusk of night. Judge found a bare patch in the jungle and closed his eyes, letting the light rejuvenate him. His stomach growled. "How much cooked meat do we have left?" he asked.

"Half a slice each," Charlotte said. "And one extra half," she added, her tone subdued.

Arjun's share. Judge's chest hurt when he thought of his lost crewmate, and he figured it was one of those wounds that would never heal, though he hoped it lessened with time. Thoughts of the ISRO Astrochemist made his insides go cold. They'd had no ceremony. Paid no respects. Said no words of prayer. Judge knew Arjun practiced Hinduism, but he had no idea how strictly he followed the tenants of his religion.

Seok scrunched his brow and pressed his lips together.

Charlotte asked, "You guys thinking of Arjun?"

Judge and Seok nodded, but said nothing.

"Should we do something? Say something?" she asked as she passed around the meat.

Nobody answered as they ate their strips of beef and drank their water.

Judge turned Charlotte's question over in his mind, searching for some middle ground, some compromise that would make him feel like he wasn't abandoning Arjun.

Bird song and buzzing insects filled the jungle with static.

After a long pause, Judge said, "I think we need to focus on getting out of here. There'll be plenty of time to mourn the dead after we take care of the living."

Psycho, Tisa and Charlotte wagged their heads.

Seok didn't. "Is there no ritual of his people? I know we don't have a body, so whatever sacraments were required aren't possible, but perhaps a prayer?"

Judge sighed. He thought religion was the biggest load of bullshit of all-time, but as he got older, and saw more strange things, it became harder and harder to chalk up every illogical occurrence as happenstance. Sometimes there appeared to be reason in the chaos, but that's what always tripped him up. Why would an all-powerful god promote—no, prefer to function—in chaos? He'd learned over the years that he had to put all those questions behind. If believing in a space fairy brought someone peace, he said let them have it. "Do you know any Hindu prayers?" he said.

Seok nodded, and said, "Something close, at least." He put out his hands, palms up. Then in a clear voice, as if preaching to a congregation, he recited, "Lead me from the unreal to the real, from darkness to light and from death to immortality or deathlessness."

When he finished, the group stood in silence, the jungle chorus going full tilt.

"Let's go," Psycho said as he led the party back into the dense underbrush.

It was slow going, and they hadn't gone far when they reached a clearing with tall grass. Large cow-like beasts with long curved horns and short tails grazed like cattle in the field, and if they knew the astronauts were there, they didn't let on. Two calves were partly hidden in the grass, and smaller animals darted in and out of the jungle, bolting into the field as if playing a game.

"We have to go around, right? The grass is tall, and we might sneak by unseen, but who knows what's in there. If we—"

The ground trembled and Psycho raised a fist and brought the team to a halt.

To the west a thin path trailed away into the jungle, and a T-rex with red stripes inched its way toward the clearing.

The grazing dinosaurs paused, their heads jerking toward the T-rex.

Out on the path the giant lizard froze, lowering its head and sniffing the ground.

The cow-like beasts didn't move. They were still as stone.

The T-rex reared back and roared, spittle spraying from its tooth-filled maw. It scratched the ground with its right claw, spoiling to run, but still the beasts in the field didn't move.

Psycho inched back into the jungle, staying low, the stock of the laser rifle at his shoulder. Judge followed, as did the others, and the five remaining adventurers from Gale Base Alpha hid behind trees.

The T-rex reached the clearing, red stripes standing out against the beast's black leathery hide. The tyrannosaurus rex turned its head, doorknob-sized eyes rotating as they searched the field.

The dino-cows hadn't moved, but as it is with children of all species, the younglings just couldn't stay still. One of the calves ran forward and huddled against its parent, and the T-rex's head jerked toward the motion. The massive lizard roared, the ground trembling as it came forward, short arms dangling from its torso. The dinosaur brought its head to the ground as it ran. It huffed and growled as its mouth slid open, revealing foot-long teeth.

That was the grazing dinosaurs' cue. The animals bolted like a herd of deer that's seen a mountain lion stalking them. The cow-like beasts bounded through the grass and disappeared into the jungle on the opposite side of the clearing.

With a roar, the T-rex followed.

The party rested, catching their breath, drinking the last of their water, and listening to their screaming stomachs, then set off again.

They hid under thick tree boughs when the afternoon rain came—Judge's underwear was finally dry—and afterward they made a last push for the center of the habitat. What they'd do once they got there, he didn't know, but he had to get there. That goal had given the team purpose. Without it, things would fray. Thinking of the future made his head hurt, but he was the leader and he had to face facts. He and his crew might be trapped in the biosphere for a long time.

"We're here," Psycho said.

They broke free of the forest and a dome made of dark glass or metal sat at the center of a clearing. The party's reflection stared back at them across a strip of hardpan separating the dome from the jungle.

A screech echoed through the habitat, and as Judge gazed at his reflection, a dark spot grew in the sky above the party.

13

The pterodactyl's reflection grew, and Judge spun as he drew his Berretta. The dragon-like beast was enormous, its massive wings folded back as it dove toward the party. It screeched, its long beak opening, teeth glinting.

"Get under cover," Psycho yelled.

Like herding cattle, Judge ran for the tree line, arms stretched out as he pushed and guided Seok and Charlotte toward the forest.

The beast screamed again, a sharp cry that sounded like fingernails being pulled across a blackboard.

Judge's awkward spacesuit boots caught on a root and he tripped, flying through the forest, and smashing headlong into a tree. He crumbled to the ground, pain shooting down his spine. Charlotte was next to him, then Tisa.

The pterodactyl banked left, making a wide circle, its shadow racing over the shining dome. The beast flapped its sail-like wings, the leathery skin snapping and cracking. Judge watched the creature's reflection as it was magnified on the dome. Jet-black eyes were set between a tall dorsal fin-like crest on the top of the beast's skull, and the eyes panned left and right, searching the forest as the dragon spiraled downward.

"I don't think it can see us," Psycho said.

Judge's head pounded, and he sat up. Blood trickled down his forehead into his eye and Tisa gasped.

"I'm ok," Judge said, rubbing the blood away with the back of his hand.

Charlotte rushed to his side, spit on her fingers, and rubbed the wound clean. She frowned, but said nothing.

No words were needed. Even a small cut could become infected, and without medical supplies or drugs, that could prove deadly. Next time it rained he'd make a little mud to cover the wound.

The great beast circled, then peeled off, dropping low and disappearing as it flew just above the tree canopy.

The party waited, the jungle song rising, blood dripping down Judge's face.

Psycho stepped out from behind a tree trunk and walked out onto the patch of hardpan that separated the forest from the dome. He gazed around, rifle stock at his shoulder. Then he let the gun drop to his side and waved the group forward.

The dome had no doors, windows, or joints of any kind. It was smooth like dark tinted glass, but hard like metal. There were no markings etched into its surface, nor were there any keypads, controls or apertures. The design aesthetic made sense to Judge. The dome looked like a larger version of the sweeper bots. With his mind already racing, he started formulating a plan to dig under the dome.

Nothing grew from the hardpan all around the dome, and jungle encroached to the strip of dirt on all sides. The party examined every inch of the dome, pounded on it, tried to climb the curved slippery sides to the top, but nothing they did gave them any clues that might help the team get inside the structure.

The party gathered under a huge hardwood tree at the edge of the jungle, their reflections staring back at them across the strip of hardpan, the dome's surface like a mirror.

Psycho bounced on his feet. "We came all this way for nothing."

Seok said, "We just arrived. Perhaps given some time we could—"

"What? Speak Friend and Enter?" Psycho mocked. "We've got no tools, no rocks to hammer the thing with, and unless a door materializes out of nowhere, I don't think we're getting inside."

Seok's eyes flicked to the laser rifle.

Psycho held the weapon up. "This might destroy whatever's inside. The brain. Would you shoot your brain with a laser rifle if you wanted it to function?"

"Taking the system down might open the airlock door," Tisa said.

Judge hadn't thought of that, and with good reason. Before he could explain why that was a bad idea, Seok said, "Psycho is correct. Taking the system down might be a very bad idea. What if life-support goes down and air stops flowing? I realize it's difficult to think of us being on Mars with all the plants and trees around, but make no mistake. We're on Mars and the environment is hostile, the air outside unbreathable."

Seok's speech made Psycho stop bouncing like a kid who's had too much sugar.

"Let's split into groups of two and search the surrounding area. Some food and water would be nice. And be silent. We don't want to alert any of the local inhabitants to our presence."

As if in answer to Judge's orders a beast roared from deep in the jungle, and somewhere above, the pterodactyl cawed.

Charlotte practically ran to Psycho's side, and Seok went with Tisa, so that left Judge alone.

"Why don't you come with us?" Charlotte said.

Judge needed five minutes alone to think, to try and wrap his noodle around the last twenty-four hours, but walking around the habitat by himself wasn't smart. Being alone, period, wasn't smart.

"Yeah, OK," Judge said.

Psycho rocked back.

Judge laughed. "What?"

"Look at you just agreeing and taking suggestions. No ball-busting questions."

"I love you, mate, but I'm beyond ball-busting at this point."

Psycho frowned.

"Can we shift the discussion from balls, please?" Charlotte said, but she was smiling. The majority of the astronauts on Mars were men, and there were no delicate flowers among the females. That didn't mean being a gentleman wasn't appreciated, and Judge tried to tone down his foul language, especially when females were around. Psycho's situation made it more important that proper language be used at all times so crewmembers didn't feel uncomfortable or harassed.

"That's on me. Very sorry," Judge said.

Psycho looked at the ground. "Actually, it's on me. Sorry, Charlotte."

Charlotte's eyes went wide and she looked at Psycho, her chin jutting out.

Psycho shrugged.

Charlotte looked at Judge and threw up her hands. "Are you kidding me?" She laughed. "Psycho, I was just grinding your stones. No worries. I..." Her voice faltered and her head tilted to the side.

Judge sighed.

"This about those rumors I heard?" she said.

Psycho blushed, but said nothing.

"Whatever," Charlotte said.

The trio found a tree with almond-type nuts hanging in clusters beneath branches with spreading crowns of deep green, six-fingered leaves. The black nuts were hard as stones, but the trio cracked them open using their boots. They ate a few each and collected a bunch more before heading back to the dome.

Seok and Tisa hadn't found water, but they did procure three coconuts and if they were careful there'd be coconut water to be had from therein.

"Do you want me to hunt? Arjun can get a fire go... Someone can get a fire going," Psycho said.

"Not tonight... not here. It's almost lights out and I don't want the sweeper bots showing up. Let's find a place to hunker down until morning light," Judge said. "I want some time to think about this thing." Judge motioned toward the dome. "Give Seok time, all of us."

Psycho nodded, his gaze shifting back to the large hardwood tree the companions had stood under earlier. "We'll need to post guards, but under that tree there looks fine."

The group got as comfortable as they could beneath the spreading boughs of the huge tree, nestling between its raised roots where they couldn't be seen by prying eyes. When the beep of nightfall arrived, the companions were eating nuts, sipping water, and drinking the coconuts' milky white liquid and eating their white flesh.

When the dome glowed like a floodlight bulb, Judge jumped to his feet. "Ouch," he yelled as he stepped on a root with his bare foot. He'd been enjoying a few moments without the clunky, hot spacesuit boots on his feet.

The jungle filled with pale light as a white pillar rose from the dome into the sky, illuminating everything within a kilometer. Shadows danced beneath the tree canopy, but the death light filled every other space like water flooded across hardpan.

Judge pulled his arm across his face, the harsh artificial light hurting his eyes. "Well, that's one question answered."

"And that answer changes things dramatically," Seok said.

"Someone care to fill us normal people in?" Tisa said.

"We originally believed the pillar of light emanated from above. If the dome is a lightbulb of a kind, that changes what could be in it," Seok said.

Judge's heart sank, and when he glanced at Charlotte, he saw she felt the same.

"Let's not jump to conclusions, though," Seok said.

Psycho turned away from the pillar of light. "Can we move to the other side of the tree, at least? Even I can't sleep with this candle lit."

The companions got to their feet and found new spots on the opposite side of the thick tree trunk in the shadows. Psycho took first watch, and he climbed into the massive tree, rifle over his shoulder, and sat on a branch, staring down at the party.

When they were settled in and Tisa's faint snoring whispered through the forest, Charlotte asked, "Seok, what do you make of the dinosaurs having red stripes?"

"Yes. Very peculiar. As you know, the dust, sand and stones on Mars get their red color from rusted minerals that formed millions of years ago and have been baking under the sun's ultraviolet rays. My guess is Mars water and soil are used to maintain this habitat. An example would be using the ice on Mars as the building block of water and moisture within the biosphere. The beasts drink this mineral rich water, then their skin cooks under this—" Seok raised a fist at the pillar of light. "Then they're exposed to artificial light during the day and at night. Given all the plants, we must assume the artificial light mimics the sun. With an odd concentration of minerals and superoxides in the soil and water, and thus in the beasts' skin, the artificial sunlight brought out the red stripes like it does when it bakes the Martian sand. Most likely this happened over hundreds of generations as the creatures in the biosphere evolved in their limited environment."

"Given it some thought, ya?" Tisa said.

"Since I saw the big boy at the airlock door."

"What now?" Psycho said.

"We take turns sleeping, and when the sun comes up, we figure out what we've missed," Judge said.

Psycho got a few winks, but the rest of the crew took their shifts at guard post and couldn't find sleep. Judge listened to his companions fidget, toss and turn, their prone forms hidden within the shadow of the massive tree.

When his watch was done, Judge lay still on the hardpan. He knew that if he concentrated on not moving, put all thought and energy toward staying completely still, he would fall asleep within fifteen minutes, but laying frozen for fifteen minutes was hard enough in his cot back on Gale Base Alpha, when nothing was crawling, slithering, or jumping on his bed pillow.

They were all exhausted the next day, and a renewed inspection of the dome revealed nothing new. Using coconut shells as shovels, the team dug a trench next to the dome, trying to get under it.

The black glass curved inward the deeper the party dug. The dome looked to be a half-buried sphere.

"No way we're getting under it," said Psycho. He tossed his coconut shovel into the forest, and birds sprayed from the jungle canopy.

"We're all in agreement shooting the dome with an M9 or the laser rifle is a mistake?" Judge said.

Nobody spoke.

"Bullshit. Speak now or—"

"A bullet wouldn't do much, I wouldn't think," Tisa said.

"And you're…" Psycho sighed, putting on a show. "You're right. We can't predict what the laser will do."

"So we're giving up?" Charlotte said. She was sitting just within the tree break cracking nuts with her boots.

To that, nobody had a response. The crew collected more coconuts and found a nasty puddle with claw prints and no dead creatures around it. They drank the foul water slowly, its thick earthy taste bitter and rank. The afternoon rains didn't come, and when the pillar of light shot into the sky like a camera flash, and Judge and company were hunkered down back at camp, raised tree roots around them, Judge allowed a small fire. Not because they needed it—they had no meat to cook and it didn't get very cold—but because it gave Psycho and Seok something to do, and he thought they all needed the comfort and familiar smell. He didn't think a small flame would bring the bots, but if it did, they'd stomp it out and hide.

Using the bow Arjun had constructed, and that Seok had dutifully salvaged from the wreckage of their vine cottage, Psycho went to work and soon a small fire crackled and popped between the astronauts, and thick white smoke rose to the sky. Seok's knife had become the axe, its blade dull but still able to split tree branches.

"Charlotte, you asked this afternoon if we were giving up," Judge said.

Psycho stopped feeding the fire, Seok looked up from his feet, which he was rubbing, and Tisa turned and brazenly stared at him. Charlotte didn't look up.

"The answer is I don't know at this point. I see no viable way to get inside the dome, and we don't even know for sure there's anything in there that will help us get out of here. It might be nothing more than a lightbulb."

Nobody spoke as the night symphony buzzed, clicked, brayed, and cawed.

"So what do we do now?" Charlotte asked as she looked up.

"We follow the water," Judge said.

14

Judge watched his crew's reflections in the dome as they receded into the jungle, Psycho on point. He felt eyes watching him as he turned and crossed the strip of hardpan, heading for the forest. He rolled his shoulders and looked back, but there was nothing there except his reflection staring back at him. The salt and pepper stubble he worked hard to make look casual was a thick tangle of tight curls, his bowl cut wild, wisps of gray hair hanging over his forehead. His blue NASA jumpsuit was dirty and torn, and the bulky spacesuit boots looked comical.

The jungle chorus was subdued, the creatures of the night giving way to the beasts of the day. Worry gnawed at Judge, the feeling that the longer they were trapped, the harder it would be to escape. His stomach gurgled and whined, and he drank the last of his water as he plunged into the underbrush.

The five astronauts left the dome in their rearview as daylight came on like a Timex, daggers of light knifing through the tree canopy. Creepers hung like tangled hair, and a thick web blocked the party's way. Spiders with footlong black jointed legs and yellow bodies clung to the web, several wriggling lumps of prey in white cocoons hanging from thick strands.

Judge shuddered. He could take giant reptiles trying to eat him, but spiders weren't his thing. They'd decided to head due west, toward where Judge and Psycho estimated the waterfall poured into the habitat. Judge believed there had to be an opening in the wall there, and the theory was that might be a good spot to gain access to the biosphere's underbelly.

The jungle thinned and opened into a clearing, creepers and weeds covering the area, a large pile of leaves at the small field's center. Psycho paused and held up a hand. The party stopped just inside the tree break, and Psycho put the stock of his rifle to a shoulder as he eased out from under the cover of the forest. Large, pointy, three-toed footprints circled the pile of leaves, and Psycho's eyes constantly shifted from the leaves to the jungle. He got low, probing the pile with the laser rifle. When nothing happened, he stood, and let the gun fall to his side.

As Judge and company joined him, Psycho said, "What the hell do you make of this?"

Judge hiked his shoulders, and Charlotte sat on the hardpan, taking a pull from her water bladder. Tisa moved in alongside Psycho, rubbing her chin.

Seok put his hands on his hips. "I think I might know what this is," he said.

Judge lifted his eyebrows and spread his hands in a "well, tell us then" gesture.

Seok ran a hand over his short-cropped hair and went to the pile. It reeked of rotting vegetation and all the leaves had turned a deep shade of brown. If it wasn't for their coarse texture, the pile could have been mistaken for dinosaur scat. Seok picked up a stick and stirred the leaves, probing for anything hidden within.

"Careful," Tisa said. "There could be giant ants, snakes, an entire animal kingdom hiding under there and stirring the pile might not be the smartest thing."

Seok paused and looked at Tisa. Then he shrugged and resumed prodding. The stick knocked on something hollow and he cleared away leaves.

Nine eggs the size of miniature footballs were mounded within the nest. They were deep purple with streaks of blood red and black, and had coarse shells that looked like stone. Seok picked one up, turning it in his hands and holding it up to the light. "It's warm," he said, and as the artificial sunlight shone through the egg, a baby dinosaur could be seen therein.

Seok smiled and handed the egg to Judge, who caressed it. Then Judge remembered where he was, and he put the egg back on the pile and backed away. Where there were eggs, there were mommies, and judging by the size of the eggs, mommy and daddy were big.

"We need to move along," Seok said, reading Judge's mind.

"Um, too late," Charlotte said.

A Brontosaurus poked its bean-like head through the ferns, its long neck extending outward over the clearing, its eyes finding the party standing around its nest. The beast's mouth slid open and it huffed and squeaked as it pushed from the jungle, four thick legs supporting a huge torso, its massive tail slapping trees as it passed.

Mommy.

Judge and crew stayed still, making no erratic moves. The dinosaur shrieked, the piggish howl ending in a high-pitched wail that sounded like a horse whinnying. The beast jerked its head up and down, stomping its right foot as if preparing to charge. It roared again, inched forward, and threw its head in the air and snorted. Judge knew these big animals were plant eaters—at least that's what the bigheads thought—but all animals became aggressive when their offspring were threatened.

To Judge's left, the trees got thicker, and the massive dinosaur wouldn't be able to fit through the filter of tree trunks. "Let's move," Judge yelled as he bolted, heading for a thick section of tall, full conifers. Psycho and the others followed, their pounding feet music to Judge's ears as he ran.

The Brontosaurus hesitated, stomping its three-toed claws and kicking up dust. The party was in the trees before the dinosaur gave chase, and a cacophony of cracking wood and exploding earth passed over the forest like a gust of wind as the creature slammed into the woods.

Judge looked back past his crew and saw the Brontosaurus' head probing the jungle, its massive torso stuck between two thick tree trunks. The beast churned forward like a machine, digging into the wood and tearing up the ground. The conifers bent and swayed, but didn't break.

A second Brontosaurus head blocked Judge's way, this one dark red with streaks of black. It was smaller than mommy, but had a long scar running down the side of its serpentine neck.

Daddy.

Judge juked right into a stand of saw palmetto, fronds lashing his face and arms, causing small paper cut-like gashes that leaked blood. The thunder of the flailing Brontosaurus faded, and the ferns thinned as Judge ran blindly through the underbrush.

The forest opened onto a large animal trail. Claw prints large and small marked the packed dirt, and several animals paused in their journeys as Judge and crew inched out onto the natural thoroughfare.

There was no sign of the Brontosaurus parents.

One by one the rest of the team stumbled onto the path and joined Judge.

Seok said, "Dad probably went to see what mommy's screaming about."

"We put the egg back," Tisa said.

Seok nodded. "Those are plant eaters. When they see their eggs are undamaged, they'll leave us be."

"Let's get off the path," Psycho said.

The party slipped back into the forest and followed the path from within the trees where it was safer. The last thing Judge wanted to do was draw attention.

"Seok, you seem to know a lot about dinosaurs. How is that? You're an engineer," Charlotte asked.

The JAXA astronaut chuckled as he ducked under a tree branch. "I've got two boys, and I studied a little paleontology in college. But it was my boys really. All the movies, books. Both of them loved Godzilla, so when I bought them books about real Godzillas, they dove right in."

"I didn't know you had children," Tisa said.

Seok sighed. "Yes, they're grown now and have families of their own."

"And your wife?" Psycho asked.

Seok's eyes shifted to the ground, and he said, "She passed seven years ago."

Psycho stopped walking and Judge bumped into him. "I... I'm sorry, Seok. I didn't know." Psycho shook his head. "Always putting my foot in it."

"No, its fine, really," Seok said.

"How'd she die?" Judge asked. He'd known Seok for years, spent months on the ship traveling to Mars, but they'd never spoken about the man's family.

"She was… murdered."

Charlotte gasped.

"Shit, I'm sorry, I mean, I shouldn't have asked. I'm such an idiot," Judge said.

"No, I said it was OK and I meant it. It's been a long time, though it still feels like yesterday, but it's good to talk about it sometimes."

A thick stand of conifers clogged the jungle, and the team paused as Psycho hacked through it with his knife-spear, bugs and small birds spraying from the vegetation.

"My boys were at school and I was away at a conference. The police think the murderers knew she was alone because my appearance was public knowledge, and everyone in town knew my boys were off at school. They broke into the house and shot her when she protested. Nobody…" Seok wiped a tear from his eye, "I didn't know for three days. I was so wrapped up in my conference, I didn't check in, and when I did…" He ran the back of his hand across his face and sniffled. "I called a neighbor, and she found her in the living room in a dried pool of her own blood."

"That's beyond horrible. Did they catch who did it?" Tisa asked, anger in her voice.

Seok shook his head no.

"That why you came to Mars?" Psycho said.

Seok looked away and didn't respond. Apparently, Judge wasn't the only one who'd run away to Mars.

The group trudged on, fighting through the underbrush along the path, staying hidden, tree branches whipping them, prickers poking skin and evergreen leaves scratching faces. Judge needed a hot shower, not only to get the dirt off, but to make him feel human. The team needed to do something normal, something to get their minds off how screwed they were.

The forest along the trail thinned as the path widened, and they lost their cover. A rumble echoed beneath the buzz of insects, like cars on a highway.

"That what I think it is?" Psycho said.

"Sounds like water flowing to me. Which way?" Tisa said.

Judge eased out onto the path, trying to see the waterfall, but all he saw was the greenery of the forest and the metal wall shining in the distance.

A roar pierced the day, and the ground trembled.

"That didn't take long," Tisa said.

The ground shook, and the insects went still, but a persistent buzz filled the habitat.

A gurgle, stomping feet, then leaves falling as a narrow head poked from the tree canopy to the south. The beast was yellow with red stripes, its small oval eyes dark red. Sail-like sheets of skin supported by teeth-like bones ran down the dinosaur's back, and as it stepped from the forest, it threw its head back and roared.

Judge pulled his M9, spinning on his toes, swinging the gun upward.

Psycho was faster, but he didn't shoot. His attention shifted from the massive beast stomping across the clearing to a drone that zipped from the forest.

The creature roared, bringing its head low to the ground, opening its mouth and revealing large white teeth covered in blood.

Psycho jerked the laser gun and fired at the drone as it dove for him, four small rotors spinning on each corner of the drone's black square fuselage. A clear dome sat atop the drone's housing, and a camera lens scoped in and out as the flying robot dipped and dodged Psycho's laser blasts.

Judge fired at the dinosaur, bullets ripping through the tent-like scales that ran down its back. The beast roared as it threw back its head, but it didn't stop coming. The ground shook as the beast came on, towering over the clearing. It stood twenty feet tall, and looked sixty feet long from its tooth-filled mouth to the tip of its long, powerful tail. Judge guessed the creature was a Spinosaurus. It was bigger than the T-rex they'd seen.

Psycho gave up trying to hit the drone and swung the rifle back toward the giant lizard. He sighted and fired, three fast bursts. Two of the three missed, but the third bolt struck home. The charge burned a hole through the beast's right leg, muscle and gristle leaking from the charred wound. The beast stumbled, the wounded leg buckling, but it managed to stay upright.

Judge saw Seok and Charlotte running for the cover of the jungle in his peripheral vision, and he heard the pop and crack of Tisa's M9 as she fired at the beast.

The drone stopped above Judge's head, its electronic eye flashing as it watched him. Judge brought up his pistol, sighted, then paused, gazing at the drone as it hovered above him.

The zap of the laser rifle snapped him from his reverie, and Judge fired at the drone.

The flying bot tilted and dipped, easily avoiding the bullet and laser blast. Then the drone's rotors cycled up and the bot tore off, buzzing past the Spinosaurus as it struggled to keep its footing. Thin arms dangled uselessly from the creature's torso, and its eyes bulged from its long narrow head.

"Take it down!" Judge yelled.

The beast stumbled forward, shrieking in pain, dark blood leaking from the burn wound on its thigh.

Psycho dropped to one knee and brought the rifle to his shoulder.

The jungle cheered the spino on, a great chirping and wailing and roaring of support that threatened to make Judge's ears bleed.

Psycho cracked his neck, sighted, and opened up with the laser rifle, burst after burst peppering the dinosaur and knocking it backward. The ground shook as the massive beast hit the hardpan in a tangle, thick clouds of dust and dirt lifting from the ground.

15

A loud sigh pushed over the field as the last of the air left the giant dinosaur's lungs, and the clouds of dirt and dust cleared away. The dead beast seemed to cave-in on itself, skin falling over ribs, its long purple-black tongue lolling between sharp teeth, glassy eyes staring at the sheet of white light above. The Spinosaurus spasmed one last time, and Judge jumped as a plume of dust rushed toward him. He covered his mouth and eyes as he was engulfed, the scent of rot and scat filling the habitat.

Above, the drone buzzed as it turned in a wide arc, its rotors clawing at the air. It steadied itself and hovered, light glinting off a lens as the robot surveyed the carnage. Everything was still for a heartbeat, and only the whine of the drone could be heard. The craft's rotors cycled up, and the drone took off over the trees.

Psycho got to his feet and tentatively inched forward, the powerful beast nothing more than a mound of skin, bone and slack muscle. Jungle noise blared as the creatures of the biosphere went about their day. No sweeper bots swarmed the scene. Psycho poked the beast on the snout with the laser rifle, but the creature didn't move.

Judge couldn't bring himself to go near the thing. His brain told him the creature was dead, but the dark eyes, two-foot teeth, curved razor-sharp talons, and thick, muscled tail all told Judge the dinosaur was waiting to strike.

The spino stayed still, and as Psycho examined the beast, some of Judge's apprehension and fear drained away.

"Looks like we've got a bit of meat, anyhow," Psycho said. He probed the corpse's back and side with his knife-spear. "The skin is tough like leather," he said.

"And it stinks," Tisa said. She and the others had emerged from their hiding spots.

A roar in the distance reminded Judge the dead creature before him was one of many, and a tingle ran down his spine, a zap telling his body it was time to get a move on. Judge said, "Gather some big leaves while Psycho and I carve off some meat." When nobody moved, he said, "Hurry! The sweeper bots might show up." He didn't really think they would, but he didn't know. Psycho had killed another dinosaur, and that may have thrown the biosphere's delicate balance out of whack.

As the team scrambled into the jungle, Psycho said, "That was close, boss. We've got to be more careful."

Judge didn't know what unnerved him more; that Psycho was preaching caution or that it had taken several shots from the rifle to bring the beast down. He nodded and put a hand on Psycho's arm. The man flinched slightly under his touch, then smiled. Placing a hand on a shoulder, or patting a back, was how Judge said you were important to him. Anyone who knew him well knew that. "Thanks for everything these last couple of days. We'd all be dead if not for you."

"Babe, I couldn't find the door, couldn't even see the floor," Psycho sang, and when Judge didn't join in, he continued, "I'd be sad and blue, if not for you."

Judge shrugged.

"Bob Dylan?"

Judge stared at Psycho, eyes wide. He wasn't a big music fan.

"You're hopeless," Psycho said.

"You're not the first to say that," Judge said.

His friend looked at the hardpan and stopped carving strips of meat off the fallen Spinosaurus. "Brenda?" he said.

Judge nodded. Psycho was the only one on Mars that knew the whole story. He hadn't even told Charlotte all of it, and they were as close as two people could get on Mars.

Turning his attention back to his work, Psycho said, "Kind of sad in a way, isn't it?"

"What's that?"

"Carving this amazing creature up like it's a turkey," Psycho said.

Judge walked around the Spinosaurus corpse, marveling at the beast's size. He paused before the open mouth. One bite was all it would have taken, and he would have been dino chow. "It certainly is incredible, and yeah, I suppose you're right. It's a shame you had to kill it. Someone... or something, went through so much trouble so it could live."

"Any thoughts on all that?"

"None that I'm comfortable saying aloud."

Psycho chuckled and looked over his shoulder as the others broke free of the jungle carrying stacks of large elephant ear leaves. Judge and Seok wrapped the meat as Psycho finished carving, and when they were done, Judge estimated they had five pounds of good meat.

"Now all we need to do is refill our water bladders," Charlotte said.

"Let's get on with it then," Judge said.

The five astronauts trekked for several hours, avoiding the larger creatures of the habitat. Judge was thankful most of the larger beasts moved like kids on the first day of school, so the company usually had ample time to avoid the creatures. The big lizards didn't appear very smart or perceptive. Psycho led, and the companions made good time as they threaded through the thick underbrush.

Judge estimated it was a couple of hours before afternoon rain, when the party entered a glade of palm trees, the ground bare and unmarred by undergrowth.

"What happened here? Looks like someone sprayed a can of weed-b-gone," Charlotte said.

Giant yellow ants trundled over the hardpan, some carrying pieces of leaves and other food.

"They look like lemon ants. Couldn't be, though," Seok said. He cocked his head, "Could it?"

"What's that got to do with there being no undergrowth?" Tisa asked.

"If they're lemon ants, or anything like them, the ants have a symbiotic relationship with the trees. They protect the trees and weed the area by biting off the stems of any new growth and spraying competing plants with formic acid," Seok said. "I've seen pictures of real lemon ants, and these look pretty close."

"Dang," Tisa said.

"In the Amazon, spots like this are called a Devil's Garden, and usually the type of tree plays a part as well," Seok said.

A low growl echoed through the jungle, followed by breaking branches. Leaves fell as a miniature dragon landed on a branch above, its beady black eyes staring down at the party like they had no business being there.

Tisa drew her M9, slowly raising the gun and sighting the creature.

The beast opened its long, curved beak, pin-like teeth standing out against pink gums. The creature gripped the tree branch it sat on with hand-like claws that ended in red talons, and as the pterosaur shifted its weight, the branch bent and swayed.

"Hold your fire," Judge said. "We're not looking to draw more attention to ourselves."

Tisa lowered her gun and Psycho pushed on, threading through the vegetation, tree trunks, bushes, huge ferns, and weeds clogging the forest.

Judge sneezed and wiped his nose, dirt and snot making a thick mud that Judge rubbed on some of his open wounds as he walked.

Beep.

The party had little time to prepare before the afternoon rain came, but it didn't matter. Judge's mouth was so dry the need for water outweighed the need to keep his jumpsuit dry, so he stripped off his boots, and threw them under a conifer. He tore a big leaf off a weed with purple spiked flowers, and found a gap in the tree canopy. He rolled the end of the giant leaf and made a funnel, turning the wide end upward to catch the rain and putting the narrow end in his mouth.

Seeing Judge, the rest of the party did the same, and before the rain ended, the companions had all drank and filled the water bladders they'd cut from their spacesuits.

"Sure could go for some of the dinosaur steak right about now," Psycho said.

"Not yet. Let's go a little further, find a good spot to camp for the night," Judge said.

"Here," Tisa said. She tossed Psycho a coconut and the Mission Specialist frowned.

The companions came upon a path that turned back on itself and headed back toward the center of the habitat. They crossed it, two large beasts trundling in the distance, kicking up dirt, but they didn't see the party as they entered a thin clearing that stretched away from the path.

In the distance the wall loomed up and shined in the harsh pseudo sunlight, the jungle wailing and buzzing. A great braying and roaring came from behind the party.

"Sounds like meat is back on the menu, boys," Judge said.

Charlotte looked confused, then nodded. "Even the big boys are food."

"The biggest. That thing was definitely a Spinosaurus, right Seok?" Judge said. He didn't know much about dinosaurs, but he'd seen Jurassic Park and read The Lost World.

Seok nodded vigorously. "Sure looked like one. The scales on the spine, the bump on the head, its size. It all matches the fossil specimens and renderings I've seen."

"They have one in the Museum of Natural History in New York, don't they?" Tisa said. "I remember seeing it as a little girl."

"They used to, I think," Seok said.

"Look." Psycho was pointing northwest, toward the wall.

Colorful dots of light sparkled like a tangled strand of Christmas lights as thick mist hovered over the forest, the sound of crashing water rising above the jungle orchestra.

"Looks like we went the right way," Psycho said.

"We've still got a ways to go," Judge said. He gazed around, searching for a place to make camp for the night, but the open field provided no cover. He'd hope to have the metal wall to his back for the night, but there was no way they'd make it before corpse light fell.

"Pick up dead wood if you see it," Judge said.

The party came over a rise in the land and Psycho stopped, gazing out on a narrow hollow.

"WTF?" Judge said.

The area was blackened by fire, and the remnants of trees stuck from the charred hardpan like black teeth. The burned vegetation wasn't what drew Judge's eye, however, but the metal support beam that ran across the ground like a fallen tree. Dirt and silt had built up on both sides of the girder, and the beam appeared undamaged.

Psycho stepped aside and let Seok and Charlotte through.

"Looks like a large amount of water was used to put out the fire. See the sediment buildup there at the edge and around the… beam?" Charlotte said.

"I agree. When the bots put out the fire, they exposed the underpinning of the habitat," Seok said.

"Not the first time," muttered Psycho.

Judge said nothing. There were clear signs that the habitat was failing. Based on what they'd discovered so far, the failing appeared noncritical, but what hadn't they seen? And why was the biosphere failing at all? He kept these thoughts to himself. His crew had enough to worry about.

A tree had fallen at the edge of the burn site, its lower half charred black, its top half free of leaves, but uncharred.

"Let's gather some leaves and branches. We can cover the top of the tree. Should hold us over until the morning," Judge said.

"And the entire area smells like an ashtray, so I don't think we need to worry about our fire tonight."

Judge nodded. "Why don't you get started on that, Psycho, while we make the shelter."

With Tisa's help, Judge cut away some of the dead branches and used them to create support beams for a roof. Charlotte and Tisa piled leaves and branches on top, and soon the roof only had a few stray beams of light knifing through it. Judge laid out five strips of meat and skewered them on sticks. Seok worked on making a bowl from a large coconut shell he hoped to season and use for cooking.

Seok reconnoitered the area, and found nothing unusual, but he did observe three peacock-like creatures munching on the large yellow and green leaves of a plant with tiny seeds hanging in bunches beneath the branches. Seok picked leaves and seeds, used coconut water and meat fat to make a dressing, and the party had salad with its dinner of dino steak.

Judge took a deep breath as he cooked, and for the first time since they'd entered the biosphere, he didn't feel like his head was being crushed in a vise. The meat smelled good, the water was clear and fresh. What more did they need? A chill ran through him as he thought of Brenda. What was she doing at that moment? Was she thinking of him? Wondering how he was doing and if he was OK? He doubted it, and the familiar sting bit him.

The evening beep resounded through the habitat and the pillar of pale light spiked into the sky to the east. Away from the dome, the pale half-light was dim, but the dusk still provided enough light to gather firewood.

Judge made himself comfortable as he watched the flames, thin tendrils of white smoke rising into the air, droplets of meat fat hitting blackened wood with a hiss. Judge's eyebrows dropped and he felt himself nodding off, the crackling of the fire lulling him toward sleep.

16

"Yo, wake up," Psycho said.

Meat roasted on sticks, and the astronauts sat around a small fire, drinking water.

"Guess I dozed off for a second," Judge said.

"More like five minutes," Charlotte said.

"Perfect timing, though. Just like an officer. All the work's done," Tisa said as she handed him a stick with a charred piece of meat on it.

Judge accepted the food and bit down on it greedily, fat and grease running down his chin. The dino-steak tasted great, but when he was done sucking down the protein, his stomach still ached with hunger. "I'm thinking we make another batch."

Everyone's head bobbed like they were puppets controlled by one hand.

Judge went about unwrapping the meat and handing it out.

The fire popped, shooting an ember across the hardpan like a fireball. Tisa got up and stomped it until it no longer glowed, and sat back down.

Seok watched where the ember had fallen, gnawing on the last of his meat then handing the stick to Judge so he could load on another. "I'm wondering why the... sweeper bots are leaving us alone," Seok said. "We've killed a raptor, a Spinosaurus, fired bullets, we've started fires, laser blasts have hit the lights." He pointed up as if to illustrate his point. "But Arjun's body was quarantined and removed like it was poison."

Nobody spoke, the fire crackled and sighed, and the jungle orchestra was tuning up for the evening performance.

"Curious, but my guess, and that's all it is because the truth is we don't know shit, my guess is fire, dinosaur deaths, and occasional system glitches are normal. No alarm sounded. No sweeper bots. Now Arjun's body, his blood. That's new," Judge said.

"True," Seok said. "But how? I mean, we just saw a drone, so maybe there are nanobots lurking around."

Judge knew what nanobots were—who didn't—but he also knew they hadn't lived up to the hype. He said, "There could be nanobots here, or something like them. That would explain a great deal."

"It certainly would, and a culture advanced enough to construct the biosphere may have taken the concept to new levels," Seok said.

"It's almost like when Marty got the sports almanac," Psycho said.

Judge and Charlotte laughed, but Tisa and Seok stared blankly at Psycho.

"Back to the Future?" Psycho said.

Crickets chirped, flies buzzed, and in the distance two great beasts fought like a couple on their fifty-year wedding anniversary.

"Come on, you guys never saw Back to the Future?" Charlotte said.

"I did," Tisa said.

"Me also, but I don't recall a sports almanac," Seok said.

Psycho's eyes narrowed, then widened with understanding. "It was in the second one."

Tisa said, "Missed that one."

Seok shrugged.

Psycho sighed and looked at Judge. "Who raises children in this century and doesn't show their kids the complete trilogy? It's a travesty. No excuse."

"Anyway…" Tisa said. "You were saying?"

"Biff snatches the time machine and goes back in time and steals a sports almanac from Marty, a book he got from the future that shows the scores of all the sporting events for the last fifty years. Very valuable in the past. The point being, things we find in here—shit, the dinosaurs themselves—have great value. In our time."

Judge hadn't thought of that, and he was proud and pissed he hadn't. He didn't get to choose when opportunity came, all he could do was decide how to respond.

"There is technology at work here that could change the human race forever," Seok said. "The ability to physically replicate an entire ecosystem. Make it self-sufficient. That alone is—"

"Let's not over speculate," Judge interrupted. "Sorry, but we don't know the biosphere is self-sufficient."

Seok looked perplexed, his hard, dark eyes finding Judge's. Seok's face softened. "Correct. We're dealing with an unknown, a series of them, so there could be lifeforms, both chemical and/or mechanical, monitoring, controlling, and protecting the habitat."

That seemed to put a period on things, at least until the team found the habitat's brain, if they ever did.

When nobody spoke, Seok added, "The real question, the only one that ever really matters, is why?"

The small fire popped and cracked and when Judge finished his second piece of meat, he tossed his skewer into the fire. He breathed in the smoke, the scent bringing him back to his childhood, and then the beach, with Brenda. He shook himself, rolling his shoulders, chasing a chill, but the unease wouldn't leave.

"Preservation's been mentioned," Psycho said. "That seems like a reasonable reason. Some unknown race built the place. Or humans from the future that went to the past. Back to the Past from the Future."

"OK, to Seok's point, why?" Charlotte asked.

Seok's head jerked up. "Because they knew the dinosaurs were going to die."

"Shit. The extinction event?" Judge said.

Seok nodded.

"Charlotte, light that joint," said Judge.

There were no protests this time, no reasons to not release the pressure that was building within all of them. Judge had gotten to know his crew in a very short time. Not unusual. People bonded faster when dealing with stressful situations. They were more understanding. More gentile and generous. He saw the stress in his crew. Even Psycho, who he thought could carry a tray of champagne flutes through a carwash without breaking a single glass.

"Wait," Judge said. He looked up and found everyone except Charlotte staring at him. She was tending to the joint which was so thin it had gotten severely bent and damaged in her jumpsuit pocket. "How could they have known?"

"Back to the Future, dude. Back to the Future," Psycho said.

"Time travel isn't possible," Seok said. "Other than regular time dilation."

"How much time on Earth will we skip being on Mars?" Tisa said.

"Not much," Seok said.

"Is this habitat possible, Seok?" Judge said. "Scratch that. Before we came through the airlock, would you have believed a place like this was possible?"

Seok shook his head no.

"Clearly we're missing puzzle pieces," Judge said.

Charlotte held up the joint. It had been straightened, then twisted tight. She handed it to Judge. "Ranking officer should do the honors, right? Just in case there's ever an inquiry." She smiled, and Judge smiled back extra wide as he accepted the thin marijuana cigarette.

"Be careful lighting that thing, Judge. You could burn half of it away with one pull," Psycho said.

Judge fished an orange ember from the edge of the fire, then used it to light the end of a thin branch. He held the makeshift match between his forefinger and thumb, and cupped his hand around the flame as he leaned in. Slowly he drew in air until the tip of the joint burned orange. He inhaled, and as he exhaled a thin stream of white smoke he said, "It's like that first sip of wine after you've crossed the desert."

Psycho took a hit and passed. "Scent of A Woman," he said.

"Bing. Bing. We have a winner," Judge said.

When the joint made it to Seok, it was half gone. He held it between two fingers, his face scrunched up like he was holding a cockroach, a thin stream of smoke trailing before his face.

"No pressure, my friend," Psycho said. "But hit or pass before that thing burns away like a moth in a flame."

"I've never…" Seok took a shallow pull off the joint, his eyes growing wide as he passed the pin'er to Judge. When he exhaled, he had a coughing fit, but then settled in, a thin smile spreading over his face.

Around the thin joint went until Psycho sucked the roach down his throat.

When the Mission Specialist didn't even cough, Charlotte said, "You did just inhale that lit roach, right?" She giggled.

"There was a speck of paper and an ember the size of a gnat," Psycho said. He lifted his chin. "Gnats back home. Not like the Mothras here."

Charlotte stared at Psycho, a smirk spreading across her face. "What the hell was that apology all about today?"

Psycho's eyes shifted to Judge, who looked at the hardpan.

Judge's muscle aches had eased, but he was hungry again, though the stomach pains had stopped. He felt at ease, imagining a frosty beer or nice glass of wine.

"What? You aren't going to tell me?" Charlotte said. She tried to take a pull off her bladder, but water dripped down her chin.

Judge laughed to himself. A little pot certainly made some people bold.

Tisa said, "What are you talking about?"

"Today, when we were out in the field, these two were talking about busting balls. Then they apologized to me for saying balls. I've heard rumors you were in trouble, that Judge here covered for you."

Psycho said nothing as he stared into the flames.

"What is she talking about?" Tisa said. She'd turned her hard stare on Psycho and he felt her eyes on him because he flinched.

"Steph said I harassed her. Meant to hurt her," Psycho said. He looked up and leaned back, as if a great weight had been lifted from his shoulders.

"Harassment? What did you do?" Charlotte said.

Psycho drew back as if avoiding a punch. "You assume I did something?"

"No, no, but I know Stephanie. Doesn't seem like a drama queen to me," Charlotte said.

"Thanks," Psycho said.

"So tell us what happened then," Tisa said.

"Steph and I were sleeping together for a while, but she had a different understanding of our arrangement than I did. We got in a fight, she went to leave, and I grabbed her arm. My bad. I apologized multiple times, admitted I was wrong."

"She filed a complaint?" Seok said.

"First crime on Mars. Thank you very much," Psycho said.

"Judge?" Tisa said.

"Commander Salis and I did independent investigations that supported each other's conclusions. There was no intent to harm, and norms had been established. Psycho left out a major part of the story. Stephanie used to grab his arm all the time. Punch him even."

"Ah," Tisa said. "No punishment?"

"Outstanding," Psycho said. "You believe me, right? That I'd never hurt Steph?"

"I know you'd never mean to... Psycho," Tisa said.

"Wow." Psycho deflated like a balloon. "And you, Charlotte? Do you feel the same?"

Charlotte stared at Judge, anger painted on her normally placid face.

"Charlotte?" Tisa said.

"You didn't say anything?" Charlotte said, her eyes shooting daggers at Judge.

"It was on a need to know. Still is," Judge said.

"Answer my question, please," Psycho said.

Charlotte tore her bloodshot eyes from Judge, and the pain on her face eased when she saw Psycho. "No, Psycho. I know you'd never abuse a woman. No way. Grab her arm, yell at her. That I can see. Intent to harm, no. And couples fight and touch each other all the time with no intent to harm. Sounds to me like she was upset about... how did you put it? 'A different understanding of your arrangement.' Non-monogamous verses monogamous? That the misunderstanding?"

"It's Mars for shits sake," Psycho said.

"You're an ass," Tisa said.

"A pig," Charlotte added.

"Yes. Agreed. An abuser, no," Psycho said.

Tisa nodded.

"Agreed," Charlotte said. "Unlike my signature youth experience." She put a hand over her mouth like she couldn't believe what she'd said.

An abrupt and harsh snore brought the conversation to a halt. One-hit Seok had fallen asleep, his head rising and falling as his chin lay on his chest.

"Why do I have a feeling this story isn't going to be nice," Judge said.

"You of all people should know," she said.

Judge felt his cheeks getting hot.

"I was abused as a young teenager," Charlotte said.

"My god, you never told me that," Judge said. Then he threw his shoulders back and his eyes went wide. She'd been very hesitant when they'd been together, almost too shy for a woman her age that had achieved what she had.

"It was an uncle. Happened over several years," Charlotte said.

The weed was making her confess, her inhibitions down. Judge rubbed her shoulder and she turned and smiled at him. "For a long time, I would've flinched if you touched me like that," Charlotte said.

"I'm sorry," Psycho said. "I didn't mean to dredge up bad feelings."

She punched him hard on the shoulder, and said, "Stop apologizing."

Psycho rubbed where she'd hit him, his smile so wide Judge thought it might split his friend's face.

"It messed me up for a long time," Charlotte said. "I still have nightmares."

"Did you tell your parents? The police?" Tisa said.

"I hadn't told anyone—ever—until just now," Charlotte said.

"How did you get it to stop?" Judge said. He felt an overwhelming urge to hug her, pull her close, protect her, tell her everything would be OK. But he couldn't. Charlotte wasn't his wife, or his girlfriend. They'd had sex twice and didn't know each other all that well.

"That's the horrible part. It went on for a few years. He'd abuse me, then cry afterward. Tell me how wrong he was, how ashamed. How he just couldn't help himself. He'd tell me what would happen to my aunt, cousins. He said if I told, he'd kill himself."

That seemed to put the conversation out of its misery, and Judge lay back and put out an arm. Charlotte eyed it, then nestled against him. Judge put his arm around her, as one would with a daughter or mother.

"I'm sorry," he said.

"Don't be. Just keep doing what you're doing."

Judge searched for a break in the roof of their lean-to, but when he found none, he closed his eyes, thinking about his cot back on base, the ship, Earth. Brenda. It always seemed to come back to that, even half a solar system away.

17

Psycho whistled and Judge came awake in the dark, his hand going to his M9. Branches creaked and cracked, leaves rustled and ripped, and grunts and growls echoed through the jungle. Judge put his back to the fallen tree trunk that made up the main wall of their lean-to, and Charlotte grabbed his arm. His first impulse was to shake her off, but instead he patted her hand.

Norms. Pain in the ass, always around, confusing and precedent setting norms. They ruled all societies, and when he'd put out his arm to Charlotte, comforted her, he'd crossed a line and established a norm. Suddenly he felt new pity for Psycho. His boisterous friend was an alpha male pig, and made no attempt to hide it. He was an open book, and any woman—person-that chose to get involved with him on a personal level, knew what they were getting. On a professional level, Psycho was indispensable, and Judge worried at the fine cracks forming in his friend's normally smooth facade.

Whatever was working its way through the forest was getting closer, the sounds of breaking branches and snarls becoming further apart.

"I think it smells us. It's moving slower, being more careful," Psycho said.

Tisa held out her M9, her hand shaking slightly. Lack of food and water had wasted her face, her normally round cheeks sunken and darker than her eye sockets.

Seok held his knife at his side, eyes shifting with each sound of movement.

"I'm gonna go see what's what. Take it out before it gets here if need be," Psycho said.

"Why is it always you?" Judge said. "I'm coming."

Nobody protested, so Judge followed Psycho out of the lean-to into the pale artificial moonlight. In the northeast, the light cone marked the center of the biosphere, the corpse light finding every crack, dark shadows hiding under every branch and behind every tree.

Psycho put up a fist and got low, bringing up his rifle.

Judge fell in next to him, M9 held in a two-handed grip. He almost felt like he knew what he was doing.

Almost.

A creature launched from the shadows, talons forward like an eagle attacking.

Judge saw it in his peripheral vision and went limp, dropping to the hardpan as the beast sailed centimeters over his head, crashing into a bush with needle-like thorns. The creature thrashed and wailed as the knife-like prickers stabbed and tore at the beast. Feathers flew, and the thing howled, squawking as it gyrated and struggled.

Judge swung the M9, sighted, and squeezed off two shots.

The first tore through the beast's left leg, severing it, and the second shattered its skull, the creature's head exploding in a hail of blood, bone, and brain. The corpse continued to thrash, then slowed, spasming every few moments before falling still.

The night symphony had gone silent, and was slowly coming back to full strength.

"We've got no business being here," Judge said.

Psycho said nothing as he eased forward, examining the corpse. "Looks like a giant eagle."

Brown and red feathers floated in the air.

"A type of raptor, maybe. Some believe they had feathers, and this guy is around the right size."

"It's no bigger than a turkey," Psycho said.

"Yeah, most were small," Judge said.

They headed back to camp and filled the others in.

"Scary stuff," Judge said.

"We can't continue to stumble around out here in the middle of the jungle. Once we get to the wall, we shouldn't leave it," Seok said.

Judge said, "When we actually make it to the wall, we can talk about staying next to it."

The team fidgeted for the rest of the night, Psycho the only one that got any sleep from what Judge could tell. Everyone was on edge. The wall loomed in the distance, and when the beep of morning light rang through the habitat the party was able to get their bearings. The team harvested and ate coconuts, and if Judge never had another pina colada in his life that'd be just fine with him.

The crash and flow of the waterfall grew louder, and the closer the companions got to the wall the more obvious it became that they were too far south. Judge called a halt and the party drank the last of their water. The regular rains could keep them going in a pinch and there appeared to be no shortage of puddles and watering holes, though most were nasty and stale.

"We can head northwest, make a direct line to the waterfall or stay the course. Shortest path to the wall," Judge said.

"Wall," Seok said.

"Whatever you think," Psycho said.

Tisa nodded at Psycho.

All eyes turned to Charlotte, and she looked at the hardpan. "I'm trying to do some fast math," she said.

"It's an extra kilometer if we go straight to the wall then turn north toward the waterfall," Seok said. "At least a kilometer."

Charlotte sighed. "We need to get out of here as soon as possible, and the waterfall is our best chance."

Judge smiled. She wanted the shortest route.

"But, given the distance and relative danger, I say we stay the course. Get the wall at our backs, and work our way north. That's my vote," Charlotte said.

Judge ran fingers through his hair. What Charlotte and Seok were preaching made a lot of sense. He looked to Psycho, who was watching him with a lopsided smile. Judge knew he wanted to go directly to the falls like a moth goes to a flame. It can't help itself.

His gaze shifted to Tisa, who stared at him with a twisted face that showed the conflict raging within her. Her tense narrow lips, brooding mouth, and crinkled worry lines revealing the fight between duty and self-preservation.

An astronaut was similar to a soldier in that their team was everything. Your fellow astronauts were like parts of your body, arms and legs, and each one served an important purpose that contributed to your ability to survive. This wasn't like normal teams. On Mars, if a teammate didn't do their job, other teammates could die.

"Psycho, continue on and take us to the wall, please," Judge said.

The Mission Specialist rolled his eyes, squeezing his lips into a tight red line. "Yes, sir."

"I had a Commander once," Judge said. "Grelly. Tough old SOB. The younger officers-and when I say younger, I'm talking dudes in their seventies-used to ask the guy what it was like to actually sail a Navy ship and he'd answer. Grelly had sailed on the USS Constitution."

Now Seok was interested. "Old Ironsides?"

"One and the same," Judge said. "For you youngsters, the Constitution is a wooden-hulled, three-masted heavy US Navy frigate. She was launched in 1797 and is the world's oldest commissioned naval vessel.

"I was new to base and there was this one building on campus where all the children and teenagers would hang out. An old barrack scheduled for rehab. They hid in there, smoked, partied, screwed. Did all the things normal kids would do, except when you're trapped on a base you don't have many location options."

"Is there a moral to this story?" Psycho said. He pushed through the underbrush, clearing a decent path for the party.

"The moral is I had to evacuate that building and half the base one night because I thought the kids had started a fire in that old building. Officers and their wives standing in the cold. Base Commander getting complaints." Judge took a breath. "Turns out it was just steam from an old heating unit, so I was expecting to get my ass reamed. Commander calls me in, and do you know what he said?"

Screeches, howls, buzzing, clicking and braying, but nobody spoke.

"He said, Judge, I'll never get mad at you for erring on the side of caution," Judge said.

"You could have just said that," Psycho chided.

"No," Seok said. "Context is important. Always."

"We're here," Psycho said.

The metal wall stood before them, and one by one the party broke free of the jungle. The pseudo-sunlight felt good on Judge's face, and he closed his eyes, letting the warmth sink in.

The waterfall thundered to the north, and didn't sound far away.

As planned, the party turned north, threading along the wall. It was much hotter without the forest canopy, and the wall served as a reflector, as well as a heat sponge. Though the wall wasn't hot to the touch, it gave off waves of heat that felt extra warm after the relative cool in the jungle.

The party hit a corner, and the wall turned slightly.

"We're at the westernmost angle of the hexagon. We're close," Psycho said.

Seok paused at the hundred-and-twenty-degree angle. "There's corrosion here," he said.

Judge joined him. Dull brown streaks ran down the wall within the angle, where the two pieces of metal came together. "From water runoff?" Judge said.

"That'd be my guess. Even the hardest metal will break down over very long periods of time when exposed to constant water pressure," Seok said.

Tisa harrumphed. "Another sign the place wasn't designed to work this long. That's what I keep wondering about. Why didn't whoever wanted to save the dinosaurs put them back where they belong after Earth had healed? Surely that was the plan, right?"

Judge had no idea what the plan had been, but what Tisa said made a lot of sense.

Seok pulled his knife and tried to scrape some of the brown corrosion from the metal, but got nothing. "Water may be discoloring the metal, but it hasn't deteriorated it, and it certainly hasn't been weakened."

A field of thick bamboo ran to the wall like a marching Army. Mist leaked through the bamboo, tiny dots of color sparkling in the water vapor. A breeze rattled the bamboo and it swayed and clicked.

Judge took a knee. "Is it just me or is this place putting up obstacles around every turn?"

"This patch of bamboo is ancient. Those stalks in the middle have a diameter of at least twenty centimeters. The stuff is thicker than trees. No way we're getting through it," Seok said.

Psycho lifted the laser rifle.

"Unless we use that," Seok said.

Mist snaked through the columns of bamboo-like smoke, the fresh scent of moisture filling the air.

"We blast through and every beast around here will know we're here. Why not just go around?" Charlotte said.

A roar brought everyone's attention back to the jungle, a deep cry of anger and pain. Another beast answered, screeching and howling.

"I've so had enough of this place," Seok said. "Live prehistoric specimens or not."

"Every paleontologist on Earth would kill to be here, right?" Tisa said.

"Be careful what you wish for," Psycho said.

"You might get it," Charlotte finished.

"Let's get to it, then. The faster we start, the faster we'll be done. I don't know about you all, but I can't wait to stand next to that waterfall with the cool mist soaking me through," Judge said.

Psycho pushed through the dense vegetation that ran up to the bamboo patch. The battle line, where the dense jungle met the unyielding bamboo, was a permanent demarcation that would occasionally shift slightly, but never in any material way.

"This is almost as hard as it would have been cutting through the bamboo," Judge said.

"So you say. We've squeezed past plenty. If we had to cut it all, we wouldn't have gone ten feet," Psycho said.

The bamboo patch only ran a quarter kilometer into the jungle, and the party was able to turn north. The rumble of the waterfall had lessoned, but it could still be heard like a snare drum beneath the jungle chorus. Animal paths crisscrossed the area, but nothing large, and creatures ranging in size from rats to small dogs scurried out of the party's way like they were dinosaurs.

The astronauts were forced to wait several times and let larger beasts trundle past, but it wasn't that difficult to avoid the stupid creatures. Unless they saw you, then they were more focused than Psycho when he caught the scent of whiskey.

The waterfall sparkled as it fell from the white sheet of light above, rainbows and stars of color bursting from the thunderous stream of water. Judge tried to see where the water was coming from, but the white and blue flow blended into the white light, clouds of mist hiding the exit point. The pristine falls spilled into a pond, which extended into a river that snaked into the jungle.

Thick forest and underbrush encroached to the water's edge, a thin patch of light brown silt separating the deep green vegetation of the jungle from the pure clarity of the life-giving H2O. A beast cried above as it circled and glided on the air currents, and Judge listened for the fans. A gentle breeze brought the scent of moisture, earth, and flowers, and Judge's nerves eased.

Something flashed on the shoreline where the waterfall spilled into the green tree canopy. Judge shielded his eyes, and jerked back, but when he focused, there was nothing there.

18

"Wow," Seok said. He headed for the lake and Judge put out an arm to stop him. Seok stared at him with frustration, but then his eyes went wide. "Did you see something?"

Judge scanned the strip of brown mud that ran around the lake and along the thin river. The waterfall spilled from the whiteness above like a faucet, pounding into the pond. Whitewater frothed on the lake, bubbles popping, lines of brown foam rippling over the water. The current flowing out of the lake was strong, and the river thinned as it twisted through the jungle.

"We need to be careful," Psycho said.

"Let's get closer to the waterfall. Maybe get behind it," Tisa said.

He'd seen plenty of movies where the secret entrance was hidden behind the waterfall, but he wasn't hopeful. So far nothing about the biosphere had been normal. That said, there might be a better view of the water's entry point.

"Good idea. Let's roll," Judge said. He hacked and cut with his knife-spear, but it still took an hour to get back to the wall. The vegetation at the base of the wall next to the waterfall was amazingly dense and tough. Vines as thick as tree trunks intertwined and snaked through a patch of bushes with stiletto-sized thorns.

"See anything of use?" Judge said. He was staring upward, trying to see whether the water was coming through the wall, or from the ceiling.

Seok shook his head. "Even if we had field glasses, I don't think it would help."

"How the hell would we get up there, anyhow?" Psycho said. "We've got no rope. The wall is smooth."

"A ladder?" Tisa said.

"You shitting… kidding me? It's at least a hundred feet tall and that's what we can see. It could be twice that," Psycho said.

"I don't think it is," Judge said. "But Psycho is right."

"What now?" Charlotte was staring into the dense underbrush they'd just come through.

"Back to the lake's edge. I need water," Tisa said.

"Maybe there's fish?" Psycho said.

"And maybe there's a fifty-foot crocodile in there. People, remember where we are," Judge said to himself as much as the rest of the team.

"Fried gator isn't bad," Psycho said.

Following the blazed trail back to the water's edge only took a few minutes, and by mid-day the five astronauts were sitting a safe distance away from the lake, sipping water and eating the last of their coconut.

"So, I've had a thought," Psycho said.

Tisa clapped and Judge whistled.

"Funny. Very funny." Psycho raised an eyebrow and waited for the taunting to cease. "Have any of you been watching the current?"

Nods, wagging heads. The thunder of the waterfall drowned out the jungle chorus, and Judge was happy for the soundtrack change.

Psycho tore a large red and yellow leaf from a nearby plant and strode to the lake's edge. He crumbled the leaf in his fist and tossed it into the pond. It jerked into motion as it was pulled toward the eastern end of the lake where the stream ran into the jungle. Judge watched the leaf disappear into the whitewater, only to be spit out toward the river.

Psycho rejoined his companions, but said nothing as he stared at the leaf until it disappeared. When it was gone, he raised his hands, palms out, in a 'see what I'm saying' gesture.

Nobody spoke, the static of water pounding into water echoing over the lake.

"You don't get it?"

Judge shrugged.

"Water don't travel up," Psycho said.

Judge still wasn't seeing it when Seok said, "You believe this water is recycled?"

"I do. Pumps, or something like that. There's no way a water reclaimer could make H2O that fast," Psycho said as he pointed at the waterfall.

"Believe it or not, waterfalls actually help oxygenate water," Seok said.

"Like Land of the Lost again. There was this one episode where they followed the river to try and escape, only to find that it reemerged on the opposite side of their habitat. If we can find where the river gets sucked back into the biosphere's infrastructure…"

"Maybe we can get into the habitat's inner workings because it won't be high up," Seok said.

"More like a drain," Psycho said.

"But will we be able to get to it?" Seok said as he stared up into the sheet of white light.

There was a splash and flash out on the pond, and all heads turned. Whitewater and foam covered most of the lake, and the turbulent water made it impossible to see what was below the surface. The sweet scent of thick moisture and earth filled the air, waves of mist rolling off the water.

Judge got to his feet, eyes never leaving the lake. "I think we've got to assume there are creatures in the water. Just like every inch of this place."

"You mean like a megalodon?" Charlotte said.

"No," Judge said. "Something like that could never live in a shallow pond like this, but there were plenty of other prehistoric beasts that lived in water. Those Brontosaurus we saw, for example. I'm sure they're down here all the time. We probably scared them away."

"There are tracks all along the river's edge. Big ones with three toes, tiny mouse feet, and everything in between," Psycho said.

A buzz like a swarm of bees rose above the pounding waterfall and the hiss of the whitewater. Judge looked up, searching the sky, but saw nothing.

"I hear it also," Charlotte said.

"Should we take cover?" Psycho said.

The buzzing got louder.

"I think we should. What do we have to lose?" Judge said.

Psycho nodded, and the party ducked beneath a conifer with thick spreading boughs, staring out through gaps in the greenery like peeping toms.

The drone came in low over the trees, banking hard and dropping into the gap in the jungle created by the river. The flying robot was bigger than the one from the prior day, and looked to be better equipped.

Two mechanical arms protruded from the black square fuselage, and four legs dangled beneath the craft. A row of lights ran atop the forward portion of the main housing, four rotors spinning on each corner of the fuselage. Silver cones, like lenses, scoped in and out on all sides, searching, documenting.

Judge whispered, "Any theories on why it's here?"

The buzzing rose in pitch as the bot flew over the lake, pausing to search the falls, then darting off north. It stopped at the tree line, as if expecting to see something, but when nothing appeared, the drone spun and headed back toward the astronauts.

"Finally figured out we're here, maybe?" Charlotte said. "You did just blast one of the largest land animals to ever exist. I'm guessing Spinosaurus don't go down in here often. Probably considered an anomaly when one of the big ones goes down unexpectedly."

"And without fighting another big guy. The sweepers may have shown up after we left. Couldn't figure out what killed the spino so the big guns came looking?" Seok said.

"Makes sense, and now they're on our ass. Great. Just great," Judge said.

"Maybe not. Look," Tisa said. Sweat ran down her beautiful brown face, her eye sockets dark and shallow, her cheeks sunken.

The drone turned again, spinning just north of the party's position, where it hovered over the spot where the lake dumped into the river. It spun one last time, cycled up its rotors, and tore off over the jungle canopy.

"That's probably a good area to catch stuff. At that confluence," Psycho said.

"Also a good spot to get eaten. Trapped between the jungle and the lake," Judge said.

"Always the pessimist," Charlotte said.

"Realist," Judge said. "Let's get a—"

A wave of water surged from the lake, a massive fist of whitewater with teeth. Two tall, floppy antennas stuck above the tumult, the pink insides of a mouth opening within the mound of lake water.

Psycho moved first, pulling the laser rifle from where it hung on his shoulder and dropping it into his hands.

The rest of the party stood rooted to the hardpan, watching the surge of water crash on shore. The open mouth disappeared within the tumult and confusion, but the two antennas still swayed and bent above the chaos.

Judge drew his M9, stepped back, and looked for his crew. He reached out and tugged on Charlotte's elbow, and yelled, "Move back. Now! Fast!"

Seok and Tisa turned tail and ran, but Charlotte still didn't move.

Judge jerked on her arm, pulling her after him as he retreated.

"Ouch," she bristled, but as she pulled her arm away, her face softened.

A high-pitched squeal pierced the day, and the scent of rot, like low tide, wafted over the lake.

The whitewater dissipated, and the creature that stood on the shoreline was straight out of an old school science fiction movie. It looked like a giant scorpion, its hard shell and dark eyes shining under the false sunlight. The creature's tail curved over its body, a red stinger at its end. Crab-like legs shuffled beneath a lobster-like torso, and as the beast inched forward its mouth eased open revealing meter-long teeth. The creature bobbed and weaved, always moving, its stinger poised to strike.

Psycho fired, three fast bursts that zapped through the air, one missing, the second severing the beast's right antenna, and the third hitting home and gashing the creature's torso.

"Sea scorpion," Seok yelled.

Judge had heard the name. Knew what it was. There was a thirty-meter fossil of one of the legendary prehistoric beasts on display back at Seok's university in Japan, though it didn't have a curved tail.

The creature wailed, leaning to one side, dark blood leaking from the charred wounds. As the beast struggled for balance, it lashed out with its stinger, its tail jerking and spearing the ground next to Psycho.

The Mission Specialist dove, bringing the rifle up as he came out of his roll.

The beast stabbed at Psycho again, and the laser rifle bleated, but Psycho flinched when the creature's tail struck the ground and the rifle shifted. That slight deviation in his aim got worse as the blast traveled, climbing upward and missing the creature by less than a meter.

The massive sea scorpion wailed, stabbing with its tail, sliding side-to-side, head bobbing like a rooster.

Judge fired the M9, aiming for the side of the creature's head. The bullets smacked into the hard shell and ricocheted off, zipping through the jungle and slapping into water.

"Save your ammo and take cover," Psycho yelled. He was back on his feet and running along the tree line.

Judge opened his mouth to yell at his friend, ask him what the hell he was doing, but Judge realized Psycho was trying to get him and the others out of his line of fire. Judge corralled Charlotte and Seok, and Tisa took the hint, and the four astronauts backed into the jungle, finding trees to shield them.

The creature reared up, its remaining antenna whipping around, blood dripping from its wounds.

Psycho turned on the creature. It was fifty meters away, standing on its hind legs, mouth open, eyes locked on Psycho.

The Mission Specialist brought the laser rifle to his shoulder, but didn't fire.

The sea scorpion lunged forward, its four front legs hitting the ground with a splash, the shoreline still wet from the surging lake water. The waterfall pounded in the background and mist rolled over the lake and jungle.

Still Psycho didn't fire. Judge stepped out from behind a tree, eyes locked on his friend. "What is he doing?" Judge took another step, the M9 shaking in his hand by his side. "Fire. What the hell is he waiting for?"

The sea scorpion scuttled toward Psycho, closing the final twenty meters faster than Judge thought possible given the beast's size. The creature roared and reared up, coiling to strike.

Psycho fired and kept firing. Zap. Zap. Zap. Zap.

The blasts hit home, the beast crumbling into the muck as its head was burned from its body, and its tail was severed. The beast's headless corpse crashed to the ground and tumbled in the mud, splashing Psycho. The corpse came to rest ten meters from where Psycho stood, shuddered with one final breath, exhaled, squeaked, and lay still.

Mist flowed off the lake, the waterfall thundered, and in the background the jungle tittered, howled and buzzed.

Psycho wiped his brow and looked around as though he didn't know where he was.

"Hey, mate, you alright?" Judge said. He stepped from just inside the tree break and headed toward his friend.

A deep mew echoed over the static of the waterfall, and a surge of water broke across the pond.

Dark eyes lifted above the surface, a narrow head rising from the depths, white teeth glinting in a half-open mouth. A thin caudal fin swayed and shifted at the end of a long tail, and four flippers stuck from the sides of a massive torso, two forward and two back, but there were no claws at the end of the appendages. The serpentine beast wiggled and dived, disappearing below a fist of whitewater.

A wave rolled toward the shore, the lake sucking outward as the miniature tsunami rolled toward the party. The charred corpse of the sea scorpion tumbled and shifted as it was sucked into the lake, and the wave grew, two rows of dagger-like teeth cutting through the clear lake water.

19

Judge spread his legs, gripped the M9 with both hands, steadied himself, and fired. Three rounds dead-on into the creature's mouth.

The beast bucked and heaved, tossing and twisting as it was carried on the fist of cresting lake water. A mournful wail pierced the day as the wave closed out, ripples of whitewater covering the lake and shoreline. The hardpan trembled as the massive beast crashed onto the shore with a slap, mud flying.

The waterfall thundered, but the insect symphony fell silent.

The creature looked half alligator, half whale. It was thirty meters long from the tip of its thin caudal fin to the end of its tooth-filled flat mouth. The beast's torso was fat and slick, red stripes zigzagging over dark gray. Four flippers slapped and churned in the mud as the creature righted itself. The reptilian head swung side to side, dark cupcake-sized eyes with sprinkles of red searching the area. It took a step forward, lowering its crocodilian head to the mud. It clicked and hissed, its breath pushing aside the vegetation of the jungle.

Psycho brought up the rifle, but Judge said, "Save your power."

The creature's eyes rolled back in its head, its flippers went limp, and the massive torso fell to the ground. The mud puckered and snapped as the beast thrashed, pulling itself from the muck before falling still. Its mouth fell open, and it gurgled, the beast's eyes already staring into the next world.

"This is getting out of hand," Psycho said. He joined Judge and the others just inside the jungle's tree break.

"Kronosaurus," Seok said. He peered out from behind a thick palm tree. "Though that caudal fin is surprising, though not really. Probably mostly cartilage."

"I'm interested, really, but I think we need to get the hell out of here. Fast," Psycho said. His eyes darted around, sweat covered his face, and he had the laser rifle at the ready.

"Yes, sorry."

"Let's retreat to the wall," Charlotte said.

"Let's follow the river," Psycho said.

Judge didn't wait to hear any other suggestions. He turned his back on the Kronosaurus corpse and plunged into the jungle, searching for a place to regroup. There were no reliable conifers, but there was a thick glade of saw palmetto with a spattering of full-grown palms. Giant ferns and thick purple stalks with elephant ear leaves with thin white flowers made up the underbrush, and Judge pushed through it until he found several stunted palmetto trees. He eased under their thick canopy, putting his back to one of the thick, bark-covered tree trunks.

When the party of five was huddled beneath a roof of palm fronds, and the jungle cacophony back at full volume, Judge asked, "Does anyone have a sip of water I can steal?"

Blank faces.

"That's priority one then. Do you think we can drink the lake water?" Judge said. They'd been drinking the rain and from watering holes, but somehow the waterfall and pond seemed different.

"It's probably OK," Seok said.

"If I go get some, will you drink it?" Psycho asked.

Seok's dark eyes turned to the hardpan. Psycho had a way of cutting through the bullshit.

"I will," Charlotte said.

Judge squinted and shook his head, his alpha male brain telling him it was his responsibility to test the water. But this was Mars, and even on Earth the norms between men and women had been turned upside down. He reigned in his well-meaning chauvinism, and said nothing.

Psycho took care of it for Judge, like so many times before, in so many situations. "You're not testing anything. Don't insult me," Psycho said.

Tisa chuckled. "Some things never change."

"No, Tisa," Psycho said. Judge could tell his friend was genuinely offended. "You can drink whatever the hell you want, OK?"

Psycho collected everyone's water bladder and pushed through the trees without another word.

"You guys better start appreciating him a little. What he does," Judge said. He sounded like a father scolding his children about not listening to their mother.

"Easy," Tisa said. "He's a big boy, and he's not the only capable person here."

"But he is always the first to step forward. Step into the void, the unknown," Seok said.

"Mostly to protect us," Charlotte said.

Tisa harrumphed and dropped her eyes to the hardpan, but said nothing.

Judge inched forward and peered through the palm fronds, watching Psycho as he held the rifle out with one hand and filled a water bladder with the other. Judge sighed. "Tisa, cover me from here, I'm going to help him." Judge didn't wait for acknowledgment, and he pushed through the palm leaves, their sharp edges biting and scraping at his arms and face.

"Give me a couple of those. You watch," Judge said.

Psycho didn't protest. He stood, dropped the water containers, and panned the laser rifle back and forth, searching the mound of whitewater that flowed over the pond. The waterfall pounded into the lake, thick mist snaking through the jungle and hanging in the air along the shoreline like steam.

Judge quickly filled the bladders, and he and Psycho inched back into the jungle and found their companions. Nobody waited, the debate about testing the water forgotten, and they all took a few sips, letting the clear water settle in their stomachs. When immediate sickness didn't come, Judge drank, the cool water sliding down his face. Waiting really served no purpose. A pathogen could take days, or weeks to incubate, and the very air they'd been breathing could be poisoning them, and they just didn't know it yet because symptoms had yet to manifest.

"It would be nice to have something to eat. Even coconut," Psycho said. He looked up at the surrounding trees, but he saw no green nuts.

"I'm sure we'll see some once we get on our way, maybe some of those berries we saw," Tisa said.

"To the wall, then?" Judge said. "I understand the follow the river argument, but based on the last couple of days I'd say the jungle is too dangerous. Seok is right. Let's keep the wall at our backs."

"To what end?" Tisa said.

"I think we should go put our spacesuits on and blast open the airlock before it's too late. We've already lost Arjun. I'd prefer we don't lose anyone else," Psycho said.

"That could flood the habitat with Martian air. Kill everything in here," Charlotte said.

"Yup. It could," Psycho said.

"Or we try and find where the river gets sucked back into the biosphere's infrastructure," Tisa said. "Does anyone see other options?"

Judge didn't.

"Maybe mess with the sweeper bots? Would that bring bigger bots, like the drones?" Tisa said.

"Why does it matter?" Judge said.

"Bigger bots, bigger doors," Seok said.

That sounded pretty thin to Judge. "Anything else?"

Nobody spoke, and the jungle trilling, hooting, braying and roaring was deafening.

The question Judge had to answer was should the party pursue both options? Judge said, "Are we still all in agreement about splitting up? Or do we want to consider doing both?"

"You know where I stand," Seok said.

"Wall," Charlotte said.

"River," Psycho said.

Tisa sighed, rolled her eyes at Psycho, and said, "River."

With the team divided, Judge had no choice but to make the call, for better or worse. This wasn't a committee decision, anyway. "I know you each have your own ideas about how to escape this ancient trap, but I'm not losing another crewmate. We follow the wall back to the airlock. Then I'll decide if we explore where the river leaves the biosphere."

"Assuming it's not another pond, with a drain at the bottom. I'm not swimming. You can count on that," Psycho said.

As the group trekked, picking through the underbrush, Judge asked, "Psycho. What's the power readout on your rifle say?"

Psycho held the gun on its side, staring at the stock. "Says thirty-eight percent. Not great. Maybe ten bursts left."

"That doesn't seem right? How many times have you fired?" Seok said.

Psycho counted in his head. "Ten-ish? So, yeah, maybe we've got a bit more. Batteries don't degrade evenly. Even these fancy things."

"Does it get hot when you fire it?" Seok asked.

"Not really. All the power is pushed outward, the housing only needs to direct the burst, not contain it," Psycho said.

The metal wall stood before the party, and as Psycho hacked through the last of the underbrush, Judge felt ill. Pain cut through him, cramps knotting his stomach. His bowels loosened and he scrunched his anus. The water was tainted, but before he could voice his concerns to his mates the pain passed, and he no longer felt like his insides were going to blow out the back end. He said, "Damn. You all feel alright? I just felt like shit for a second."

"I'm fine," Seok said, and the rest of the party nodded and hiked their shoulders.

Judge's nerves jumped, the shiny metal wall standing before him.

The thunder of the waterfall was to the north, so Judge stepped past Psycho and threaded along the base of the wall, trying not to disturb the vegetation and not leave a path. He twisted, avoiding vines and tree limbs.

"Oh," Charlotte said. She stopped and bent over, holding her stomach.

Judge put a hand on her shoulder.

"I'm OK. I'm OK."

None of the other astronauts had a reaction to the water, but still Judge's brain was conjuring all kinds of colorful scenarios involving little bacteria eating him from the inside out. "Thanks to our trek to the dome, we have a good sense of the size of the habitat. Even though sticking with the wall means we have to walk further, we're already moving faster," Judge said. The vegetation didn't grow to the wall in most spots, and the team was able to follow the natural path, their eastern flank protected.

The party trudged on, and when the sharp beep marked the coming of afternoon rain, Judge was the first to get his boots off. The water felt good on his skin, in his mouth. He stared up into the white light, sparkling dots of color dancing in the rain. He used a leaf to fill his water bladder, and when the rain stopped, he felt better. Steam rolled off the metal wall as the harsh light burnt away the moisture, the smack and pop of spacesuit boots pulling from the mud echoing off the wall.

"Careful here," Judge said. He was still on point, and as he avoided a huge anthill, a tree branched slapped him in the face.

"Who's on first?" Psycho said.

"What?" Tisa said.

"No, what's on second. Who's on first?"

"Enough, you just outdated yourself by about four generations," Judge said. "And the three stooges weren't that funny to begin with."

"You're lucky my father isn't here. You would've caught a beatin' for that blasphemy," Psycho said.

When evening beep brought the pillar of light, and the pale pseudo moonlight, Judge felt like he'd been walking for days. A beast roared in the distance. Another answered, and this alpha ritual silenced the smaller creatures of the habitat, and reminded Judge it was almost lights out.

The companions harvested four coconuts, spent entirely too much energy cracking them open, then pressed their backs to the metal wall and ate and drank. A flock of bat-like creatures fluttered past overhead, the snap of their wings and their sharp cries bouncing off the wall like it was a stereo speaker.

"I'll take first watch," Judge said. Nobody argued.

Judge repositioned himself so he was behind a large fan of palm fronds, trying to shield himself from the corpse light, but it leaked through the habitat like sewage in clear water. He felt himself drifting, retracing his steps all the way back to Gale Base Alpha. It seemed like so long ago.

Seok snored, and the puff and sigh of Psycho's breathing rose and fell along with the night symphony, like he was part of it. Judge supposed he was, they all were. So far, they'd lived off the land, what the habitat provided. What would happen if they took more? Damaged the biosphere beyond poaching a few of its specimens? Psycho wanted to blast a hole in the airlock, but maybe they didn't need to go that extreme.

Judge's eyes slid closed, the night chorus pulling him in, the scent of earth and plants filling his nostrils. His stomach grumbled and he forced his eyes open, staring into the shadows beneath the jungle canopy. The pillar of light shined in the distance, and a creature brayed, and was answered by another. Judge thought of Brenda, wondered what she was doing, imagined her face. Her lips. His brother's face filled his mind and he rolled his shoulders, trying to crack his neck, but no relief came. His eyes slid closed and sleep took him.

Beep.

The morning light snapped on and Judge came awake, the neck of his jumpsuit drenched with sweat. In the vegetation, peering out from behind a tree branch, two red eyes watched him.

20

Judge didn't move, and didn't know if he could. Fear ran through him like electricity, pain shooting to the tips of his toes and the ends of his fingers. He was afraid to breathe, show any sign he was anything more than a stone, a small pebble on a rock-strewn beach. The eyes panned the astronauts like searchlights, the rest of the beast hidden in the thick jungle undergrowth, its head blending into the dense vegetation. Huge ferns and stunted palms filled every empty space beneath the tall trees with gray trunks and red leaves that were packed with life.

He considered going for his gun, but decided against it. Any movement could trigger the creature, and since it was content sitting still, why pull on its tail?

Leaves exploded from the jungle, and the creature flashed before Judge, its green body covered in thin scar-like red lines. The beast grabbed Tisa's arm, and yanked her from where she lay sleeping against the wall.

The dinosaur walked on four thick legs, a ten-meter tail tapering back like a whip. The beast looked like a giant monitor lizard, except for the Spinosaurus-like scales running down its back. Narrow jaws locked down on Tisa and she screamed. The creature moved like a spider being chased with a broom, shifting and dodging, moving so fast it was hard to keep track of it.

Judge drew down, swinging the M9 up in his fury, but he was too late.

The beast darted into the jungle, tearing leaves and breaking branches as it blended into the undergrowth.

Tisa screamed, gurgled, and yelped as she was dragged through the jungle, grasping for trees and vegetation as she twisted and fought.

Psycho came awake with a start, scanned the scene, launched to his feet, and snarled.

The rest of the party sat rooted to the hardpan, looking around, rubbing sleep from their eyes. When Charlotte saw the trail of blood leading into the jungle, she gasped. Her eyes darted to her companions, and when she realized Tisa was gone, she wept.

Seok stared at Judge with expectant eyes.

Judge had been on watch. "It... It happened so fast," he said. "Morning bell woke me, and I saw eyes in the jungle, watching me. Then it just attacked. Bolted through camp, took Tisa, and disappeared before I even knew what the hell was happening. I... Tisa. Oh, shit. Not another one." Judge fell to his ass and let his head fall into his hands.

Charlotte went to him and rubbed his back.

"You fell asleep? I'm gonna go fix it," Psycho said. He grabbed the laser rifle and plunged into the jungle.

Being left behind, along with his sleeping while on watch, sent a surge of adrenaline and guilt through Judge. He vaulted to his feet and plunged into the jungle behind Psycho. "Wait here," he said to Seok and Charlotte.

Tree branches whipped his face as he pushed through the forest, the thin trail of blood getting thicker with each step. He went around a large conifer, its broad boughs spreading twenty meters around its trunk, and he found Psycho kneeling over a puddle of blood.

Tisa's cries rose above the jungle noise.

"This blood is going to bring the sweeper bots. We've got to move fast," Psycho said. "Keep up."

Judge stayed right behind Psycho, ducking under branches, dodging tree trunks and bushes, and trying not to get snagged by every thorn and pricker bush. The trail of blood thinned, then stopped. Psycho paused, fading into the shadows beneath a thick cottonwood tree with spreading branches.

Nothing moved in the forest, the strangled cries of Tisa fading. Psycho listened for a few seconds, then turned to Judge and hiked his shoulders.

Judge nodded.

Psycho sprang into the undergrowth, pushing through weeds and ferns. Insects and flies covered him, but he didn't stop. Psycho was on the one-yard line, the rock was in his hands, and he was getting into the end zone.

A loud clicking rose above the jungle chorus, the sweeper bots swarming over the jungle.

The pair broke free of the forest into a narrow clearing that looked to be part path, part grazing area. Tall grass swayed in the gentle breeze, and in the center of the field a reptilian head bobbed up and down, appearing and disappearing in the grass.

Psycho sighted the laser rifle and fired.

The dinosaur's head disappeared in a spray of blood and bone. Its body stood tall for a few seconds, unaware of management's termination, then the corpse flopped forward onto Tisa.

Judge slid around Psycho and went to Tisa, the clicking and scuttling of a trillion cockroaches filling the habitat.

Most of Tisa's torso had been chewed away, and both legs dangled from thin strands of gristle. Her face was cut and smashed, beautiful dark eyes staring blankly up at the sheet of white LED-like light. One arm had been completely severed and it lay on the hardpan next to the corpse, and the other arm had been gnawed off to the elbow.

"Shit!" Judge yelled. He fired the M9 in his fury, his eyes blurring with tears.

"Not now. Not now," Psycho said. He was pulling on Judge's elbow.

The sweeper bots were close, their clicks and whirs drowning out the insects and calls of the wild.

Judge let Psycho pull him away, his eyes never leaving Tisa's corpse. Arjun had been dragged away so fast he hardly remembered what the man's dead body looked like. Tisa's final moments, the image of her destroyed body, seemed worse.

Judge and Psycho watched from the cover of the jungle as the sweeper bots swarmed the clearing, covering Tisa's remains, scrubbing her from existence.

"Should I try and get one?" Psycho asked.

"For what?"

Psycho hiked his shoulders.

"No. We've got enough to deal with."

Red lights shined atop the miniature robots and they froze for a second before disappearing back the way they'd come. All signs of Tisa's death had been removed, and nothing remained except the dinosaur corpse and a trail of broken branches and crushed leaves.

"Shit. I can't do shit right," Judge said.

"If you'd been awake, would anything have changed? You saw the thing, right? It was watching camp, waiting?"

"It was watching. Don't know about the waiting part. I was only awake a few seconds," Judge said.

"Maybe you could've gotten a shot off, but don't beat yourself up. I was an ass saying what I did. None of this is your fault."

That wasn't true, and Judge knew it. He'd been the chief champion of the mission, helped hand-pick the team, supervised the prep. No, this was his mission, his responsibility, and there was no way he'd ever shed those feelings.

The pair backtracked, following the broken branches and trail of fallen leaves. The drips of blood were gone, but Judge still saw them in his mind's eye, a constant reminder of what had happened. The sweeper bots might be able to remove all the physical evidence, but the mental blemishes remained, nagging at Judge, making his nerves dance and his stomach ache.

When they got back to the wall, Seok and Charlotte were gone.

✳✳✳

"I told them to stay here. Why the hell would they leave?" Judge was angry. Now the team was separated. Exactly what he'd been doing everything he could to avoid.

"Maybe a beastie showed-up and they had to run? We didn't give them a weapon when we took off on them," Psycho said.

"Tisa had the third gun. You think it's out there in the jungle someplace?"

"I didn't see the sweepers take it."

"Doesn't matter. What the hell are we going to do now? Yell for them?" Judge said.

"Might draw unwanted attention."

Judge sighed. "They know how to get back to the airlock, right? All they have to do is follow the wall."

"True. They'll be a few minutes in front of us. Or behind."

"I hope so." If something had happened to them while he and Psycho were running through the jungle, and the sweeper bots took care of their remains, Psycho and Judge could be alone. They'd heard no screams other than Tisa's, no cries for help, so Judge pushed his fears deep, tried to summon some hope. Psycho was right. They had to run, and he'd probably find them sitting under their conifer.

Judge and Psycho threaded along the wall, and half the day burned away. They saw no footprints, no signs of their friends, and that worried Judge, but there was nothing else he could do. He had to press on, and if they weren't at the airlock camp, then they'd have to find them.

"Screech. Screech." A giant bat-like creature swooped down from the white light and perched itself at the end of a long tree branch. The limb bent under the beast's weight as it stared at Judge and Psycho as they threaded along the wall. "Screech. Screech. Screech." The creature's black marble eyes tracked the companions' every move, shifting from one talon to another as it inched closer to the tree trunk.

Judge eased the M9 from his pocket. He whispered, "Should I take it? We need the meat."

Psycho shook his head no. "There's nothing on that thing. It's skin and bones, and the gunshot might alert others to our presence."

"Like Seok and Charlotte."

Psycho wagged his head in a 'you've got a point' gesture.

Judge brought up the gun, the creature watching him with its glassy eyes, leathery wings tucked at its side. It looked comfortable sitting on the branch, no sense of urgency that Judge could see.

Psycho started walking again, slowly moving away from the beast.

It screeched at him, its long narrow beak opening, pin-like teeth glinting in the harsh white light.

Judge backed away, but had only taken two steps when the beast dropped from its perch, wings opening, mouth cracked in a toothy grin as it came at them.

Judge blew the beast from the sky, blood and guts splattering the metal wall, the corpse falling to the ground with a thud. The shot echoed through the habitat, ringing off the walls like a bell.

"If they didn't hear that, then I don't know what to say," Psycho said. "Good shot, by the way."

Judge stared at the creature's corpse, sorrow washing over him. He wasn't a hunter, and could count on one hand the number of things he'd killed, insects notwithstanding. He didn't like the feeling, and even though he knew the beast was attacking him, it didn't make him feel any better to see the dead animal, a beast from a lost time, a lost world, gone forever. Judge slipped the gun away, hoping he wouldn't need it again soon.

"You alright?" Psycho said.

Judge nodded, but said nothing.

"It'll be OK," Psycho said.

Now Judge was really worried. Psycho the positive one? "I just... we have no control in here."

"Funny control," Psycho said. "Don't really notice you have any until you have none at all."

"When did you become so wise?" Judge said. For all he knew about his friend, there was much he didn't know.

"Something my dad used to say. 'Control is an illusion. Chaos rules.'" Psycho looked at the hardpan. "Come on," he said as he started walking again, slipping beneath a vine that ran from the jungle and was climbing up the metal wall.

Judge held out a hand and let the vine's leaves run through his fingers as he passed it. Odd. They'd seen no vegetation clinging to the wall in any other areas. "What do you make of this thing?" Judge stopped and gazed up at the vine as it trailed over the smooth metal.

"Sweepers haven't gotten to it yet?" Psycho said. "It is odd, though."

The party of two continued on, Psycho leading Judge around plants, roots, and vines, always keeping the wall to his back.

Relief flooded through Judge when they found their mark on the wall and knew they weren't far from camp. Voices floated through the jungle as Psycho and Judge wove in and out of conifers.

"Yo," Psycho called when they got close, and the chatter ceased like a T-rex had arrived. "It's us. No worries."

Seok and Charlotte pushed through the underbrush and the four astronauts took turns embracing.

"What happened? Why did you leave?" Judge said.

"We had a... friend to deal with, and we heard the gunshots, the sweeper bots, so we figured it was time to take cover, so we did," Charlotte said.

"Then when the commotion died down, we'd lost our way, so we went to the wall and backtracked here, figuring you'd do the same," Seok said.

Judge nodded.

"Where's Tisa?" Charlotte asked, the folds of pain running over her face and squinting eyes revealing she knew the answer to her question.

"She… didn't make it," Judge said.

Seok's chin fell to his chest and Charlotte cried, leaning against the wall, her red hair falling across her face. She was scratched, bruised, and streaked with grime, her eyes red cinders set in slick black sockets, cheeks shallow, dark bags below bloodshot eyes.

They sat in silence until afternoon rain.

The team filled their bladders and Seok and Psycho gathered some nuts and found odd green fruit that looked like avocado, but tasted more like a sour apple. The stuff was horrible, but it was food and they hadn't needed to hunt.

When darkness came, Judge was happy for it, though his nerves danced on a wire.

Now they were four.

21

When Judge was roused by Charlotte for his watch the jungle chatter was subdued, corpse light leaking through the conifer's thick boughs. The rhythm of the forest slowed as dawn approached, many of the night creatures heading home before the early risers came looking for breakfast. Even the insects seemed part of the rhythm, and as Judge listened, he could make out specific calls and hoots, the constant static of braying and buzzing having been replaced with a less frantic tune. He blinked as he looked up at the underside of the makeshift platform that hid the spacesuits. He rubbed his eyes. He was thankful for the short nap, but now that he'd gotten a little sleep, it was clear he needed much more. He yawned and stretched.

Charlotte was on watch.

"You see anything of note?" Judge asked.

"Didn't see anything, but—"

A roar echoed over the jungle, and it was answered by a hiss and yowl.

"But I heard a bunch. Good thing the big ones don't seem to smell us. Something ran past about an hour ago. Something bigger chasing it. I thought they might run right through camp," Charlotte said.

"Sound is weird in here because of the echo. Especially close to the wall," Judge said. He got to his feet as quietly as he could. "I'll let you guys sleep as long as I can."

She nodded.

Judge checked his M9 and pushed out into the virtual night. Moving through the forest was like having a pale spotlight shining through the trees at an odd angle. It reminded him of the woods behind his house back home, the way the floodlight over the deck would leak into the forest. Shadows danced behind tree trunks, bushes, and underbrush, but no small animals scuttled about. Shift change was underway.

The beep of morning light woke his companions and they ate the last of their fruit and drank some water. The party hadn't found a watering hole in the area, so there'd be no refills until afternoon rain, which hopefully would come. Their second day in the habitat the rain hadn't come, and Judge knew that was part of a cycle that would eventually leave them without water. At that point they could plan better, but currently he had no idea what the skip pattern was.

"I was thinking we should take another look at the airlock. Maybe something has changed," Seok said.

"Agreed. It's close and we can hunt and gather along the way," Psycho said.

The party threaded through the glade of conifers to the wall, where they made a left and headed east. Their footprints were easy to see in the soil along the wall, and within five minutes they stood before the airlock, gazing up at it as though it were a monument.

Nothing had changed. Controls hadn't appeared. There was no instruction manual hanging from the wall next to the door, no signs at all. Psycho probed the center of the door, but it didn't iris open.

"This metal is different than the wall," Seok said.

"The way it peels back and folds, I'm thinking it's softer?" Judge said.

"I don't know about that. Less brittle, maybe." Seok turned his penetrating gaze on Psycho. "You really think the laser rifle can get through that?"

Psycho nodded emphatically. "Yup. Only question is how much power will it take? I might have to blast the thing several times."

The party's heads all jerked toward the jungle at the sound of breaking branches. Growling and huffing echoed off the wall. Something big was threading through the forest. An animal path led due north from the airlock, but there was no dust floating above it, no signs any creatures had passed that way recently.

Judge said, "I don't think disabling the airlock is smart. I'm with Seok. If the Martian atmosphere gets in here…"

"We get in our SEV, go back to base, and roll in red sand like it's money," Psycho said. "I don't want to destroy this place. Hell, the almanac, remember? But I also don't want to die. I say we take the chance, and if—"

A creature bounded onto the path to the north, huffing and braying as it clawed the ground.

Judge drew his M9 and Psycho sighted the laser rifle. "Don't use that unless you absolutely have to. We need the juice," Judge said.

Psycho nodded.

The beast's head was armored, three horns protruding at odd angles, dark eyes locking on the party as they stood before the airlock. The creature looked part rhino.

"Odd," Seok said.

The party stared at him.

"The beast must be frightened, because that's a triceratops," Seok said.

When he didn't elaborate, Psycho said, "And?"

"It's a herbivore, at least that's what we think…"

The dinosaur snorted, its head pumping up and down, thick legs pounding the hardpan. Dense muscles bulged beneath gray armored skin as the beast surged down the path. Red spots dotted the creature, a large red stain like a red wine spill cutting across its head armor and climbing up its center horn.

The creature was twenty meters off when Judge fired, three fast shots that smacked into the beast's forward headshield and didn't even slow the creature down. It was huge, standing three meters tall and stretching five meters in length.

"No way that thing can get through the thick jungle to the east of here. Then there's the palm grove. Follow me," Judge said.

Judge ran along the wall, Charlotte and Seok behind him, Psycho watching their rear. The triceratops wailed and cried as it thundered down the path, sliding to a halt before the airlock and wailing.

Palm trees began appearing interspersed with the conifers and saw palmetto. Judge cut sharply north, knifing into the forest and leaving the wall behind. He moved fast, ducking under tree branches, around thorn bushes, always working northeast toward the palm forest.

The tall palm trees grew in unordered rows, and as the conifers fell away, the palms grew closer together and before long Judge and his companions were pushing through tight spaces. The sounds of pursuit lessoned, but Judge didn't stop until he had a thick patch of palm trees between himself and the dinosaur. The party waited in silence, gasping for air. Running in the bulky and awkward spacesuit boots was hard, and they were all winded from their dash.

The triceratops wailed and cried as it gave up, and the creature passed to the south, probably following the wall.

"That was close," Charlotte said.

"Too close," Psycho said. "Still want to mess around?"

They harvested coconuts and headed back to the airlock.

"Do you see that?" Seok was just emerging from the jungle, and he was pointing up at the wall.

Judge looked up, the harsh light reflecting off the metal wall hurting his eyes. The smooth gray metal disappeared in the whiteness. There were no seams, rivets, nothing... except.

A rectangle a much darker shade of gray than the wall stood out thirty meters up, just where the wall blended into the fake sunlight.

"I see it," Psycho said. "An air vent?"

"Could be," Judge said. "The HVAC system has to circulate the air somehow. It's probably darker because of dirt and dust build-up over a long period of time."

"Why hasn't it been cleaned by the sweepers?" Seok said.

"Too bad we can't get a closer look," Judge said.

"Who said we can't," Psycho said.

Judge chuckled. "Unless you've got some special skills I'm unaware of, or you've got twenty-five meter stilts hidden in the jungle, I don't see how we can get up there."

Psycho said, "You of little faith. Remember that vine we saw?"

"Yeah? So? Even if it can be used as rope, how the heck is that going to help us?" Charlotte said. "The wall is too smooth for any of us to climb."

"All true. But I've got an idea," Psycho said. "Seok and Charlotte, get me the longest piece of vine you can. Not thicker than one inch in diameter. Live vine would work best."

Seok shook his head. "But I don't see how—"

"You will."

Judge rolled his eyes, and said, "You gonna share it with us?"

"I'm still working on it, but I know I need the vine," Psycho said, and he plunged into the jungle, examining the trees closest to the wall.

"Do you mind going?" Judge said. "I think I know what he's thinking. If we can cut down a tree close to the wall, get it to fall in the right spot, maybe we'd be able to climb up there."

"And he needs the vine to guide the tree," Charlotte said.

"Just a guess," Judge said.

"But a good one," Seok said. "Can I take the gun? Since Psycho has the rifle."

Judge phished the weapon from his pocket and handed it to Seok. "There's not much ammo left. Only use it if you have to."

"10-4," Seok said as he and Charlotte headed west along the wall.

Judge followed Psycho and he found the man standing next to a conifer that stood fifteen meters tall. Brown spiked leaves covered the hardpan, and the air smelled of pine, earth and moisture.

"This one will work if we can guide it right," Psycho said. "Don't you think?"

Judge chuckled and stared at his friend. Psycho was the only person on Mars that could predict what he was thinking. The only other person who could do that was on Earth. He said, "How the hell are you going to cut that thing down? You can hack at that trunk with your knife until you're eighty and you'll get nowhere."

"Fire," Psycho said.

"Fire? The sweeper bots will come running."

"Not if I keep it small and clean. I'll get it going now so we have plenty of time to do it slow."

Judge sighed. "And if it falls before Seok and Charlotte get back with the vine-rope?"

"We wing it," Psycho said. He clapped Judge on the back and started gathering dead evergreen branches and dried leaves.

The day dragged on, the hours slipping away as Psycho and Judge tended the small fire at the base of the conifer. The base of the trunk was getting red, but there was still a very long way to go.

The afternoon rain came, and it actually helped by knocking down the smoke. The flame itself was protected by the dense boughs of the conifer, and the fire weathered the few drops of water easily while the four astronauts drank their fill.

With a couple of hours of daylight left, Psycho climbed up the tree a little, the trunk creaking and cracking. He tied off one end of the vine and dropped the other end down to Seok who threaded through the jungle toward the wall. With the vine in place they waited, feeding the fire, never taking their attention off the base of the tree.

"I just had a horrible thought," Charlotte said. "Won't the sweeper bots come?"

"Eventually," Seok said. "Though we've seen little dead vegetation and not many dead branches and fallen trees, the vine growing on the habitat wall proves overgrowth and natural plant death aren't top priority. Think of it like Spring and Fall cleanup. I hope."

The trunk popped and creaked with each push of wind, and about an hour after lights out, the tree started to crack.

Scrambling in the pale light was difficult, but Judge could see well enough. Psycho ran through the jungle, picking up the vine and putting his back to the wall beneath the vent. As soon as the tree tipped, he'd hightail it into the jungle, getting out of the path of the tree.

Judge and Seok braced themselves against the tree trunk, pushing it toward the wall.

Charlotte stood behind them, cheering them on. There was no room for her hands on the tree.

Two cracks, like the snap and pop of gunshots, echoed over the jungle as the tree began its fall. It tipped southeast, toward Psycho, and Judge saw his friend dart through the underbrush. He was clear before the tree let go completely.

The conifer came down, crashing through limbs, crushing small trees, and coming to rest against the metal wall.

Psycho hooted and hollered. "That's work, bitches!"

Dust rose from the hardpan, and the tree rolled, wedging itself firmly against the wall, a Y branch supporting the massive trunk.

"Looks good," Judge said as he walked alongside the fallen tree to the wall. The conifer's densely covered branches flattened everything next to its thick trunk, and limbs stuck out like spokes on a bike wheel as the trunk tapered down and leaned against the wall.

Darkness pressed in on them, shadows danced, and with the night's main event over, the larger creatures of the habitat went back to their nightly tussles.

The party settled in under the fallen tree, the pillar of light sending daggers of pale light through the dense branches.

"I'll take first watch," Judge said. There was no way he could sleep, at least not until his heart stopped galloping. The night felt hotter than normal, and Judge used his hand to fan his face. He gazed up through the branches of the fallen tree. Had they blocked the airflow in their immediate area? There'd be many such vents, so getting oxygen wasn't a worry, but it could explain the increased temperature. Judge sighed. Everything they did here affected something, threw some delicate system out of balance. Eventually, that would catch up with them.

22

After a breakfast of coconuts and water, Psycho set off up the fallen tree. His mission was exploratory, and he'd left the laser rifle, fire starter bow, and spacesuit boots behind. He carried a length of vine-rope, and planned to tie off a safety line.

"That bark looks pretty rough, Psycho," Judge said. "I know the boots are bulky, but your feet are going to get torn to hell."

"I've got my socks," the Mission Specialist said, but as he mounted the tree trunk just beyond its break point, he stopped, staring at the fallen conifer. "You're right." He retrieved his spacesuit boots and slipped them on. He threw the loop of vine over a shoulder and climbed. Judge, Seok and Charlotte watched as he inched through the fallen tree, going branch to branch, being careful not to move too fast and shift the tree.

He was halfway up when several limbs pressed between the wall and tree trunk snapped, and the tree moved. Psycho gripped a branch as the trunk rolled, and he quickly stepped up onto the next limb, then another, and as the conifer settled, Psycho resumed his ascent.

"Any thoughts on how to get this thing open? If it's what we assume it is?" Judge said to his companions.

Charlotte looked at Seok who hiked his shoulders and said, "We've got nothing to pry it with, even if there's a gap. It's like this entire place is one piece, like it was poured into a mold. The lack of seams, rivets or bolts. I'm not hopeful."

"But there's dirt and grime on the vent, right? That's why it's dark, so there has to be gaps. How else would the air get in?" Charlotte said. She seemed to think she'd scored a point.

Seok shook his head. "It could be like a filter, or that buried water thing we found."

Psycho slowed. The fallen tree was bouncing and shifting as the trunk tapered down and Psycho got closer to its end. He paused, hanging the vine on a branch, twisting his head and surveying the area.

"He's looking for a place to tie off," Judge said.

Psycho didn't find a good spot to tie a safety line. If the fallen tree slipped the rest of the way to the hardpan it wouldn't matter anyway. He continued climbing, peeling off the main trunk and sliding down a branch that took him to the front of the vent.

Judge and the others strode forward until they stood below him. "What we got?" Judge shouted. His voice rang off the metal wall and echoed over the jungle, and the insect trilling ceased for two heartbeats.

Psycho's legs were wrapped around the branch, and he held on with his right hand while reaching out with his left. He rubbed the grate, letting his fingers inspect every groove and slit. "It's a vent for sure," Psycho said. "The intake openings are very fine, and I can't see inside."

"Any way to get it off?" Seok said.

"Not that I can see. There's no gap around the edges, no place to pry it off even if we had something to do that with. No screws, trim... nothing." Psycho sounded frustrated.

"Alright, come on back down," Judge yelled.

"Time to let Psycho fry something?" Charlotte said.

"Seems like the smart thing. What's the downside?" Judge said. "Unlike the airlock door, if we damage or destroy the vent and related ductwork there are plenty of other vents to feed the habitat."

Seok nodded. "I don't see any other option at this point."

"He seemed confident he could do it," Charlotte said. "That realistic?"

"Yes," Seok said. "I'd think we'd need to be ready to move fast."

"Why's that?" said Psycho as he dropped from the fallen tree trunk. He pushed along the fallen conifer, wiping his brow with the back of his hand.

"When you blast that thing, the sweepers might come. This will be a different kind of damage. Especially, if we set fire to the place," Seok said.

Psycho went and got the laser rifle and Judge and the others followed.

"We'll need to shield ourselves. There could be a ricochet, or the metal might burn or splash as it melts," Charlotte said.

"Unlikely on both counts," Psycho said. "I'm going to try and position myself behind the trunk. Reach over it and fire."

Charlotte said nothing.

"You're wrong, though," Seok said. "Charlotte is right. We know nothing about what the metal wall is made of or the vent, and we haven't fired at either before."

Psycho nodded. "You're right. Sorry. Amped up right now."

Charlotte smacked him on the back. "Just trying to keep your ass alive."

"And I appreciate that," Psycho said.

Then he smiled at Charlotte, his 'how you doin' smile, and Charlotte smiled back. Judge felt anger race through him, the tickle of jealousy, then he remembered he hadn't wanted a relationship. He'd told Charlotte he couldn't get past Brenda, though she didn't know the worst of it. Now here he was not wanting her to be with another man. Cake meet mouth.

A roar echoed over the jungle and the companions exchanged furtive glances.

"Sounds like our buddy from the gate. Big boy T-rex," Judge said.

"He's a ways off. "Let's get on with it," Psycho said.

Judge considered protesting, and was going to suggest they wait until they were sure the T-rex had moved on before Psycho tried to blast the vent, but then he remembered in the biosphere there was no good time or safe haven. Danger lurked under every branch and behind every tree trunk.

Psycho's second climb was much faster. He'd tied the vine off where the tree met the wall, and he'd already tested all his footholds and handholds. When he was ten meters from the vent, he climbed onto a branch that stuck off the bottom of the tree trunk, the laser rifle dangling from its shoulder strap.

Using the branch like rope, he twisted his legs around the limb as he held tight. When he was steady, he grabbed the branch with one arm, his legs pressed together and wrapped around the limb, and used his other arm to lift the laser rifle and place its barrel on the tree trunk.

"I see now," Judge said to himself.

Seok said, "I'd fall like a leaf."

Psycho twisted his free arm and wrapped the shoulder strap around his forearm to steady the weapon. Then he shifted the gun, aiming it at the vent.

"Take cover," Psycho yelled. "Firing in five, four…"

Judge and the others scuttled behind tree trunks.

"Three, two, one."

The laser rifle trilled, and the bolt hit the vent with a twang and sizzle. The bolt ricocheted, and ripped through the jungle and smacked into the hardpan, a thin tendril of white smoke lifting from the charred vegetation, but there was no flame.

The vent was blackened, dented, and slightly bent, but it had held.

A roar thundered over the forest.

"Hurry, Psycho," Judge urged.

Psycho fired the laser rifle again, but his arm was tired, and the gun bounced. The shot rebounded off the vent and planted itself in a tree trunk four meters from where Judge stood.

Psycho struggled to keep from falling, wrapping both arms around the tree trunk. The laser rifle fell, dangling from Psycho's arm from its shoulder strap. He cursed, the vent blacker, more bent, but still no hole big enough to squirm through.

Tree branches bent and cracked as a T-rex pushed through the underbrush. The beast threw back its head and roared, meter-long teeth glinting in the fake sunlight. Slime mixed with blood dripped from massive jaws, doorknob-sized black eyes searching the fallen tree. It raked the hardpan with its claws, muscles rippling down the beast's two thick legs.

Psycho steadied himself, pulled tight to the conifer limb, and swung the rifle back up onto the tree trunk. He braced himself, aimed, and fired, thankful the laser rifle didn't recoil.

He slipped as he fired, but held fast, and the shot didn't rebound.

The vent was charred, metal dripping down the side of the wall like candle wax. The blast area glowed orange and white, but was quickly fading to black.

There was a hole in the vent big enough to scramble through.

The T-rex roared and surged forward, and the ground trembled with each footfall as the massive beast trundled toward the fallen tree, Psycho in its sights.

Judge opened his mouth to yell to his friend, but Psycho didn't need a warning. He was frantically pulling and clawing his way back to the top of the fallen tree, struggling up branches, the laser rifle dangling at his elbow.

Judge rolled his shoulders and said, "Seok, give me back the M9."

Seok slapped the weapon into Judge's hand and he arced it upward, sighted, and fired. No hesitation, cool as ice and smooth as silk.

The bullet smacked into the side of the T-rex's face and the creature bellowed, jerking back as if punched by a giant unseen hand. It teetered on its two legs, shifting side to side, blood dripping from the wound on its head.

The buzz of a drone rose above the chaos.

"We've got company," Judge yelled.

The T-rex looked from the fallen tree to the jungle where the rest of the company hid, its glassy eyes barren of intelligence.

"Oh what I wouldn't give for a stone to throw into the forest," Charlotte said.

Judge knew what he needed to do, but didn't want to do it. He yelled, "Here! Over here!" Then he turned and bolted away into the jungle.

The beast roared and thundered as the ground shook and trees creaked and snapped.

Judge wove through the forest like a running back through a secondary, weaving between tree trunks, avoiding thorn bushes, slipping through vines, and jumping over roots and anthills. He spared a glance over his shoulder, and the jungle swayed and shook as the T-rex gave chase.

He ran on, tree limbs smacking his face, creatures fleeing before him, the commotion behind him lessoning as the T-rex gave up. He'd bought Psycho and his crew valuable time, and hopefully they'd used it well.

The buzzing of the drone intensified as Judge worked his way back to his companions. He hid behind a thick fern and examined the fallen tree and the surrounding area. The drone hovered, cameras rotating. It was a smaller drone, and it appeared focused on the fallen tree, but when its mechanical eye caught sight of the damage on the wall, its rotors cycled up and it darted toward the vent. It hovered there, then spun and flew up and down the tree, did three circles of the area from above, then disappeared over the jungle canopy.

Judge revealed himself, walking toward the fallen tree.

Psycho appeared out of the underbrush, followed by the others.

"Everyone OK?" Judge asked.

Nods and wagging heads.

Beep.

Afternoon rain came, and the companions drank and filled their bladders.

"We've got a couple of hours to prepare before it gets dark. I'm going to climb up there and take a look. Psycho, do you think you can hunt? Get us some meat to cook?" Judge said.

Psycho nodded.

"Seok and Charlotte, gather as many nuts and coconuts as you can. No idea how long it will be before we can get more food and water," Judge said. That was a scary thought he didn't want to dwell on. If they got lost searching the habitat's infrastructure, they could starve to death while they looked for a way out.

The companions went about their tasks, and Judge climbed the fallen tree. Waves of heat rolled off the burnt vent as he approached, the metal still glowing faintly around the edges of the hole. It would take hours before the metal cooled enough to squeeze through.

Beyond the grate a white tube stretched into the distance. It wasn't big enough to stand in, but the party could crawl, or walk hunched over. The ductwork appeared to be made of some type of fiberglass, and there were fine black streaks running through the white.

He climbed back down, and moved away from the fallen tree. If the T-rex, sweepers or drones decided to check things out he didn't want to be around. He found a thick patch of bushes with long thorns and started piling branches, making a teepee-like shelter. Judge heard Psycho coming through the underbrush and he called out to let Psycho know where he was.

Judge was finishing stacking branches when Psycho appeared carrying two rodents the size of small dogs. They looked like pigs, but had horns and were speckled with red and green dots.

"Those look good," Judge said

"Nice shelter. I'll get a fire going. Can you butcher these?" Psycho said.

"10-4."

Psycho collected dried wood and went to work with his fire making bow, and Judge skinned and gutted the two dinosaurs.

"We can cook some and smoke some. Might be awhile before we get food again."

"I was just thinking about that," Judge said.

Charlotte pushed through the trees with Seok in tow. She was covered in spiderwebs, but held an armful of coconuts, and a bunch of smaller nuts in a giant folded leaf.

"You found us," Psycho said.

"Looks like we're set," Charlotte said.

The evening beep sounded, the whiteness above blinked out, and the pillar of corpse light rose like a sword.

"We'll see what the new day brings," Judge said.

23

Morning came like a flashbulb, and the party ate, took care of personal business, and prepared to climb the fallen tree. The air vent had cooled, the thin hole charred black. Morning birds sang, insects buzzed, and it seemed like a normal day in the habitat, if being underground in an artificial biosphere on Mars could ever be normal. Judge cracked his knuckles and took a sip of water. Even though they'd eaten the prior night his stomach still grumbled, his mind constantly conjuring fantasies of burgers, vodka and bread. What he wouldn't give for a slice of Italian bread, and maybe a little sauce to sop up.

"You OK?" Charlotte asked. "You look like you were used hard and put away wet."

Judge chuckled. "My dad used to say that."

"Mine too," she said. Her normally smooth face was creased with carelines, her eyes narrowed, even though she was forcing a smile.

"Let's get on with this before something comes to fix that hole," Judge said.

"Surprised that hasn't happened yet," Seok said.

Judge had worried about that. Something wasn't right.

Carrying the supplies proved to be an issue, but as usual Psycho came through with a solution. Charlotte smiled ear to ear as Psycho cut off the top of his jumpsuit, his toned abs making Judge feel a hundred kilos overweight, even though he'd probably lost five in the last three days. He made a rucksack by tying off the arms to the neck hole and using the arms as straps. They packed the sack with nuts, cooked meat wrapped in leaves, and rations of coconut, and tied the top off with vine. Climbing with the pack on was going to be difficult, so Seok suggested tying it to the safety line and hauling it up.

Charlotte's eyes flicked to Psycho's bare chest often enough to raise Judge's hackles. He rolled his shoulders and rubbed his eyes. "Fabio, you're on point with the M9."

Psycho's eyebrows lifted, but he exchanged weapons with Judge.

"Seok, Charlotte, then me. When you get to the top, take your time. Some of those edges might be sharp. We'll go slow. Wait until we're all up there—"

A roar pierced the morning and everyone's head jerked to the west toward the airlock door.

"When you get inside inch forward, but wait for me. There's no rush. If you get stuck, don't panic. Just let us know. Normal voice should do it in there with the echo."

Nods of agreement.

"Lastly," Judge said, "I know this doesn't need to be said, but there was that seminar... What was his name? He said repeat important shit many times. So far, we've been 'in the environment' if you will. An oddity, yes, but just another creature under the dome. Now we're going where we're not supposed to be, and we have no idea what measures the biosphere systems might take."

"Yes," Seok said. "So far I think everything has been preprogrammed protocol. Documenting, prioritizing in a computer-type way. When we enter the inner workings, there's no way to know what we might activate."

"And what about air?" Charlotte said. "I still think we should at least bring our spacesuits."

"No," Judge said. "If we get to a point where we think we're leaving an oxygen environment, we'll backtrack. Those suits are too important. We'd have to wear them, and they're bulky and we have no idea how much space we'll have. If we stay in the air supply system the ducts should get bigger, lead to a chase way. Beyond that..." Beyond that Judge didn't have a clue.

The ground trembled slightly, and growling and barking echoed along the wall.

"It's getting closer," Seok said.

"Let's get to it then. Be out of here before it gets here," Psycho said.

He vaulted onto a branch and started climbing. The route to the vent had been climbed several times and Seok and Charlotte had no problems following the beaten path.

Leaves rustled and branches creaked and cracked. A T-rex head poked through the foliage, a thin dark line of blood running down the side of its face onto its muscled torso. The beast lowered its head, dark eyes searching.

The team froze, watching the dinosaur as it stepped forward, the fallen tree shaking.

"Go," Judge whispered. "We have to." Worry leaked through him. Nobody had squeezed through the hole yet, and they had no idea how long that might take. What if he couldn't fit? He was the biggest, which was why he put himself last. Worst case they could go on and explore and he could stay behind.

The T-rex roared, but still hadn't seen them.

Psycho reached the vent and slid through, no issues. Same for Seok and Charlotte.

Judge felt better knowing they were safe, but that idea made him laugh as he climbed, pulling himself from limb to limb. He stepped on a sucker branch as he dropped down onto the limb that led to the hole, and it snapped.

The T-rex stopped moving, its narrow reptilian head turning in Judge's direction. Hockey puck-sized eyes locked on Judge, the beast's mouth falling open a crack as it gurgled.

Judge slipped as he climbed toward the vent, and he was forced to hug the branch, laser rifle hanging from its strap, small green needle-like leaves piercing his face, chest, arms and legs. He was almost to the vent. Psycho peered through the blackened hole as he pulled his makeshift rucksack into the duct.

The tree shook violently, and Judge looked over his shoulder.

The T-rex had spun around and was battering the tree with its thick tail, slamming it over and over.

Judge dove for the vent hole, and Psycho caught him, helping him ease carefully into the tube. The edge of the charred hole was sharp in spots, and he felt no relief until he was safely inside the white tube.

He sprawled next to Psycho, staring out the hole.

The tree crashed to the ground, and the dinosaur roared, stomping its feet, its massive tooth-filled jaws smacking.

Psycho coiled the vine rope and lay it next to the hole. "We can always climb down if need be," he said. His voice echoed and carried, the *womp womp* of fans turning filling the tube.

The duct the astronauts sat in had a diameter of roughly a meter and a half. They couldn't stand up fully, but there was plenty of room to crawl, stoop, or slide. The white tube with black stripes was clean and smooth, and it ran straight on into darkness.

"OK, let's do this," Judge said.

Pushing the rucksack before him, Psycho half crawled, half walked through the duct. Seok walked hunched over and so did Charlotte, but before long they were monkey crawling like Judge.

As he inched through the tube, Judge tried to relax, but with the danger behind him he had a minute to think, to clear his head, to remind himself he was in a thin little tube, below the surface of Mars. His claustrophobia came back like the flu, and cold dread seeped through him and he felt sick and hot.

He slowed, breathing heavy. The others disappeared into the gloom in front of him.

The fans pounded, air flowing like wind, and below it all there was a series of creaks, taps, beeps, titters and whistles.

He took a deep breath and that cleared his mind, like he'd taken a sip of wine. Did the air smell odd?

"Judge, get a move on." It was Charlotte. She'd waited for him.

"Sorry, it's hot in here."

"Yup."

As they went on, the stray light from the habitat faded and blackness filled the tunnel. As the airflow increased, light decreased, and before long the companions found themselves pushing against a steady gale in impenetrable darkness. They were keeping within touching distance of the person in front of them, and putting his hand on Charlotte's spacesuit boot every few seconds helped Judge steady his nerves and slow his heartrate.

"Come out to the coast. I'll show you around. We'll have a few laughs," Psycho said.

Judge cackled.

"You guys are worse than an old married couple with the private jokes," Charlotte said.

"Private?" Psycho said. "Die Hard? Ever hear of it? It's the best Christmas movie ever."

"It's not a Christmas movie," Seok said.

"It kind of is," Judge said.

"Talking films at the heart of Mars. Cool podcast," Psycho said.

"I'm in," Judge said.

"There's something up here," Psycho said. "Slow up."

Judge crowded in behind his companions, peering into the darkness.

The tube connected with a chase way fifteen meters square. The air flow surged through the duct, its scent oddly chemical. Giant fans thumped, and as Judge followed the team into the chase way, the heavy airflow pushed him back.

"Air smells strange," Seok said. "Could explain things. Nutrients and other chemicals in the air."

"Doesn't appear to have hurt us," Charlotte said.

Judge remembered how a couple of deep breaths brought his stamina back like he was a marathon runner. How they'd all been hiking like Olympians without enough food and water. Out in the habitat he hadn't noticed the scent, but in the vents, where the air was condensed was a different story.

The shaft was dimly lit by a pale green light that emanated from the walls, and above cables crisscrossed like a spider's web. Judge jumped when something moved next to him. He inched toward the wall, hand out. Tubes running along the duct walls that Judge had assumed were plumbing and power, were undulating and pulsing like veins, and closer inspection revealed thin capillary-like vessels spidering out over the chase way walls.

"It looks... alive," Seok said. In the green light the veins looked yellow. "They're probably red."

"What?" Psycho froze.

"Green light mixed with red makes yellow," Seok said.

The pipes undulated and shifted as something passed through them. The veins were covered in small pustules, and Judge almost jumped out of his skin when one of them hissed and pissed air into the chase way.

"Amazing," Seok said. He was examining the piping closely, his face centimeters from a moving vein.

"That could be waste removal you know," Judge said.

Seok jerked away and chuckled, but he didn't smile.

The webbing of natural pipes twisted and snaked down the walls of the chase way, both directions ending in blackness. The pounding of the fan seemed to be coming from the party's right, so Judge went that way.

Faint lines that looked to have been made by wheels streaked the smooth floor, but none of the supply veins or related capillary-like pipes encroached on the chase way floor. Like the primary habitat, the duct was in perfect balance. A steady wind blew through the chase way, and to Judge it had the sharp, tangy, bread thick smell of a brewery.

"What do you make of the hanging cables on the ceiling?" Psycho said.

When nobody spoke, Seok said, "They look like stainless steel, but the way they sag looks like rope. I would think power lines wouldn't hang like that."

Psycho held up a fist as he came to a halt.

Tiny metal spiders swarmed over a bulge in one of the pipes. Green ooze streaked with red dripped from a rip in the vein, and the miniature robotic spiders spun metal webs around the breach. The bots squeaked and tittered, eight triple-jointed legs fine as angel hair spaghetti spreading out from a kidney bean-sized torso. Red eyes glowed at the ends of hair-like stalks, and they swayed slightly in the air rushing through the duct. The droids didn't appear to notice the party, and when Psycho continued down the chase way, the robots didn't pause in their work and not a single red eye strayed in their direction.

"Like the sweeper bots," Psycho whispered.

"Amazing how small they are. The finery and detail required to make metal parts of that size is incredibly difficult," Seok said.

"Could... could we make something like that?" Judge asked.

Seok didn't hesitate. "No, most certainly not. We've imagined things like that. We're developing tech that will one day allow us to build things like the spiders. But now? Not even close."

"Makes me think of what you said before about nanobots," Charlotte said.

"Yes," Seok said. "Things we see here and think of as biological could actually be technological."

Air whished through the chase way, and Judge cracked his knuckles. The pounding of the fan was getting louder, like a helicopter approaching.

"You mean like cyborgs?" Psycho said.

"Not exactly, but yeah," Seok said. "Living things merging with technology is nothing new. Are your nieces and nephews chipped?"

"They are," Judge said. It was a big debate for expecting parents. Should they allow the government to put a chip inside their infant? The selling points were many: it would stop kidnapping, was the ultimate way to store medical records, and could save the child's life should they become lost. And for a small additional fee, guaranteed removal services could be purchased along with the installation, so the child could have the chip taken out when they reached the appropriate age should they choose.

"Artificial organs save tons of people," Charlotte said.

She'd been quiet and the three men turned to look at her.

She smiled, but Judge could tell her heart wasn't in it.

After forty-five minutes of fighting their way into the steady wind, the party came to an intersection. The chase way they'd been walking in continued on and curved away, and a new shaft jutted off on the left at a right angle. A massive fan filled the new duct, and it spun rhythmically, pushing air.

Womp. Womp. Womp.

Womp. Womp. Womp.

Beyond the fan something sparkled in the dim light.

24

Judge stood before the huge fan, mouth hanging open, hair blowing in the steady airstream, eyes watering. He peered past the spinning blades, trying to see what lay in the chamber beyond, but it was dark and shadowy. Red light leaked into the space, but there appeared to be no other light. Unease raced up Judge's spine and he shook himself and rolled his shoulders.

The faint roar of a dinosaur echoed above the howling wind.

Vein-pipes clung to the walls around the fan, their tiny capillaries creeping to the edges of the fan blade's radius. Tiny pustules along the veins spit air into the fan, and Judge shivered.

"It's cold," Charlotte said.

The pipes farted and bellowed, rank steam joining the chilled air provided by the fan.

Psycho leaned in, his eyes tracking the motion of the fan blade. "The chamber beyond is probably an air handler."

"What's that?" Judge said. He thought he knew, but wasn't sure.

"Really just a large sealed area where air is mixed and its temperature and composition are adjusted prior to dispersal," Psycho said.

"Could be where the oxygen mix is created," Seok said.

"Are you thinking ice?" Charlotte asked.

"I am," Seok said.

"Can you fill us in, please?" Psycho said.

"Figure out how to turn off that fan and we can see for ourselves," Judge said.

Psycho started counting on his hand, then aloud. "One, two, three. One, two, three."

"Don't even think about it," Judge said.

"I think it's moving slow enough," Psycho said. "The fan is so big there's a solid second to step through."

"You, sir, are out of your mind," Seok said.

"Count it off. You'll see," Psycho said.

Seok sighed loudly, his eyes going hard, chin out. It was his 'I don't suffer fools lightly' face. He gazed at the fan, eyes locked on its base. His head bobbed as he counted. He straightened and turned. "You might have a point, but you're still nuts."

Psycho braced himself before the fan and started counting. "One, two, three. One, two, three.

"Wait," Judge said. "Even if you get through, what if the rest—"

"One, two, three!" On three, Psycho casually stepped through the fan, slipping between the huge blades as they spun.

Judge started. It was like Psycho had disappeared. There were no screams of pain, no blood splatters. "Psycho?" Judge crooned.

The pounding fan, the whistling airstream, but no Psycho.

Sweat dripped down his back and Judge felt the walls closing in around him.

"Psycho," Charlotte yelled, much louder than Judge had.

"Yo," Psycho screamed. "All good."

Then Psycho was back on Judge's side of the fan, as if he'd reappeared at a magician's request.

"Did you… You just…" Judge stammered.

"It's easy once you get the timing down. Focus until the blades slow in your mind. It's easy," Psycho said as he stepped through the fan again.

Judge's heart leapt and pain shot down his legs.

It took Seok longer than Charlotte to build up his courage, but both were able to step through, leaving Judge alone in the chase way. Screeches and howls echoed up the shaft, and Judge looked back the way they'd come. The large duct curved away, the occasional puff of air coming from the pipe-veins like steam release valves. He breathed deep and shivered, but felt better than he had in a long time, despite his lack of food and water.

"When you get through the air current is strong. The fan is pulling air into the chase way. So as soon as you step through, go to your right or left. Get out of the airstream," Psycho said.

Judge stood frozen, cold perspiration covering his face and drenching the neckline of his jumpsuit.

"You OK over there?" It was Charlotte. "Or you've finally chosen your moment to abandon us?"

"Just taking a last look around over here," Judge yelled. "How's the air over there?"

"Cold, but you'll see why. We were right about the ice," Seok said.

"You've got light?" Judge said.

"Just get over here, will you?" Psycho said. "Don't make me disparage a superior officer."

"Oh, has something changed? You follow a different code underground, mole boy?" Judge said.

"Nooooo," Psycho said. "But if you're gonna be a powderpuff, I'm calling you out on it. This is—"

"My god!" Charlotte shouted. "You two are worse than sisters."

"I think you just insulted all sisters," Seok said.

No more stalling. Judge focused, counting in his head, watching the blades spin. He stood there for several minutes counting, gathering his courage, then he stepped through.

Judge couldn't believe he'd done it, and he smiled as he fought his way to the side, out of the fan's airflow. For a brief instant he felt the fan grab hold of him, pull him toward its chomping teeth, but he lowered his shoulder and pressed into the gale until he stood with his crewmates.

Red light beamed from odd fixtures along the walls, and Judge felt like he was standing in a ray of yellow sunlight, the green light leaking through the fan mixing with the red. The brewery scent had become more earthy, and Judge's nose tickled.

The chamber was carved from the Martian bedrock, and dark streaks that looked black in the red light crisscrossed the cavern walls.

The companions stood with their backs to the wall on a service access ledge that ran around the chamber. Below, a massive machine unlike anything Judge had ever seen sat in the center of the space, robots of various sizes and shapes buzzing around, their headlamps cutting through the murky red light. Chunks of ice speckled with Martian soil entered the top of the machine via a clear tube. A netting of veins covered the apparatus, and metal and rubber could be seen in the gaps. Tiny bots like sweepers swarmed over the machine, and large vents, like the pustules on the pipe-veins covered the odd device. The vents spit and puffed, filling the chamber with mist.

"Well now we know where the air comes from," Judge said. "Martian ice."

"I'd love to know how the machine works. What chemicals they add to the mix. There any way we can get a sample?" Seok said.

All heads turned his way. Seok's eyes were even darker in the red light. "Sorry," he said.

"No need to be. We just don't stop being scientists," Charlotte said.

"You figure that big vei... pipe at the bottom is for water?" Psycho said.

"Probably," Seok said. "Or what will become water."

"Ice is water, no?" Charlotte said.

"Sure. Yes," Seok said. "But we don't know what, if anything, they treat it with."

"Can we take a closer look?" Charlotte said.

Judge stepped forward and looked over the ledge. "We'll have to climb."

"On?" Charlotte said.

Judge reached out and stroked a pipe that clung to the wall. It didn't move or react in any way.

"Oh, hell no," Charlotte said.

"We've got no choice, unless we go back," Judge said.

"I don't see another way out of here, but there must be passageways for the bots down there," Seok said.

"What do you make of the pipe bringing in the ice?" Judge said. "It looks sealed."

"Yeah, we're still in system. The air is fine in here," Psycho said.

"But if we have to pass through a door, how will we know the atmospheric conditions of the space we're entering?" Charlotte asked. "Bots don't need air. Would cyborgs?"

To that nobody had anything to say.

Judge closed his eyes, listening to the howling wind, the beeping and tapping of the bots, and the rhythmic pounding of the giant fan. He opened his eyes and took a deep breath.

There appeared to be other fans farther along the wall, though it was hard to see them in the dim red light. "The chamber looks to be carved from the Martian bedrock, and I know bots don't need oxygen, so Charlotte is right. We come across any closed doors, I think we need to backtrack, which makes the question should we bother to climb down valid."

"I agree i.e. the bedrock," Seok said. "When the first rovers took pictures on Mars' surface, few rocks were visible, but we've seen bedrock exposed in craters. When examined the bedrock was found to be sedimentary stone with a high concentration of sulfur in the form of calcium and magnesium sulfates, along with the telltale red stripes indicative of odd concentrations of minerals and superoxides."

The giant machine puffed and bellowed, steam spitting from the spider work of veins.

"The bots are like ants," Psycho said. "There's got to be a way for them to come and go. Go back to the queen."

"Maybe," Judge said. He was still examining the walls, not relishing the idea of climbing on the veins. What if they ruptured? What if the stuff inside was toxic? Not likely, but there was no way to be sure. "What does going back buy us?"

Nobody spoke.

"Let's climb then," Judge said.

"Too bad we don't have the vine," Seok said.

"Where would you tie it off?" Psycho said.

Seok looked around, and hiked his shoulders.

Judge examined the web of veins clinging to the chamber wall, running his fingers over the pulsing pipes. "The larger ones feel hard. All of them are warm."

"Warm?" Psycho said.

"Makes sense. To modulate the temperature as the ice is converted," Seok said.

Judge nodded but said nothing.

"It's not that far down," Charlotte said.

Judge sighed. "I'll go first."

The ledge was thirty meters from the floor of the chamber, and bots skittered and rolled beneath them.

"Stay close to the wall," Psycho said.

"Thanks for the advice." Judge rolled onto his stomach, letting his legs hang over the edge. He pushed off, gripping a thick pipe-vein. His spacesuit boots made it difficult to wrap his legs, but it didn't matter. He was sliding, and small capillaries snapped and bled as he fought for purchase, mist pissing from the vein's pores. He grasped at pipes to slow his fall, and came to rest on the stone floor. Judge vaulted to his feet, put his back to the wall, and looked up. Psycho's face stared down at him through the red light. Judge gave a thumbs up.

Psycho returned the thumbs up and within minutes Seok, Charlotte and Psycho stood next to Judge, their backs to the wall the same way they'd done it above. Ant-like metal bots the size of small dogs tore around, antennas waving, headlamps slicing through the red light as they performed maintenance on the giant machine and cleaned the space, the faint sound of suction and brushes whirring like a rhythm guitar to the machine's lead and the fan's drumming.

Up close the massive device looked like the most advanced jet engine Judge had ever seen. That is if said engine was covered in living red spiderwebs. Beneath the web of veins and capillaries, metal pipes, glass cylinders, and black stone-like bricks made up the machine. The device constantly puffed and coughed as it supplied air to the chamber, which in turn was supplied to the habitat.

"A machine like that could reverse pollution on Earth," Charlotte said.

"Almanac," Psycho said. "Marty's almanac."

"Look there," Seok said. He was pointing to a stream of bots disappearing into the wall.

"Stay close," Judge said as he and his companions inched along, staying as close to the wall as possible while not disturbing the pipe-veins as they heaved and twisted. Damaging them would bring spider bots.

Judge reached to his side and felt the laser rifle hanging from its strap and was reassured. Psycho had the M9 in his hand, and he pointed it at the floor.

Squeaks, pops, and beeps rose above the flowing air as the party got closer to where the bots streamed in and out of a small doorway. There was no way the party could get through without being trampled or seen. Judge and crew paused in the shadows, the red glow and headlights of the bots cutting through the darkness.

"We could blast our way out," Psycho said. "But that'll bring more. You think they'll notice us if we just crawl through along with them?"

"They're moving fast," Charlotte said.

"The question isn't will they notice, but will they do anything? The drones didn't," Seok said.

The giant engine sputtered and coughed. A piece of ice had become stuck in the supply tube, and chunks were backing up like falling dominoes.

Grinding filled the chamber, rocks being crushed against rocks. The red lights pulsed, and a beeping alarm sounded, but it wasn't a steady, rhythmic beat. It was an assortment of beeps, clicks, and buzzes that sounded oddly like speech and Judge flashed back to his childhood and R2-D2.

Red lights strobed atop all the bots and they swarmed the engine as if controlled by one mind. The robots climbed the clear tube, their headlights cutting through the red glow. The bots shook and massaged the clear tube, pushing and pounding on it.

Judge didn't wait to see if the blockage was cleared. "We'll never have a better chance. Let's go," he said. He eased along the wall, hands shaking, a clammy sweat breaking-out on his back. Bots rushed to the machine's rescue, and Judge looked back one last time before darting through the red light toward the doorway and whatever lay beyond.

25

Dancing red light filled the passageway, dark shadows writhing and twisting on the metal walls like a mirrored funhouse. Daggers of white light pierced the gloom, bouncing off the tunnel walls, creating starbursts in the red glow. The passage was tight, five meters across, and Judge kept his back to the wall, holding Charlotte's hand. She held Psycho's, who held Seok's. They moved fast, shuffling along in their dirty spacesuit boots, guns at the ready, a rectangle of yellow light visible at the end of the tunnel.

A line of bots entered the passageway, moving together as one, their headlamps filling the tunnel with harsh white light.

Judge and his companions pressed themselves to the wall as the robots passed. There wasn't much clearance, but if the bots saw them, they hadn't reacted.

Judge and crew shuffled forward and broke free of the passageway into a vast chamber that stretched on into darkness in every direction.

"Another air handler?" Charlotte said.

"I don't think so. Wish I had some light," Seok said.

A pinkish glow spilled from the passageway, but its cloud didn't spread far. Judge took several hesitant steps into the gloom and stopped after ten meters when he couldn't see his hand in front of his face.

"Let's follow along the wall," Judge said.

"That does seem to be our default strategy," Psycho said.

"You got a better idea, smartass?" Judge said.

Psycho's head jerked back in mock insult. "Allow me to retort."

"Please don't," Seok said.

Psycho said nothing.

"Which way, Psycho? Since you seem to be complaining like a mother whose children forgot Mother's Day. Right or left?" Judge said.

Psycho harrumphed and went right.

Judge trailed his hand along the wall as he walked, and he felt no piping, veins, or anything other than what felt like smooth, cool metal. The ceiling could be ten meters high or a hundred, there was no way to know. But there was.

"Hold up a second," Judge said, and he heard Psycho grumble to a halt before him. "Hello," he yelled at a medium volume. No echo. Nothing except the faint pounding of the giant fans and the push of the airstream. Judge yelled louder. Then louder. Nothing.

"WTF?" Psycho said.

"Nothing for the sound waves to bounce off, or…" Seok said.

"Or?" Judge said.

"Or, the metal walls are somehow absorbing the sound, but that is very unlikely."

"Why very?" Charlotte said. "I thought you said we don't really know shit about anything in here?"

"Not exactly what I said," Seok said. "But I'm basing my opinion on what I see."

"Maybe whoever-or whatever-built this place doesn't hear," Psycho said. "At least the way we think of it."

To that nobody had anything to say, and the party continued to follow the wall until they came to a closed metal door twice the size of the tunnel that led to the ice crushing machine. Two lights blinked alternately above the door, one yellow and one red.

Judge stopped before the door.

Beep.

The door slid open.

Judge reeled, throwing himself backward, his lungs on fire as air got sucked through the opening.

Psycho grabbed Judge under his arms and pulled him away as Martian air spilled through the open door. The two men crab-walked backward, and when they were two meters from the door, it hissed closed.

Judge lay on the floor fighting for breath, his lungs on fire, eyes burning. Slowly he came back to himself, and his breathing steadied as he sat up.

"There must be motion sensors on the doors in here," Seok said.

"You just breathed Martian atmosphere?" Charlotte said.

"No.... clue... but it sure... wasn't oxygen," Judge said.

The party had some water, ate some cooked meat, and rested.

"If my bearings are right—and that's a big if given our situation—the passageway beyond the door you just opened might lead to the ice mine," Seok said.

"That would certainly explain why it's 'out-of-system' as you might say," Judge said.

Seok nodded. "Mine the ice from Mars' crust, pulverize it and dump it into a bin that feeds the machine through the tube we saw."

"There are probably many machines like that, right?" Charlotte said.

Seok nodded.

"And the way they're... alive. Explains how this place has survived so long," Charlotte said. "Or at least we think it has, crazy time travel theories notwithstanding."

"Do you hear that?" Psycho said.

"No, but I feel it," Charlotte said. "Like a heartbeat running through the deck."

"Where's it coming from?" Judge said.

"Hang-on a minute," Psycho said.

"What are you doing?" Seok asked, the tone of his voice leaving no doubts about his level of confidence with Psycho when it came to unapproved actions.

"Nothing. Just sit tight a second," Psycho said.

The airflow had lessoned, as had the thrum of the fans, and Judge's ears rang in the partial silence. He heard Charlotte's sharp breathing, and Seok's faint sniffle and wheeze. The three astronauts from Gale Base Alpha waited in the stillness, time stretching out like tax day. Judge's knees ached, a thin spike of pain ran through his head, and his stomach was tap dancing with his bowels.

"I think—" came a voice from the darkness.

Seok gasped and Judge jumped.

"Sorry, I'm back," Psycho said.

"Oh, joy for us," Charlotte said.

Judge smirked in the darkness. Even when the team was facing constant danger, leave it to jealousy to brighten Judge's day. Whatever luster Charlotte had seen on Psycho was peeling faster than paint applied to wet wood.

"I think it's coming from the center of this space," Psycho said. "I saw light, and the beat got louder and stronger the deeper in I went."

"You're saying we should leave the wall? Plunge into complete darkness where we can get lost?" Seok said.

"Lost?" Psycho said. "Are you shitting me right now? Lost? Define what you mean by lost. Because if lost means being halfway across the solar system buried under a trillion metric tons of red sand and stone, I'd think—"

"Knock it off," Judge yelled. He was done thinking. He took a step forward, intending to trek to the center of the chamber, but his years of training held him back. Things done without thinking in space-on Mars-led to death. They'd have to go slow. "I'll use the laser rifle like a cane to probe the darkness. Take a hand."

Judge wrapped the rifle strap around his arm and held it out before him like a lance. He swung it in a wide arc, bringing the tip of its barrel close to the deck. Then he took Charlotte's arm with his other hand. Charlotte took Seok's hand, and Psycho watched their backs.

The team inched through the blackness like a flock of blind birds for an hour, Judge probing the area before him. The floor thrummed with a steady beat that got louder as they walked on, and when Judge saw the green glow of light in the darkness ahead, his heart soared and the tightness in his chest eased for the first time since they'd drilled open the doors on the Martian surface.

They walked on, and it felt like miles, but like a beacon at the end of a long journey the green light grew in strength, the heartbeat rising above the fans and airflow.

As the party entered the green cloud of light, they were careful to avoid damaging the webbing of veins and capillaries crisscrossing the floor. The source of the light was a shaft that delved into the Martian surface. Heaving veins and massive cord-like black vines speckled with metals of various colors snaked from the hole like giant power cables. All around the edges of the shaft clear crystals grew, like rock candy or salt building on an ocean stone.

Judge let go of Charlotte's hand and slung the rifle over his shoulder, searching the shadows for bots.

Seok and Psycho walked to the edge of the shaft, peering down into its vast maw, but Charlotte hung back, shielding herself behind Judge as he inched forward like a child afraid of a dog he just had to pet.

Metal cables like netting trailed from the shaft into the darkness above and crawled across the chamber's floor. At the edge of the shaft there was a control board with a series of knobs, buttons and levers, but there were no traditional display screens. The panel was dark and covered with dust and silt. Beneath the controls a series of small shelves similar to the cubby holes you'd find in a nursery school were filled with what looked like metal computer disks.

Judge and Charlotte joined Seok and Psycho at the edge of the shaft.

Thick wires intertwined with undulating veins ran through the shaft, terminating in an odd machine that reminded Judge of a fancy bicycle pump.

A massive black box with a cylinder sticking from its top sat at the bottom of the shaft. It was covered in pulsing veins, and a shiny metal tank sat beside it. Thick heaving pipes entered the tank, and the vine-like wire speckled with metal trailed away from the black machine.

"The veins are going in and the wires out," Charlotte said. "Looks like."

The pounding of the machine pulsed through the chamber, the deck shaking.

"I think I know what this place is," Seok said. "Power generation room. The heart of this place." He looked up into the blackness, as if expecting to see something.

"Geothermal?" Charlotte questioned. "Or, Mars-thermal?"

Seok nodded, and said, "I'm sure you all know the basic principles. Geothermal energy originates from the formation of the planet and the radioactive decay of minerals in the planet's crust. Since thermal energy determines the temperature of matter, all types of manipulations are possible."

"This is infinitely more advanced, of course, but the machine down there does resemble an enhanced geothermal pump," Charlotte said.

Seok nodded vigorously. "Yes. On Earth we pump water into wells to be heated or cooled and it's pumped back out."

"This would explain how the biosphere has been maintained for millions of years. An inexhaustible supply of Martian ice that provides air and water, and infinite supply of power generated by Mars' natural never-ending cycles. The symbiosis of it all is truly amazing," Charlotte said.

"Which proves our theory," Psycho said. When none of his companions spoke, he added, "There has to be a brain controlling all this."

"But where?" Seok said. He gazed upward again.

None of the veins or pipes had pustules, and no steam spit and puffed from them. "Looks like a closed system," Judge said. "These supply lines could be coming from anywhere. I'm figuring we've only seen a fraction of the place." His stomach gurgled and Charlotte looked at him funny. Exploring had put their real troubles on the back burner. Outside in the habitat the day would be waning, and so far, they'd found nothing to help them escape. They were running low on food and water, and if something didn't break their way soon, they'd have to retreat. He saw no other choice.

Green light sparkled off the crystals growing around the edges of the shaft, and white rays of light shot from the odd shaped glass-like rocks. Judge wondered if they were like diamonds. Psycho's almanac idea flashed in his mind. The ability to manufacture diamonds would be the most valuable process in the galaxy. In the past, diamonds were mainly used for jewelry and some electronic equipment, and dust and shavings for blades and other industrial uses, but the new order of electronics utilized diamonds as part of their matrix, and their value continued to skyrocket.

Judge bent and broke off a piece of clear crystal from around the edge of the shaft. That ruled out diamonds. He held the shard up to the green light, and silver and black dots sparkled therein. "What do you make of this stuff? Waste? Residue from a chemical process?"

"Here, let me see it," Seok said. He reached out his hand and Judge extended the shard of crystal.

Seok received the crystal, but it slipped in his hand and he overreacted, jerking awkwardly and tossing the shard in the air. He grabbed at it, missed, grabbed lower, and managed to hit the crystal and knock it into the shaft.

The shard of glass-like rock sparkled in the green light as it fell, spinning and turning, and finally it smashed into the machine below and shattered with a pop and tinkle.

White lightning spidered from the device, crackling and popping as it reached out its thin white fingers and spread up the shaft. The electricity geysered from the hole, shooting into the air, momentarily illuminating the area.

A column of light stretched into darkness, and above the shaft continued into blackness. Veins and cables climbed the walls, crisscrossing through the shaft, and spilling out onto the ceiling. Static crackled and snapped as the lightning died away and the thump and rattle of the machine below filled the chamber.

There was a screech far off, like metal scraping on metal.

"Great," Psycho said. "Throw yourself in next time."

Seok frowned and looked at the floor.

The skitter, beeps, and clicks of approaching bots echoed through the chamber.

26

Headlight beams shone in the distance like eyes as they knifed through the darkness. Judge brought up the laser rifle and spun around, searching for… what he didn't know. The skittering and squeaks of the droids rose above the thump of the machine, like rain tapping on a tin roof. It was impossible to tell how many robots were on the way, but it was a safe guess it was more than one.

"Psycho," Judge yelled.

"Boss." The Mission Specialist was at Judge's side in a heartbeat.

"Here." Judge handed Psycho the laser rifle.

Psycho accepted it and drew the M9. "I kinda liked having an old school gun in my hand." He held it out like Judge might bite him.

Judge took the weapon and nodded.

The oncoming lights pushed away the darkness, the beeps and scrapes of the bots filling the chamber.

"Take positions behind the control console," Judge said. It was the only cover, and it wasn't much.

The four astronauts packed behind the control panel, Judge and Psycho on the ends, weapons trained on the approaching lights.

"Where the hell did those things come from anyway? We walked a few kilometers. Right? How the hell did they get here so fast?" Charlotte said.

"We probably missed all types of things in the dark. For all we know, we walked right by them," Seok said.

The bots that emerged into the green light were unlike anything the party had seen so far.

The machines were conical, their wide end floating centimeters above the deck, a red light panning back and forth at the uppermost tip. Standing at four meters tall, with triple jointed metal arms ending in tools of various types, the robots looked menacing as they broke formation and surrounded the shaft.

The whir of a drone rose above the heartbeat of the machine and the buzzing and chittering of the maintenance bots.

The droids paused when they were evenly spaced around the shaft. There were sixteen of them, and the red lights atop the droids rotated like cyclopean eyes, but they didn't appear to notice the party.

The flying drone buzzed into the cone of green light, banking sharply left and cutting around the hole. It cut in, hovering above the shaft, small rotors spinning on each corner of the fuselage, camera lens scoping.

"Do you think they see us?" whispered Psycho.

"I don't know," Judge said.

"Probably," Seok said.

The drone's rotors cycled up and it darted forward, angling sharply as it plunged down into the shaft. The pounding of the drone's rotors echoed from the hole, shadows dancing in the green haze. Several seconds passed, Judge's heart falling into rhythm with the machine.

The drone rose from the shaft, zipping upward and disappearing through the web of pipe-veins and vine-wires into the shaft above.

"Doing a diagnostic?" Charlotte asked.

"A red flag popped up somewhere when the crystal hit the machine and caused that reaction. The way those veins are heaving around the edge, I can't imagine crystals haven't fallen into the pit before now, but my guess is this is a high priority area."

The sixteen bots around the shaft hadn't moved, the red lights atop their frames steady.

The drone descended from the shaft and hung in the green light, the headlamps of the sixteen droids cutting through the gloom. The flying bot rotated, its primary camera eye panning the area. It froze when its electronic eye fell on the control console.

Psycho did his best Scooby-doo impression. "Ruh, roh."

The red lights atop the robots all rotated in the party's direction.

The drone chirped and sang, and the bots charged.

Psycho vaporized the two droids closest to the console with two blasts from the laser rifle.

"Stay between us," Judge yelled. He fired the M9, squeezing off shots slow and easy. His hand jerked, and he took the gun in a double handed grip. Bullets plunked into the oncoming bots, but it wasn't enough to stop them.

The drone darted forward, rotors whirring, and hung over the mayhem, its camera eye zooming.

Psycho screamed, a battle cry that fell dead in the heavy blackness. He swung the rifle and fired, flashes zipping from the weapon. Sparks, white light, fire and smoke spouted from the bots as Psycho zapped them like he was playing a video game.

Judge pocketed the M9 and gathered Charlotte in his arms. They got low, putting their backs to the control console. Seok joined them, the man's dark eyes darting around so fast Judge couldn't see his pupils, fear tearing at his face, lips drawn into a thin red line.

Psycho stood before them, picking off bots like ducks at a carnival, sparks and smoke filling the air. Metal clanked and bent as droids were blown apart and vaporized, arms and other parts dropping to the floor like forlorn toys.

A sharp, continuous beep rang through the space, and Psycho yelled as he fired, but the blasts were getting weak.

The laser rifle spat out one last charge, and fell silent.

There were two droids left and they came on like Psycho hadn't just pulverized fourteen of their siblings.

Judge vaulted to his feet and leveled the M9.

Psycho flipped the laser rifle in his hands, turning the solar system's most advanced handheld weapon into mankind's most primitive: a club. He swung the rifle at the oncoming bot, jumping a little and extending his arms as far as he could as if reaching for a fast ball. The gun connected with the top of the robot, and it pitched to the side. Psycho kept swinging, yelling and cursing, taking all the frustrations of the last few days out on the bot. He swung and swung, and finally the bot's red light faded to black.

The last bot veered toward Judge, avoiding Psycho as he swung the rifle.

Judge braced himself and fired, squeezing the trigger as fast as he could. Bullets pinged and ricocheted off the bot, but it slowed as he fired. The gun bounced in his hand, the crack and pop of gunpowder expanding, and the whiz of bullets leaving the barrel and streaking through the air the only sounds he heard.

The robot froze four meters from Judge, static electricity running over the machine like it had shorted out. Then the bot inched forward, as if crawling, arms extended and reaching out for Judge. The red light dimmed.

Then Psycho was there, swinging the rifle, pounding on the droid like it was the last cockroach alive. He huffed and sucked air, the gun smacking the bot, throwing sparks. The rifle made an odd sound, and a piece fell to the floor with a clang, but Psycho didn't pause. He was possessed, lost in the fog of battle, and he didn't stop until the bot's red electronic eye went dark.

Psycho collapsed next to the crushed bots, sucking for air.

"Thanks, Psycho," Charlotte said.

"We're not out of this yet," Seok said.

The drone still hovered above the scene, rotors spinning lazily as it hung in the green light. It backed off, spinning around as if looking for its friends. A red light atop the fuselage flashed three times as the bot glided up into the shaft. As the drone disappeared, the red flashing light went steady, the red glow disappearing into the darkness above.

"What the hell do you make of that?" Judge said.

"Almost like it wants us to follow," Seok said.

Psycho got to his feet and dusted off his jumpsuit. "I don't see or hear more droids on the way. Wouldn't 'the brain' send reinforcements?"

"You would think," Seok said, his gaze straying upward again.

"You think we should climb up there?" Judge asked.

Seok hiked his shoulders, but said nothing.

"Why? Other than the drone?" Charlotte asked. She was eyeing the tangle of piping and veins like it had teeth.

"A hunch," Seok said.

Psycho lifted an eyebrow. "You get those?"

Judge strode forward until he stood at the edge of the shaft. Below, the machine thrummed away, veins heaving and twisting, wires and pipes pushing water and pulling power. Judge wasn't an engineer, but it looked to him as though everything was working the way it had been.

He gazed up at the vein-pipes and vine-wires as they disappeared into the dark shaft above. When he looked back toward his companions, they were all staring at him.

"We go up or back. I can't see wandering in this darkness with no light. I think we were lucky to make it here," Judge said.

Charlotte asked, "Do you think we can even find our way back through the darkness to the passageway if we wanted to?" The tone of her voice revealed her skepticism.

"She's got a point," Seok said. "We had the green light as a guidepost most of the way here. Getting back to the passageway would be akin to finding a needle in a haystack."

"I hate that analogy," Psycho said. "Has anyone, ever, in the history of the universe had to find a needle in a haystack?"

Judge ignored him and said, "Looks like we're climbing."

"What about this?" Psycho held up the spent laser rifle.

"Can you climb with it? If not, leave it behind, though it was useful as a club," Judge said.

Psycho dropped the gun and it clattered on the deck.

Charlotte held out the last wrapped leaf containing two pieces of cooked dinosaur meat and a chunk of nasty coconut flesh.

"Might as well finish it off, but save some water," Judge said.

The companions shared the remaining food in silence, passing the meat and coconut around, all pretenses of germs and social norms forgotten. To some extent, every astronaut on Mars was used to having no privacy, sharing everything they owned, and being physically close to everyone they knew. There was no social distancing on Mars, not until you went out on the surface, then there was nothing but distance.

When they were done eating, the team mounted the vein-pipe, wire-vine webbing that extended upward into the shaft. The companions didn't talk as they pulled themselves from vein to vine, pipe to wire. Judge moved slowly in the faint green light, making sure of his footing before moving on. Charlotte was next to him, Psycho and Seok below.

They'd been climbing for ten minutes when a loud beep resounded, and the shaft filled with white light.

Judge covered his eyes with the back of a hand, and he heard Charlotte whimper and Seok suck in a deep breath. A rectangle of white light filled the top of the shaft.

The vein-like piping looked different under the harsh artificial light, and they sizzled with static. Shadows danced below, red and green light leaking up the shaft like forlorn Christmas lights.

The meat and coconut sat in Judge's stomach like stones, and he was still starving. Images of steak, beer, potatoes, fries, and martinis filled his head. His mouth watered, and sorrow washed over him. The idea that he might never have a martini again. Might never again partake in the basic pleasures he'd taken for granted. Brenda's face filled his mind. He'd become resigned to the idea that they couldn't be together, and that they'd most likely never see each other again, yet the possibility that they might had sustained him during the long journey, the cold and lonely nights lying in his bunk, wishing he was half a solar system away.

The rectangle of light grew as the party climbed, stopping to rest twice and drink some water from their EVA suit bladders. Judge had about five mouthfuls left, and when that was gone the clock would start ticking. Three days. If they didn't find water within three days they'd die, and their bodies would be swept away like they'd never existed. What would Houston back on Earth think when they didn't report in? What were they thinking now? Judge was way overdue to report back to the Commander, and emergency planning was certainly underway to launch a rescue mission and investigation, but that could take a week, and what would they find when they arrived?

Psycho was the first to the top, and he patted the air behind him with an open palm in a 'hold-up' gesture.

Wire-vines spilled over the rim of the shaft into the chamber beyond, and Psycho used one to pull himself out of the shaft.

Judge closed his eyes, waiting for the all clear, but Psycho said nothing. Below, the machine thrummed, and a gentle breeze pushed up the shaft. It was then Judge noticed the drone was gone. There were no whirring rotors, no servos pumping and squeaking.

"You better get up here," Psycho said.

Judge pulled himself onto a thick vein that bent vertical before spilling onto the floor beyond. He grasped it, planting his spacesuit boot between two bulging wires, and yanked himself upward onto his stomach. He rolled over and got to his feet, white light blinding him for an instant.

Judge rubbed his eyes.

Dark glass-like walls curved upward into white light, and beyond the cloudy walls, Judge saw dark jungle under fake moonlight.

"We're under the dome at the center of the habitat," Psycho said.

Judge's smile ran away from his face when he saw the figure at the center of the chamber.

27

A mound of clear crystals like those around the geothermal pit, but larger, shone with a bright light that emanated from below. An intense, focused white streak shining through the formation as though it was a lens. The pile of crystals was stacked in uneven, disorganized rows, and the formation stretched up into whiteness. A path five meters wide ran around the pile, and there were cuts, bumps and scratches in the hardpan where bots had passed.

Embedded in the face of the crystal formation was a monstrosity of integration between living tissue and the mechanical. The thing had no real form, and resembled a machine that had been taken apart, yet there appeared to be sinew and muscle holding the pieces together. A giant white and red blob-like mass sat at the center of it all. The form heaved and bubbled, and wires thin as hair ran from it into various parts of the creature.

"Is it a cyborg?" Charlotte asked.

"More like a bio-machine," Seok said.

Metal tanks, large glass-like tubes, and circuit boards surrounded the globular mass like organs. They were tied into the brain via vine wires and vein pipes that trailed up through the clear crystals into the bio-machine.

Judge stepped forward, his hand out before him. "It's... amazing."

Next to the creature, an odd machine protruded from the crystals. It looked like an open umbrella with no canvas stretched over the frame, its handle stuck in the formation. Ten red suction cup-like tips stuck from the ends of ten thin pieces of needle fine metal, each with a different color wire connecting it to the bio-machine.

"What do you make of this?" Judge asked, pointing at the odd umbrella-like device.

"It appears to be a probe of some kind," Seok said. "Why there are so ma—"

A dinosaur roared outside, its harsh cry echoing through the habitat and filling the dome.

The drone appeared, its rotors cycling up as it floated above the bio-machine. It darted forward, heading for the glass wall.

"It's gonna crash," Psycho said.

The drone zipped on, and an instant before it smashed into the dome, a small doorway appeared in the glass, and the drone flew through it.

Psycho lunged toward the opening, throwing himself more than running, arms out.

The door closed and Psycho skidded to a halt, sliding into the dome like it was a catcher protecting home plate.

Judge started, tracking the drone as it sailed into shadow. Through the tinted glass walls the light pillar blasted the jungle with corpse light. Judge stared through the glass, and saw the party's footprints in the hardpan outside the dome and the hole they'd dug trying to gain access. Had the AI seen them? It must have, so why had it left them alone?

Judge turned back to his friends, all of whom were standing before the bio-machine, and he joined them.

"Hello?" Charlotte said, looking around as if ghosts might answer.

"Hello!" Psycho yelled, his voice bouncing around the dome.

The blob at the center of the bio-machine said nothing. There were no signs it was alive other than its slight movements and the pumping of the vein-pipes.

"If this thing is the biosphere's AI, how are we going to talk to it?" Judge said.

"Talk to it?" Charlotte sounded like Judge had just said he was the best-looking guy on Mars.

"Ask for help," Seok said.

"Start with the universal language? Math?" Charlotte said.

"How? Where are the inputs? How do we wake the thing up?" Psycho said.

Judge shook his head.

"You're missing a key point," Seok said. "An extensive understanding of any alien language, beyond basic vocabulary and underlying architecture, would require knowledge of their culture. There could be many cultural interpretations of even the simplest phrases. That's why conversation is so difficult, especially for people with different native languages and cultures. Hell, it's hard to have a conversation with someone even when you know them and speak the same language."

"But asking basic questions and getting yes or no answers based on binary or some fancy equation isn't conversation," Psycho said. "Can we do that?"

"Think of the consequences if we screw up," Charlotte said. "We could start an interstellar war."

Seok stared at the device with ten thin metal arms. "Humans can't communicate with any other species on Earth, which makes it unlikely that we'd be able to communicate with extraterrestrial life. Not without... extraordinary measures," Seok said.

"You're telling me that aliens with the ability to construct this place, make the devices we've seen, transport or recreate the dinosaurs and ecosystem of Earth's past, can't understand cavemen like us?" Psycho paused and took his last pull of water, the fizzle and gurgle from him sucking the final drops from his bladder echoing through the dome.

"He's got a point. Any race with a level of tech required to build all this, should have some basis for at least limited communication," Charlotte said.

Seok tore his gaze away from the ten-armed device, and said, "Perhaps. I do believe some type of basic communication should be possible between humans and aliens, unless things that we think are common to all languages—situating in time and space, talking about participants, etc.—are so diverse that the human language provides no starting point."

Shadows danced outside, and the team rested and pondered their situation as the pseudo night slipped away.

Judge jumped when the morning beep rang through the habitat. "Damn," he said as he covered his ears.

The pillar of light blinked out, the LED sky came to life, and the dome went clear, the jungle outside coming into full view as a new day began. Judge's dancing nerves took a break, the sight of the conifers, giant ferns, and palm trees oddly soothing.

With no on switch visible, the team searched the interior of the dome again, but found nothing new. Outside the dome, beasts of all sizes roamed in and out of view, none of them paying any attention to the dome, which from the jungle POV was a black reflective bubble.

"I've got an idea, but it could bring trouble," Charlotte said.

When nobody spoke, she said, "What if we poke it?"

"I'm sorry?" Seok said.

"Touch Big Brain there." Charlotte seemed confident.

Judge drew in a long breath, and almost laughed. It wasn't that crazy, was it? Judge nodded and stepped forward, positioning himself before the red and white globular mass Charlotte had named Big Brain. He looked back at his crewmates, then leaned forward and brushed the back of his hand over the undulating red and white mass.

The crystal formation flashed red three times and the tinted walls darkened, blackness creeping over the interior of the dome.

The suction cups at the tips of the umbrella contraption's arms glowed.

Seok took a hesitant step toward the machine. "It's communicating."

"Tell me you don't think it's telling you to let that thing attach itself to you," Psycho said.

Seok said nothing as he inched forward.

"Judge, you going to let this happen?" Psycho said.

"I think he's right," Judge said. "If that thing can... read our minds, communicate telepathically, we might get out of here after all."

Seok paused and slowly turned in Judge's direction.

"Telepathy? Really?" Psycho said.

"Why not?" Charlotte said.

Psycho harrumphed and crossed his arms over his chest.

"If it's got to be done, I'll do it," Judge said.

Seok stepped forward and blocked Judge's way. "Respectfully, sir, but I believe my knowledge of linguistics makes me more qualified for the... connection," he said.

"Yoo Lee, you're saying you're smarter than me?" Judge yelled in his best drill sergeant voice, but he couldn't keep a smile from slipping over his face.

"Sir, no sir," Seok said.

"Well get to it then," Judge said.

Seok nodded and Charlotte patted his shoulder. He inched forward, less eager now that he had the approval of the group. He paused beneath the outstretched needle arms, looking up like a lost child.

A low baritone hum blasted through the dome, and the device's arms writhed and twisted as they surrounded Seok's head. He didn't move, his eyes darting about, sweat dripping down his face. Then with a suddenness that made Judge jump, all ten arms darted forward at once, the tiny suction cups attaching themselves to Seok's face, forehead and neck.

Seok spasmed, his body rocking as a series of beeps and clicks preceded another loud hum. Seok's face twisted and his eyes closed, his head falling back like his neck was broken.

Psycho stepped forward, but Judge put up a hand.

"My name is Yoo Lee Seok. We're from Earth," Seok said.

The faint rattle of dead leaves rustling against the dome.

"Yes, that one. Who are you?" Seok asked.

Nothing. Nobody spoke and Charlotte sniffled.

"Who made this place?" Seok asked. Then, "Why?"

Outside, the jungle night symphony hummed and buzzed. Psycho cracked his knuckles and Judge listened hard, like the monstrosity in the crystal would whisper the answer to him. They could hear the questions Seok was asking but not the answers. Time stretched out, Seok's eyes darting around beneath his closed eyelids, jungle life continuing beyond the dome as if nothing was happening within.

"How long ago? Why is the habitat deteriorating? We saw multiple failures. Why didn't you send the sweepers to deal with us? You made a decision? Why no rocks in the habitat? Why didn't the creators come back? Finish the job?" Seok's questions went on as the day waned outside. Judge's stomach rumbled and Charlotte chuckled.

"How many bullets you got in that gun?" Psycho asked.

Judge pulled the M9 and released the clip into his palm. He thumbed out the shells, shiny brass bullets falling into his hand. "Eight," he said as he pushed the rounds back into the magazine.

Psycho whistled. "Eight bullets. We better save them for hunting."

Without a beep or warning, the walls lightened, and LED-like light filled the inside of the dome. The crystal formation flashed red, and several of the vein-pipes connecting to the AI farted and puffed steam.

The suction cups popped as they broke free of Seok's skin, the thin metal arms retracting, the device folding like an umbrella.

Seok stood silent, staring forward at the mound of crystals, forehead scrunched, shoulders hunched, eyes glassy with tears.

"You alright?" Judge said.

Seok nodded. "Water. Need water." He pulled his bladder tube free and sucked down the last of his water. He breathed, pulling in a deep breath and exhaling. He sat on an outcrop of crystal below the creature, Big Brain puffing and heaving as if nothing had happened.

"So, we only heard your side of things," Charlotte said.

Seok nodded vigorously, the color coming back to his face. "The connection allowed us to speak, well, it to speak really. It read my mind, sifted through my memories, which gave our encounter context." When nobody spoke, he continued, "It's an AI, as we surmised. It oversees the complex biosphere we've seen, controls the population, the bots, keeps everything in balance."

"So, the million-dollar question," Judge said. "Who and why?"

"The builders of this place, as we've guessed, were aliens. They were from so far away I couldn't comprehend the distance, or how they got here, or if their physical forms actually traveled here. Different timelines spun in my head depicting multiple outcomes from the same events. I never did acid, but based on the descriptions I've read and have heard I had a bad trip." Seok paused and rubbed his temples with the tips of his fingers. "The extraterrestrials are called the Toro Ki', and they had... slaves that resembled octopi, except they had two short arms along with their eight legs. That's why there are climbing cables all over the place. Their purpose here was the preservation of the creatures of Earth. Protecting them from the extinction level event that occurred 66,819,231 Martian years ago."

"Dang," Judge said.

"How'd they know?" Psycho said.

"The aliens had been hurt badly by meteors, and they tracked the rock that caused the extinction event that killed the dinosaurs," Seok said. "Based on the vectors and their advanced tech they were able to predict the asteroid's path within a .0000000001 percent error factor. They can travel in time on a very limited basis, sometimes see possible futures depending on the time currents," Seok said. "So, they put a beacon on Earth to monitor the extinction event, but the creatures of the Age of Reptiles were-are-unique in all the galaxy, so they devised a plan to preserve them."

"By transporting them here?" Psycho said.

"Then putting them back on Earth after it recovered," Seok said.

"Sooooo," Psycho said. "Why didn't that happen?"

"The AI doesn't know," Seok said. "It's had no communication from the Toro Ki' in 38,724,019 Martian years."

Silence fell as the company pondered that scary thought. The jungle outside the dome went still, and Judge wondered if all the astronauts on Mars had also just paused in their daily routine, some unknown metaphysical connection alerting his mates.

"Maybe they lost their funding," Judge said. He chuckled sardonically. Popularity, and thus funding, for the space program had faltered four years prior after a space cloud anomaly had passed through the solar system without fanfare, the exception being the disappearance/destruction of the International Space Station. Price tags to fund space operations didn't mesh with most Americans' vision of conservative taxation, but innovation was innovation. Mankind's quests into space were inevitable and ultimately profitable, and Mars was Earth's first waystation to more distant journeys and bigger profits.

"That's too realistic," said Charlotte.

28

Psycho laughed. "Maybe the aliens died out? Virus, or some shit. Maybe they blew each other up? Got destroyed by another race?"

"Maybe they elected a reality star as their leader," Charlotte said. "Maybe there's a—" Charlotte stared out at the jungle.

Judge and the others turned.

A magnificent beast emerged from the conifers onto the strip of hardpan that separated the jungle from the dome. The beast sniffed the ground where the astronauts had walked, and sauntered over to the hole they'd dug.

"Stegosaurus," Seok said. "It's a herbivore."

The beast was ten meters long from the tip of its long tail to the front of its flat snout. The heavily built quadruped had a rounded back, two long, powerful hind legs, and two shorter and thinner fore limbs. The beast's dark skin glistened, and red upright spikes and plates ran down the center of the creature's back and out to the tip of its tail, shrinking in size along with the tail's girth. The beast inched forward, its golf ball-sized eyes staring at the dome.

"Do you think it senses us?" Judge asked.

"I don't know," Seok said, as if in a daze.

The Stegosaurus froze, its narrow head jerking east.

A roar thundered over the jungle, and the Stegosaurus lumbered into the forest, disappearing into a thick stand of conifers.

"To get back on topic," Judge said, "you're saying the AI has no clue why the Toro Ki' didn't come back?"

"Correct. The biosphere was brought here more than eighty million years ago and mothballed, awaiting extraction of specimen dinosaurs that were to be transported here by spaceship from Earth," Seok said.

"Brought here? All this is a ship?" Judge said.

"No," Seok said. "Units of this type are manufactured then transported and tied into local resources."

"Local resources like water, ice, power. Those things I can understand." Psycho pointed at Big Brain, and said, "That, I don't understand. Is it one of them?"

"No," Seok said.

"What the hell is it then?" Charlotte asked.

"It is AI. That's all it knows," Seok said.

"Does it know how it… grew its living parts?" Judge said.

"Its current state is all it has ever known," Seok said.

"This all makes so much sense," Judge said. "They place the biosphere in the center of Gale crater, and over millions of years Martian soil covers it."

"Explaining the presence of Aeolis Mons," Seok said.

"This all sounds so fantastic, but as we've seen, things in the habitat aren't perfect. I heard you ask why the habitat was deteriorating? You told it we saw multiple failures," Charlotte said.

Seok sighed. "Yes, it rambled on about this question for some time. I—"

"Rambled?" Psycho said.

"More on that in a minute," Seok said. "The AI described how the habitat was designed to be self-sufficient and function for fifty million years."

Judge hiked his shoulders. "So, the biosphere is well beyond its useful life."

"Indeed," Seok said. "The biosphere is currently functioning at 89.61789 percent efficiency. The AI estimates that catastrophic habitat failure will begin in 500 years, plus or minus one percent."

Judge turned back to the glass wall of the dome, gazing at the vibrant jungle beyond. It was all so perfect until you left the water running for too long and things started to break and leak. "When did Big Brain detect our presence?"

"The moment we entered the airlock," Seok said.

Judge turned back to his crewmates. "Why didn't the AI send the sweepers to deal with us?"

"Ah, now you hit upon the most curious part of my… connection," Seok said. "And it speaks to Psycho's question when I referred to the AI as rambling." He paused and took a breath. "When I asked why the AI let us be, it said because its primary mission was to protect exotic life."

"Like the dinosaurs," Charlotte said.

"Correct, but that's not what made imaginary spiders crawl up my spine," Seok said. "When I pressed, the AI admitted it sent the drones to check us out, but didn't send the sweepers because… it was curious."

Nobody spoke, the faint jungle chorus filling the silence.

"It made a decision? So it's aware?" Charlotte asked.

"Not exactly," Seok said. "But it's well on its way. My guess is that's the real reason it didn't remove us from the habitat."

"What do you mean?" Judge said.

"It's learned all it can. It can't evolve further without learning, and it saw six astronauts as a way to do that," Seok said. "It said it was sorry about our friends. That also scared the shit out of me."

"It understands sorrow? Fear?" Psycho asked.

"No. It only knows the words. What they mean, not the actual feeling associated with the words," Seok said. "But give it a couple of thousand more years and it'll get there."

"It doesn't have a couple of thousand years. Does it understand that?" Judge asked.

"It appears to, but I think it hopes... yes, I said hopes because I think it's crossed the awareness threshold there. I think it hopes the Toro Ki' will show up, and that being late fifty million years was just a minor scheduling snafu," Seok said.

"I heard you ask about rocks. Not that it matters, but why the hell aren't there any?" Psycho said. "I need shit to throw, bang stuff with. It's like half my toolbox is empty."

"I asked because I found that oddity particularly interesting myself, Psycho. The AI said no rocks or sedimentary formations were necessary because essential elements normally provided by mountains and tectonic shifts were provided elsewhere. Another major concern was weight. Even the Toro Ki' must have had transportation costs."

"Those essential elements. Did they cause the red markings on the dinosaurs like you thought?" Judge said.

Seok nodded.

"And the air?" Judge said.

"Yes, you aren't going nuts. The air is enhanced with a variety of elements to create an exotic air mix that allows for the enclosed environment."

Psycho yawned, and as if on cue, the evening beep chimed and the sheet of light above blinked out and the crystal formation blossomed like a white explosion, the pillar of light knifing into the dark sky. The harsh light filled the jungle around the dome like a klieg light, and the beasts of the habitat scurried away into shadows.

"I need to get some rest," Judge said. "We're safe in here and should be able to sleep without worrying for the first time in a long time. If you can handle the light."

"I think I can sleep on the sun," Psycho said. "We'll be fine as long as the sweepers don't decide to come run the vacuum."

"Seok," Judge said. "Tell me you got an answer to your last question?"

"Yes, there is a failsafe to open the airlock," Seok said.

The collective exhalation of breath and the ensuing hugs was the only celebration the astronauts could afford. They needed rest, and then they were going to get the hell out of the habitat.

The party slept like stones, even with the pillar of light and Psycho snoring so loud dinosaurs wandered out of the jungle a few times to investigate. The dark glass pressed in around Judge at first, his friend

Claustro reminding him he didn't like being confined. He brushed the thought away, and that was becoming easier each time he did it.

The morning beep brought Judge awake, the dome walls went opaque, the sky turning bright white.

With no water or food there was nothing to do except get out of dodge. Judge said, "Let's have it, Seok."

"This better work," Psycho said.

"It has to," Judge said. Seok said the failsafe was for the airlock and he'd forgotten to ask about access to the dome.

Seok said, "If it doesn't, I'll let it poke me again. It wasn't that bad. A second time I might be able to…"

"What?" Psycho said.

"See some of its memories," Seok finished.

"You mean what it's got stored in its memory banks?" Judge said.

Seok closed his eyes and began to sing an unintelligible string of hisses, burps, farts, whistles and grunts that got louder and faster as he chanted. He ceased abruptly, his eyes snapping open like they'd been pasted shut waiting for a surprise.

At first, nothing happened, then an opening appeared in the dome, a square five meters across. Jungle sounds floated through the opening along with the scent of moisture, rotting vegetation, and flowers. Birds squawked, insects buzzed, and for a minute, Judge enjoyed the sounds.

For a minute.

"Let's go before it changes its mind," Charlotte said, and she was the first one to step through the doorway onto the hardpan surrounding the dome.

A dinosaur roared three times, each time getting louder.

"Our timing is for shit," Judge said as he followed Charlotte.

"True that," Psycho said. "But it sounds far off."

When all four astronauts stood outside the dome, staring at their dirty, haggard reflections in the smooth, tinted glass, the door dissipated.

"That's a neat trick," Judge said.

"The Toro Ki' can manipulate elements in ways I couldn't even begin to understand," Seok said.

"They got transporters? Like on Star Trek?" Psycho said.

Seok chuckled, and it was a welcome sound. "Sort of, yes. They can't transform all matter, though."

The four remaining astronauts plunged into the jungle for the last time, following their tracks and the marks they'd left on trees the first time they'd trekked to the dome. Occasional broken branches, sliced leaves, and trampled anthills marked their passage, and Judge found himself wondering if he was going to miss the place. Insects buzzed and hummed, dinosaurs growled and roared, and above, a great pterodactyl banked across the white sky, its brown leathery wings rippling as it coasted and screamed.

They came upon the area where Arjun had been killed and Judge went cold. The old shelter had been destroyed and the raptor corpse was gone, a faint black stain all that remained.

When afternoon rain came it was welcome, and the four companions stripped off their jumpsuits and clunky EVA boots and lay on their backs, drinking and staring up into the whiteness.

At lights out, the party made camp under a conifer, the metal wall marking the edge of the habitat looming in the distance. They ate coconut and sat around a small fire, Judge with his back to the trunk of a tall evergreen. They had no worries of sweeper bots. The AI had let them come so far, see so much, but what would it do when it saw its last chance to ascend leaving the biosphere? Judge asked, "Seok, how'd you leave things with the AI?"

Seok stared at the fire and didn't respond. A beast roared and he looked up, his gaze straying in the direction of the airlock. "We have to deal with him before we do anything."

Psycho laughed. "Yeah, us and our eight bullets."

Seok's eyes went back to the fire.

"How did you leave things? Why did the AI break the connection?" A worm of worry grew in Judge's stomach.

Seok turned his dark eyes on Judge, sorrow painted on his face. "The AI saw us. What we are."

"What the hell does that mean?" Psycho said.

"My memories. It saw everything I know, everything I think," Seok said.

"It's afraid?" Charlotte said. "Of us?"

"Maybe," Seok said.

"There was no training for this shit." Judge sighed and threw back his head. "I don't even like space, and I hate the cold!"

The others laughed, and Charlotte said, "Why the hell did you come to Mars then?"

The laughter died away and Psycho coughed. A gentle breeze pushed through the jungle and leaves rattled, knives of corpse light cutting through the conifer's boughs.

"I was afraid," Judge said.

A night beast cawed and mewed.

"Are you still afraid?" Charlotte asked.

Judge took her hand. "No."

Psycho stared up into the darkness and Seok focused on the fire.

"I came here because it was the farthest I could get from Brenda. I knew if I was close enough to get on a plane, I would. That I wouldn't be able to stop myself and I'd ruin her life," Judge said.

"Why would you ruin her life?" Seok asked. "If she didn't want you, you walk away. But not addressing it, leaving it out there like a festering wound will lead to bigger problems." His eyes lifted from the fire and stared toward the pillar of light.

"Because those bigger problems aren't worth whatever happiness I might find," Judge said.

"That's a bit fatalistic," Charlotte said.

"Brenda is my brother's wife," Judge blurted. His head jerked back, and he sucked his lips.

Psycho sighed. "Doesn't it feel better to have it off your chest?"

"No, not really." Judge stole a glance at Charlotte, whose eyes were locked on him like laser sights. "It was never meant to happen. Any of it."

"But..." Charlotte said.

"But it did, and she wanted to break things off with my brother," Judge said. "He's an adult, but even if I could take the guilt, they've got two kids." He sighed. "So I ran."

"To Mars," Charlotte said.

Judge nodded in the darkness.

29

The party trekked through the jungle, making a last push for the airlock and their spacesuits. Conversation was subdued and superficial, Judge's revelation of the prior night still sitting out there like a fart in church. He could tell Charlotte wanted to be angry, but was having trouble. Her face shifted between anger, frustration, and pity. It was difficult to tell what Seok was thinking, his cold demeanor showing no signs of a thaw or sympathy. Psycho was the one who kept patting Judge on the back, telling him to buck up. He was a friend, and Judge needed him more than he wanted to admit.

Depression washed over Judge, and he concentrated on putting one foot in front of the other, carefully avoiding roots, anthills, and tree branches. He'd lost two crewmembers on his watch, and it didn't matter what the circumstances were. When he got back to base, he'd have to send out messages to the families of Arjun and Tisa. The thought of it turned his stomach, as did the idea of having to explain all this. Judge saw the Commander's face in his mind's eye, saw the contempt bordering on humor, Salas not believing him at first. What would happen after that, Judge didn't know.

The heat beneath the jungle canopy was stifling, and mist snaked between the underbrush. The forest chorus was ringing at full volume, and the larger beasts brayed, roared, chuffed and growled. Judge was almost used to the constant ruckus, though he sometimes longed for the solitude of the base, or the ship. Maybe it was time to go home?

"Something up there in the trees. Let's give it some space." Psycho was on point, and he paused, gazing through the thick underbrush. "Looks like a watering hole."

"Yup, that nasty little puddle we found. Remember?" Judge said.

"Aye," Psycho said. "Quiet. Let's go take a look."

Psycho inched through the foliage, pushing aside giant fern leaves and avoiding the sharp edges of saw palmetto fronds. He dropped to a knee and held up a fist.

Two creatures drank timidly from the dirty pool of water, ears flicking like deer, tails wagging.

"You guys can see those, right?" Psycho said.

"Yeah, why?" Judge said.

"It looks like a thestral," Psycho said.

"I'm not familiar with that breed of dinosaur," Seok said.

"That's because they're not dinosaurs," Psycho said. "Who raised you?"

Seok lifted an eyebrow.

"A thestral can only be seen by someone who's seen death," Psycho said.

"You OK?" Judge asked.

"Harry Potter?" Psycho said.

Nobody spoke.

"The creatures Luna and Harry see? They pull the carriages to the castle?"

Nothing except the braying of the jungle.

"You're all hopeless," Psycho said.

"And you're an ass," Charlotte said.

The creature looked like an emaciated pony with translucent wings which had thin red skeletal bones spidering through them. Judge did a double-take and rubbed his eyes. The beast's dark skin had red spots of various sizes and shapes, and its long brown mane flopped over the side of its horse-like head and ran down the beast's back. Dark eyes focused on the puddle, ears twitching, tongue lapping up dirty water.

"It might be a dracorex," Seok said. "The fossils never showed wings, but it's possible they fully disintegrated over time."

"Bones in wings tend to be cartilage and very thin," Charlotte said.

"Thing looks like a Jersey Devil," Judge said.

"A what now?" Charlotte said.

"A cryptid creature that people claimed to have seen in the Meadowlands of New Jersey," Judge said. He'd seen a picture once that almost made him believe.

The ground trembled.

"There's a debate as to whether dracorex ever existed as its own genus. Only a skull and four vertebrae were found, which had led some to speculate that perhaps the dracorex was nothing more than an adolescent of another genus."

The ground shook a bit harder.

"Sounds like our T-rex friend is still hanging around the airlock," Judge said.

"These things don't appear to notice," Charlotte said.

The creatures had moved away from the muddy puddle and were tearing foliage off a nearby bush, chomping the leaves and thin branches.

The buzz of a drone preceded its arrival, and the black flying robot circled the watering hole, then paused and hovered, its cameras turned west.

The ground shook, and the footsteps were getting closer together as the approaching dinosaur picked up speed.

"Why's the drone here?" Charlotte asked.

Psycho leaned forward, craning his neck to see, and putting his weight on a thin tree branch. It snapped with a loud crack, and Psycho fell onto the hardpan.

The grazing dinosaurs froze, heads jerking toward the sound like deer. Leaves fell like rain as a cluster of pterosaurs sprayed from the tree canopy, shrieking and swarming the party as they fought to find cover.

Judge swung up the M9, but there were too many, he only had eight bullets left, and the creatures were flying erratically, dipping and diving, darting through the trees, searching.

The drone's rotors cycled up and the flying robot darted forward, cutting a line through the cloud of pterosaurs. Long, narrow beaks snapped at the machine as it zipped past, needle-sharp teeth glinting in the harsh artificial light. The creatures brayed and yelled, flying around like gnats.

Judge and company cowered beneath a conifer branch, watching the cloud of dinosaurs snap and avoid each other.

"Come on," Psycho said. He ducked under a branch and disappeared into the jungle.

Judge sighed and looked at Charlotte, who hiked her shoulders. Seok gave no sign.

The braying of the beasts reached a fever pitch, and the ground trembled and shook. A mighty roar echoed over the forest, and the tittering and screeching of the pterosaurs ceased for a heartbeat.

"We stay here and they're going to see us," Judge said as he plunged into the jungle without another word.

Psycho moved from tree to tree, moving fast, but carefully. Judge followed, Charlotte and Seok on his tail. Stray pterosaurs wove through the tree canopy, screeching and calling.

A thin, horrible cry rang over the forest.

They'd been spotted.

A group of four pterosaurs missiled toward the party, cutting around branches, tearing off leaves.

Judge sighted the M9 and fired, two fast shots that missed, wood splintering and cracking as the bullets smacked into branches. Only six shells left.

"Give me that damn thing before you waste all the—"

A pterosaur burst from the tree boughs, claws forward, mouth open in a toothy grin, wet eyes gleaming.

Judge swung the gun and fired. The bullet zipped past Seok's head and thumped into the beast's breast. The pterosaur was blasted backward, a ball of blood and torn flesh tumbling into the underbrush.

The party ran, cutting through the forest, tree branches whipping their faces, vines grabbing at them, pricker bushes tangling them up, tree roots looking to take them down with each step.

Nearby, the T-rex roared, the ground shook, and Psycho changed direction, plowing through a dense line of conifers and breaking free into a stand of palms.

Psycho pulled up short, skidding to a halt.

Two fifteen-foot raptors blocked their way, glassy eyes focused, serpentine tongues lolling out, heads bobbing. One of the creatures wailed, as if letting all the beasts of the habitat know the location of the intruders.

The drone hissed past, but Judge couldn't see it because it was above the tree canopy. He aimed the M9 but it was too late; the raptors were already moving.

The beasts circled the party, clicking and gurgling, slime dripping from their tooth-filled maws. The larger of the two creatures kept lunging forward, and pulling back, its powerful legs clawing at the hardpan.

Judge waved his hand and Charlotte and Seok dropped to the ground. Judge fired again, and this time he caught the larger beast in the upper thigh of its right leg.

The raptor yelled, an earsplitting wail that echoed off the biosphere's walls and rang over the habitat. The beast fell back, hissing, blood dripping from the wound.

The smaller raptor attacked, launching itself at Psycho, and they went to the hardpan in a tangle.

Judge sighted the M9. If he missed, he could hit Psycho. Five bullets left.

The wounded dinosaur had recovered, limping in a circle, sizing-up Charlotte and Seok.

Judge swung the Beretta toward the wounded beast and put a bullet between its eyes.

The raptor stood for a second, blood geysering from its shattered forehead, doorknob-sized eyes rolling back in its head. The creature took a step toward Seok, spasmed, and fell over.

Judge swung the gun back toward Psycho, who was pinned beneath the remaining raptor. The beast's head darted in and out, pecking like a chicken as Psycho moved and slithered, avoiding the strikes.

Judge struggled to aim, the gun barrel moving in small circles as he tried to hold the weapon steady. Psycho was too close, and he wasn't a good enough shot.

Psycho screamed, lashing out with his knife in an effort to break free. Blood dripped from his mouth as the raptor pressed him to the ground, its talons digging into his chest. Psycho gashed one of the beast's small forearms, and the creature roared when the knife hit bone, dark blood leaking across the creature's torso as it thrashed and bit.

Judge moved to his right, shifting his position as he aimed the M9. If he missed...

The raptor's jaws clamped down on Psycho's torso and the Mission Specialist screamed, blood pouring from his mouth, arms outstretched in a posture of defense as he and the beast tumbled over the hardpan. The sound of meat being torn from bone, the ripping of muscle and snapping of bones echoed over the jungle.

Psycho rolled, blood pouring from his mouth as he fought to free himself. He lashed out with his knife, slashing wildly, but the creature was faster.

The dinosaur bit down on his head, severing it from his body with a rip and pop that Judge would never forget.

Charlotte screamed, and Seok gagged, spitting up bile and what remained of the coconut and water he'd had for breakfast.

Psycho's corpse fell to the ground, gristle, spinal cord, blood and tattered esophagus hanging from the corpse's neck. The astronaut's skull cracked and popped as it was crushed in the raptor's tooth-filled jaws, brain and blood leaking onto the hardpan.

Judge let loose with a primal scream of rage so loud his vocal cords burned, and heat ran through him. He took two fast steps, closing half the distance between himself and the raptor.

"No, don't go near it!" yelled Seok, but Judge was gone, lost in the fog of battle, eyes red with anger, a burning need for revenge driving him forward.

He took two more fast steps toward the raptor.

The beast looked up from its dining and turned its wet black eyes on Judge.

"Time to die," Judge said. He leveled the Beretta, pointblank range, and squeezed the trigger until the gun was empty, planting four shells between the raptor's eyes, blowing out the back of its head. Blood, brain, and bone splattered the underbrush, and the beast toppled to the ground, its eyes still locked on Judge, a piece of Psycho's arm impaled on one of its teeth.

"No!" Charlotte yelled as she ran to help Psycho.

Judge put out an arm.

The click and scrape of the sweeper bots filled the forest and Seok and Judge dragged Charlotte back as the trees bent and creaked, leaves fell, and tree branches snapped as the bots came on.

Tears leaked from Judge's eyes as he watched the sweepers swarm from the jungle like locusts, covering Psycho's remains and scrubbing him from existence. The bots chirped and beeped as they worked, the whir of the drone's rotors as it watched from above completing the ensemble.

When the sweeper bots were done, the drone's rotors slowed, and it hovered while the bots surrounded the party.

"Um, what the hell is this?" Charlotte said.

Judge was lost in his grief, staring at the dull brown spot where Psycho's corpse had been. "I don't know what I'm going to do without him," Judge said.

"Look," Seok said.

The sweeper bots had formed a perfect circle around the three remaining astronauts, each bot evenly spaced from the one on each side of it. Then they froze, the red lights atop their housings blinking three times, then going solid.

"AI?" Charlotte said.

Seok waved, and the drone's rotors cycled up and it darted away, disappearing over the trees. The sweepers stayed frozen for another ten seconds, then scurried off into the jungle one by one, dipping as if bowing as they went.

The forest chorus returned, and a roar thundered through the habitat.

"Best get out of here before everyone comes for lunch," Seok said.

Judge nodded, tears leaking from his eyes as he stared at the dead raptors.

Back on the trail, Judge retreated into himself. He didn't know how he was going to get by all this, didn't know if he could.

"What's that?" Charlotte said.

Judge's head jerked up. Charlotte pointed at something white in the boughs of the tree they were walking under. Judge mounted a branch and climbed, pulling himself up. He'd only gone up ten meters when he gasped; anger, frustration and fear fighting for control of his emotions.

Hanging from a broken tree limb, twisting in the gentle breeze, was a piece of fabric from one of the EVA suits.

30

"OK, let's not panic," Judge said, but screaming and pulling out his hair was exactly what he wanted to do.

"Could be one piece from one suit," Charlotte said.

"But something's found the suits," Seok said. "Not good."

"No," Judge said. "It isn't, Mr. Obvious. Let's try and worry about the problems we know exist, not the ones that might."

Seok and Charlotte looked at one another, then down at the ground.

He knew he was reaching. Wasn't that his job? Go down with the ship. Leave no man behind and all that. He had to get Seok and Charlotte out alive. That's all that mattered. He wouldn't have any more blood on his hands, and if that meant he had to be Sunny Sally to keep his team's morale up, then so be it.

They had another kilometer to go before they got to the conifer base camp, the wall disappearing into the whiteness above to the south. Pain arced through Judge's legs and feet with each step, his back throbbing, stomach stabbing him, reminding him it was in need of supplies.

He was on point, and when he looked over and saw the sullen faces of his two remaining crewmates, sorrow washed over him; the sweats of despair, the cold chills of fear and frustration. The feelings that made Judge question why he thought he could run half a solar system away to escape Brenda. A galaxy wouldn't be far enough, because she'd always be in his head. That's what needed to change.

"You thinking about Psycho?" Charlotte said.

A brief stab of guilt knifed through Judge, but he mustered the courage to lie anyway. "Yeah. I just can't believe I'm never going to see him again. I always thought... I thought..."

"You'd sit on a beach someday, when you were old and wrinkly, drinking beer, telling anyone who'd listen about how you walked on another planet," Charlotte said.

Judge said nothing.

"Probably a good way to get chicks," Seok said.

Judge and Charlotte both stopped walking and stared at Seok.

"Just figured that's what Psycho would have said." Seok smiled. A rare sight.

A roar thundered through the jungle.

"We're real close now," Judge said.

The forest thinned ahead and through the dense underbrush Judge saw the gap in the tree canopy that marked the animal path that led to the airlock. He inched forward, slipping under fern leaves, traversing saw palmetto and giant weeds with broad purple leaves and ice cream cone-like flowers of various colors sticking from their longest stalks. The air was fragrant with earth, moisture, and pine.

Judge paused behind a giant elephant ear leaf, peering around its edge, Seok and Charlotte looking over his shoulder.

The ground trembled, and dust rose from the path and blew into the jungle, mixing with the moisture and mist, creating a brown haze that snaked through the forest. A rumbling gurgle echoed down the path, like the largest kitchen drain in history was spitting bubbles and rank air.

The beast's head broke through the clouds of dust, its head low to the hardpan, swaying back and forth, red eyes scanning the forest. Its long muscular tail was out straight, the muscles along its flanks rippling and spasming.

The T-rex lumbered past, the ground shook, then slowly went still as it headed west along the wall.

"Shit," Charlotte said. She'd wandered back into the jungle a few meters and something sparkled at her feet.

Judge and Seok joined her, and the three astronauts stood dumbstruck, staring at a spacesuit helmet, its top cracked and its faceplate broken.

"That's Arjun's," Charlotte said. "It's got a JAXA sticker on it."

"We're so screwed," Seok said, and smiled.

"What are you smiling about?" Judge said. He didn't think there was anything humorous about their situation.

"Psycho," Seok said.

The three companions laughed, remembering their friend.

Another roar pierced the day.

Judge said, "Whatever's happened to the suits, we'll know soon enough."

As the three survivors made their way to the spot where they'd hidden the spacesuits, pieces of cloth, hose, flecks of paint, small shards of metal, and patches of fabric littered the jungle like toys in a child's sandbox.

The party arrived at the conifer base tree to find its lower boughs torn away, the area rutted and torn up, and the platform they'd built destroyed, its pieces littering the forest. The remains of the EVA suits lay scattered about like candy wrappers after a piñata party, forlorn and useless.

Judge dropped to his butt and let his head fall in his hands. With no suits, there was no point to opening the airlock. No going back to the station. No going home.

Home. The idea of going home kept asserting itself in his mind, yapping about facing his fears. He rolled his shoulders, trying to shake his unease, but failed. His tension sat in his stomach like old cheese, fighting to get out.

Charlotte dropped to the ground next to him and Seok stood over them, looking around as if searching for an undamaged suit.

"Seok, what the hell are you looking for? Magic beans?" Judge said.

Seok stared at him, eyebrows furrowed.

"I'm sorry. Jack and the Bean Stalk?"

Nothing.

"Just figured that's what Psycho would have said," Judge said.

"The magic beans grew the bean stalk?" Seok said.

"Very intuitive of you," Judge said. "But I'm just busting your shoes because you've given me an idea."

Charlotte vaulted to her feet. "You've got a plan?"

"Maybe. But first we need to know how bad things are," Judge said.

Seok's gaze panned over the remains of the spacesuits, but he said nothing.

"I'll take from here to the wall. Seok, you go northeast, Charlotte northwest. Bring back every suit piece you find, no matter how small, and grab food and water if you can."

Seok and Charlotte nodded and disappeared into the jungle. When Judge was alone, he pulled the empty M9 from his pocket and laid it on the ground. He got to his feet and rubbed his back as he scanned the desolation. He sighed and started collecting spacesuit pieces.

By afternoon rain, the companions had what they'd found of the six EVA suits and their related gloves and helmets laid out on the ground like pieces of a destroyed airliner during a crash investigation. Two of the suits only had helmets and gloves, most of the others were in pieces.

"Those damn flying rats could have dragged stuff kilometers away from here," Charlotte said.

"We're screwed. It's confirmed," Judge said.

"Maybe not," Seok said. He strode forward and pulled Tisa's undamaged helmet from her pile, then collected gloves and pieces of suits, laying it all together like he was putting together a puzzle. When he was done, there was a complete suit, though it was in multiple pieces, and one leg was longer than the other.

"If we only had a needle and thread," Charlotte said.

"Maybe we do," Judge said.

Seok lifted an eyebrow.

"Use Arjun's bow and get a fire going. I'm going to get us some meat," Judge said.

"Food?" Charlotte said.

Judge shook his head no. "A needle and thread."

He left his bewildered friends and trekked into the jungle a few meters before climbing a conifer at the edge of a thin animal path. The footprints of passing rodents and other small creatures crisscrossed the hardpan, flowing in and out of the forest.

Judge heard Psycho in his head. "Any of the small ones you get won't be worth the effort. All skin, bones and muscle." Judge laughed and said aloud, "That's what I'm counting on, my friend."

It only took half an hour for a bunny-like quadruped to mosey by, and Judge nailed it easily with his remade knife-spear.

When Judge got back to camp, the disappointment on Charlotte's face was palpable, but Seok didn't seem surprised. They watched with curiosity as Judge skinned the beast. The creature's paws had thin talons that arced away from its padded feet. Judge chopped the longest one off and held it up. "I was going to use a bone fragment, but this is better."

"The needle is the easy part," Seok said.

Judge raised his hand. "Watch and learn."

He took a strong stick he'd scavenged and made a crude point at its end with his knife. The straight branch was about an inch around, and Judge wedged it into the ground for a spindle. He cut a thin slit into the white sinew that held the corpse's rear legs tight to its muscles, and he pulled a strand free, tying its end to the stick. Then he pulled sinew thread.

"Where the hell did you learn to do that?" Charlotte said.

"A&E," Judge said.

Charlotte laughed, but Seok looked lost. "TV," she said.

Judge worked for about an hour, and when the lights blinked out and the pillar of light rose into the sky, he had ten meters of thick twine made from muscle sinew.

Charlotte said, "Not to be sexist, but I made my own clothes in High School. I'm thinking I can take over from here while you help Seok with the backpack."

They'd scavenged all six of the life-support backpacks, but two were crushed and clearly couldn't be repaired. Two others were badly banged up, and Seok's preliminary tests showed issues he couldn't fix. The remaining two were functional, though only with multiple error overrides. Seok thought he could make one decent backpack from the two functioning ones.

The fire popped and crackled as Charlotte sewed and Seok worked on the backpack. Without tools there wasn't much he could do, but swapping hoses, fittings and wiring brought one backpack—Psycho's, as fate would have it—to eighty-four percent efficiency. With one complete EVA suit, Judge could go back to the SEV and retrieve the back-up suit. In two trips, all three of the astronauts would be safe in the rover.

"Too bad the SEV can't make it up that slope. You could pull it into the airlock," Charlotte said.

Judge nodded but said nothing.

Seok cleared his throat. "The smallest person should wear the suit."

"What?" Judge said. "To the SEV?"

Seok nodded in the firelight.

"I'm going," Judge said. "This is my task. My responsibility."

"I understand, but aside from the fact that both Charlotte and I also feel a sense of responsibility, the suit itself is mostly mine," Seok said. "Helmet and glove couplings and the like are standard, but the EVA suits are fitted to an astronaut's body specifications, though people of similar size can use each other's suits. Judge, you're the largest among us. The oxygen scrubber is working, heat and cooling are fine, though the patchwork suit only has one functioning fan, instead of three."

"I know, but it'll be fine. I tried the thing on and it fits, even if it's a little tight. I'll breathe shallow, and I don't have far to go," Judge said.

"Sir, I—"

"No!" Judge was surprised at how loud he'd yelled. "I'm not losing anyone else." He turned away from Seok and Charlotte and lay on his side, ants trundling by, insects buzzing. "Goodnight." He said, and closed his eyes.

There were no arguments the next morning. The party of three trudged through the early morning mist to the airlock door. All was quiet there, the faint hum of the early day a welcome respite from the constant chatter and buzz.

Judge stripped off his boots and pulled on the ragdoll spacesuit with Charlotte's help. They went slow, easing past patches and sinew-sown seams.

Seok stood before the huge airlock door, rubbing his chin.

"How's that thread going to hold up in the Martian atmosphere?" Charlotte said.

"The suit only needs to hold until the airlock pressurizes with me inside. There's duct tape in the supply chest, and I can use that to shore up the repairs and there's another roll in the rover."

"You sure you don't want to carry a helmet?" She looked back with longing in the direction of their conifer base where they'd left the cracked helmets. The comm in the uncracked helmet Judge was to wear was busted, and without tools, Seok was unable to transfer a functioning comm into an uncracked helmet. Judge suggested he carry a helmet with a functioning comm, but hearing and having a conversation with his helmet on would be difficult, so they'd decided not to burden Judge further.

"What the hell can we do anyway if you run into trouble?" Seok said.

"Good point," Judge said. That sentiment applied to the entire Mars mission, didn't it? They had safety protocols, back-up plans to back-up plans, all to provide a false sense of security and control. Every astronaut since Yuri Gagarin sat on a stick of dynamite has understood the dangers of their journeys, but they took the risk anyway.

A roar thundered over the forest and Judge rolled his shoulders. "OK, let's go," he said.

Charlotte lifted the suit helmet, placed it over Judge's head, and dogged down the hasps. She placed her palms on the helmet's clear faceplate, attempted to shake and move it, but when it held fast, she gave a thumbs up.

Judge called up his display and saw the suit was functioning at eighty-two percent capacity. It had been stripped of its water reservoir and patch kit, and several red maintenance icons flashed red, but the status light was green, and that's all he cared about.

He gave a thumbs up and Charlotte smiled.

Seok sang his mournful tune of sighs, toots and whistles, and the giant door opened, revealing the airlock beyond.

A roar echoed over the biosphere.

31

Judge stepped into the half-light that filled the airlock. The headlamp on the cobbled together EVA suit was broken, but light spilled in from the habitat. Silver lines, like rope, crisscrossed the ceiling, and twenty meters into the airlock, the stainless-steel hinges of the supply chest glinted. The jungle symphony echoed through the airlock, the scent of earth and scat fading as Judge inched forward into the gloom. He looked back, and Seok and Charlotte stood backlit by the biosphere's pseudo sunlight, watching him. Charlotte waved, and he waved back.

When he'd gone ten meters, the door behind him irised closed with a hiss and plunged the airlock into total darkness.

Judge stood in the blackness, frozen, trying to call up a mental picture of the airlock and recall the exact location of the supply trunk. There was a flashlight in there along with the duct tape, and if he could get it, things would go much faster. He checked his suit display. A new warning light indicating emanant containment failure blinked yellow, but the suit was at seventy-nine percent, status green.

In the blackness, Judge's heart pumped, his nerves dancing on a wire. Sweat rolled down his back and forehead, though the suit's interior temperature was sixty-four degrees. His harsh breathing echoed in the helmet, and his stomach screamed, his muscles tight and rigid.

Why hadn't the AI turned on the lights for him? Was it having second thoughts about letting them leave?

He put out a hand like a blind man and shuffled through the darkness, moving slow, though he knew there was nothing in his way. He felt imaginary things around him, sensed the unseen breath of invisible creatures lurking in the blackness. No shadows danced, and not so much as a pinprick of light broke the void-like gloom.

Judge went another ten meters and bumped into the chest. His sigh of relief sounded like a gust of wind in the closed airlock, and he went to work opening the trunk in the darkness.

A faint dinosaur roar made Judge look over his shoulder, but there was nothing but hollow nothingness. "Seok should have learned how to turn on the damn lights." Judge chuckled in the darkness, the sound bouncing around the airlock.

The chest opened with a pop and a puff of air like an ancient tomb. Judge leaned in and felt around. There were rations, a length of polypropylene rope, bullets, clothes… finally his hand found the flashlight. He pulled it free.

The airlock's main lights snapped on.

Judge covered his eyes as he dropped the flashlight back into the chest. "Took you long enough," Judge said as he gazed around, searching for ghosts. Why the AI hadn't turned the lights on when the door opened was yet another example of how even the habitat's AI wasn't functioning properly. Or was it that the AI didn't want Judge to leave? Maybe it was arguing with itself, growing and evolving every second, and it was undecided?

He quickly used most of the tape to add additional strength to the EVA suit's repairs. When he stood before the door, he paused, his nerves no longer bouncing off his bones. If the door didn't open the way he thought it should, with a simple poke, then maybe the AI would help.

Judge took a deep breath as he checked the EVA suit's readouts one last time, and was still a go. He reached out and tapped the center of the door, and as it opened, wind pushed a stream of red sand through the widening hole like a sandblaster.

Visibility on the Martian surface was five meters, and Judge stepped out into a sandstorm. This was Mars. What the hell had he been thinking? His suit beeped and screamed as new indicator lights went yellow. A sense of urgency jolted him, and Judge darted into the sandstorm, knifing toward the rover's last known location.

A gust of wind caught him and lifted him from the ground and tossed him backward. Judge tumbled in the maelstrom, and smashed into the destroyed drill.

The EVA suit chimed like it was going to explode, all lights red. The suit had been breached, and he had no repair kit. He struggled to his feet, and pushed forward, fighting the wind, arm raised before his face shield in a vain attempt to clear his vision, which was blurring.

He paused in the chaos and tore a piece of duct tape off a seal he'd wrapped several times. The tape got gunked with sand, but he was able to partially seal the tear. The suit didn't care and continued to yell, but its efficiency jumped thirty-eight percent after the repair.

He fell to his knees and crawled forward, the air currents along the ground less harsh. The Martian surface rose to his right, and that meant the SEV was to the left. He put one hand in front of the other, focusing on the next five meters, and when he saw the tops of the rover's slotted wheels, joy spread through him. He was going to make it. After everything, he was going home. He was done with space. Maybe he'd meet a new woman, and he'd never see Brenda again.

The SEV was half buried in red sand, but the main door popped open and Judge hurried inside, closing the door quickly behind him. He dropped into the command chair and looked around. It felt like years since the six astronauts had sat in the SEV, chatting and arguing about the mundane. He reached out to pressurize the cabin, but figured that would just waste time.

Then he realized he had a major problem.

With only two functioning suits, how would they depressurize the SEV for access after the second trip? Judge sat in the pale light as the SEV was blasted with sand, his mind spinning. How had he missed this? How had Seok? The answer was, Seok didn't miss it. No way.

Judge glanced around the cabin and his eyes went wide when they found the research module at the rear of the SEV. It could be detached, which meant it could house an astronaut while the other two entered and unpressurized and re-pressurized the SEV.

Relief flooded through him as he grabbed a roll of silver duct tape from under his seat. The rip and tear of the tape as he reinforced his suit, and the tinkling of sand pelting the rover filled the cabin.

Judge packed the spare EVA suit, and headed back out into the sandstorm. He'd bring Charlotte back first, and on his way, he'd grab the rope from the supply trunk so he could run a guideline to the rover from the airlock. That would make things safer, easier and speed things up. The airlock door irised open and Judge moved quickly, the door closing behind him. The sounds of the jungle chorus grew as he got closer to the habitat's entrance.

As he approached the far door, a great braying and hooting thundered through the airlock, followed by a mighty roar.

The door opened before him.

The T-rex with the red stripe running down the center of its head stood silhouetted in the doorway. The beast threw back its head and roared, its tail smacking trees, slime dripping from its open jaws, powerful legs stomping the hardpan.

Judge dropped the suit and sprang forward, wishing he hadn't left the gun in the woods under their conifer. There was ammo in the supply trunk.

"Here!" It was Charlotte. She and Seok hid behind a thick tree, watching the T-rex prance around.

Judge slid to a stop and eased back into the mouth of the airlock.

The T-rex growled and came at the open airlock door, sensing Judge's movements.

A knife-spear struck the dinosaur on its left flank and fell harmlessly to the ground, not leaving a scratch. It did get the attention of the stupid T-rex, and the beast's head jerked toward where Seok hid behind a large fern.

Charlotte ran for it, closing the thirty meters between her hiding place and the airlock in twenty harrowing seconds. When she reached Judge, she threw her arms around him.

She smelled of sweat, fear, and something else. Judge kind of liked it.

The T-rex, realizing it had been duped, stomped and clawed at the vegetation, searching for Seok.

Judge and Charlotte backed into the airlock.

Seok ran across the animal path, moving away from the T-rex. Judge smiled. He was going to make it.

The T-rex growled and stomped, nose still digging through the underbrush, swinging its massive tail.

Seok gave a thumbs up, but even as he ran the last few meters to safety, the beast's tail whipped and cracked, and it caught Seok in the torso and wiped him from the ground like an ant.

Charlotte screamed and headed back toward the habitat.

Judge grabbed her arm and pulled her away, backing through the airlock, and the door before them hissed closed.

Judge clawed at Charlotte to follow, but she cried and pulled from his grasp. "We need to help him."

"There's nothing we can do right now."

Charlotte stopped struggling. "You think he's dead?"

"You saw what I saw," Judge said.

Guilt gnawed at Judge as the pair made their way back to the rover. When he and Charlotte sat safe inside the SEV, still in their suits, Judge said, "I've got to go back."

Charlotte nodded.

Judge brought up the SEV's cabin pressure and Charlotte stripped out of her EVA suit and packed it up. She pecked Judge on the cheek and said, "Good luck." Then she disappeared into the research section and sealed it off as though it was being detached from the SEV.

Judge reached out and put his ungloved hand on the barrier that separated him from Charlotte. He didn't like the feeling of not being by her side. "You OK in there?"

She tapped on the barrier twice.

Judge put his helmet and gloves on, grabbed the second suit, and depressurized the SEV. The wind howled as he exited onto the Martian surface, backtracking to the habitat using the guide rope he'd put in place. Once in the airlock, he paused at the supply chest and put the spare bullets in with the extra suit.

When he stood fifteen meters from the biosphere's entrance, he stopped, straining to hear what was happening beyond the door.

He stepped forward and the door irised open.

Judge got low, scanning the path and the jungle beyond. Clouds of dust and dirt still floated in the air, but the jungle chorus was going full tilt and there was no sign of the T-rex.

"Here!" Seok called out.

A drone hovered above the tree canopy and Judge ran toward it, and when he arrived, Seok had his back to a tree, massaging his ankle.

"You alright?" Judge said. "It looked like you got smashed."

"Knocked the wind out of me real good, but I landed on a conifer, and its boughs cushioned my fall."

If Judge never saw another evergreen tree, he'd be OK with that, though the trees had saved the party so many times he knew that wasn't fair. Someday when he had a house, a place to hang his hat, he'd plant conifers all over the place. Maybe Charlotte would help him.

"Can you walk?" Judge asked.

Seok nodded and got to his feet.

Back at the SEV, with Charlotte and Seok safely tucked away in the research portion of the rover, Judge used the spare suit and dug out the SEV. He was exhausted, but thanks to the rations from the supply trunk, they had a feast.

Between bites of reconstituted chicken, Judge said, "So. The almanac."

Seok nodded. "We possess the knowledge to control the habitat, and possibly repair it. The technology within is worth trillions of dollars, but what are our rights? We work for NASA, governments on Earth fund all this. It's not ours, is it?"

"I hate to channel my dead friend Psycho, but that depends on what we say and how we say it," Judge said.

Seok lifted an eyebrow.

Judge stared at the three empty seats.

Charlotte said, "And who knows what the morons back on Earth might want to do with the habitat and the beasts in it. Knowing the US government, they'll want to turn the dinosaurs and AI into weapons."

"What proof do we have, anyway?" Judge said. The motherboard which controlled the data in Arjun's suit had been destroyed, and the only proof was the footage shot before entering the airlock that was relayed back to the rover, which only showed the doors and the Martian surface. "Would the big heads even believe us?"

Seok's eyes went wide, and his mouth opened like he was going to say something, but didn't.

Judge's eyes flicked over the three empty seats again.

Charlotte said, "We've got to explain the death of astronauts."

Nobody spoke.

"Let's get moving before we get buried again," Judge said.

Seok nodded as he engaged the rover's engine and the SEV jerked into motion.

"Any luck raising Gale Base?" Judge asked.

Seok shook his head no. "The storm is pretty bad. Probably be a few hours."

Judge nodded, but said nothing. He needed the time to think.

The desolate plain of Aeolis Palus stretched into the distance in every direction, the rover's thick wheels kicking-up red sand, thick clouds lifting from the Martian surface like smoke.

***

On a forsaken, war ravaged planet 3.19 parsecs from Mars, a cosmic alarm activates. A preprogrammed failsafe kicks in, and an AI that's been powered down for millennia awakes.

The End

Other Severed Press books by Edward J. McFadden III: Drop Off, Jurassic Ark, Keepers of the Flame, Throwback, Sea Tremors, Primeval Valley, Shadow of the Abyss (#1 Amazon Bestseller), Awake, and The Breach (#1 Amazon Bestseller, Amazon #1 Hot New Audio Release). His other novels include Quick Sands – A Theo Ramage Thriller, Dogs Get Ten Lives, The Black Death of Babylon and HOAXERS. Ed is also the author/editor of: Anywhere But Here, Lucky 13, Jigsaw Nation, Deconstructing Tolkien: A Fundamental Analysis of The Lord of the Rings (re-released in eBook format Fall 2012 – Amazon Bestseller), Time Capsule, Epitaphs (W/ Tom Piccirilli), The Second Coming, Thoughts of Christmas, and The Best of Pirate Writings. His short stories have appeared in over 75 magazines and anthologies. He lives on Long Island with his wife Dawn, and their daughter Samantha.

CHECK OUT OTHER GREAT DINOSAUR THRILLERS

JURASSIC ISLAND
by Viktor Zarkov

Guided by satellite photos and modern technology a ragtag group of survivalists and scientists travel to an uncharted island in the remote South Indian Ocean. Things go to hell in a hurry once the team reaches the island and the massive megalodon that attacked their boats is only the beginning of their desperate fight for survival.

Nothing could have prepared billionaire explorer Joseph Thornton and washed up archaeologist Christopher "Colt" McKinnon for the terrifying prehistoric creatures that wait for them on JURASSIC ISLAND!

K-REX
by L.Z. Hunter

Deep within the Congo jungle, Circuitz Mining employs mercenaries as security for its Coltan mining site. Armed with assault rifles and decades of experience, nothing should go wrong. However, the dangers within the jungle stretch beyond venomous snakes and poisonous spiders. There is more to fear than guerrillas and vicious animals. Undetected, something lurks under the expansive treetop canopy . . .

Something ancient.

Something dangerous.

Kasai Rex!

CHECK OUT OTHER GREAT DINOSAUR THRILLERS

WRITTEN IN STONE
by David Rhodes

Charles Dawson is trapped 100 million years in the past. Trying to survive from day to day in a world of dinosaurs he devises a plan to change his fate. As he begins to write messages in the soft mud of a nearby stream, he can only hope they will be found by someone who can stop his time travel. Professor Ron Fontana and Professor Ray Taggit, scientists with opposing views, each discover the fossilized messages. While attempting to save Charles, Professor Fontana, his daughter Lauren and their friend Danny are forced to join Taggit and his group of mercenaries. Taggit does not intend to rescue Charles Dawson, but to force Dawson to travel back in time to gather samples for Taggit's fame and fortune. As the two groups jump through time they find they must work together to make it back alive as this fast-paced thriller climaxes at the very moment the age of dinosaurs is ending.

HARD TIME
by Alex Laybourne

Rookie officer Peter Malone and his heavily armed team are sent on a deadly mission to extract a dangerous criminal from a classified prison world. A Kruger Correctional facility where only the hardest, most vicious criminals are sent to fend for themselves, never to return.

But when the team come face to face with ancient beasts from a lost world, their mission is changed. The new objective: Survive.

CHECK OUT OTHER GREAT DINOSAUR THRILLERS

SPINOSAURUS
by Hugo Navikov

Brett Russell is a hunter of the rarest game. His targets are cryptids, animals denied by science. But they are well known by those living on the edges of civilization, where monsters attack and devour their animals and children and lay ruin to their shantytowns.

When a shadowy organization sends Brett to the Congo in search of the legendary dinosaur cryptid Kasai Rex, he will face much more than a terrifying monster from the past. Spinosaurus is a dinosaur thriller packed with intrigue, action and giant prehistoric predators.

LAND OF DEATH
by Eric S Brown & Alex Laybourne

A group of American soldiers, fleeing an organized attack on their base camp in the Middle East, encounter a storm unlike anything they've seen before. When the storm subsides, they wake up to find themselves no longer in the desert and perhaps not even on Earth. The jungle they've been deposited in is a place ruled by prehistoric creatures long extinct. Each day is a struggle to survive as their ammo begins to run low and virtually everything they encounter, in this land they've been hurled into, is a deadly threat.

www.ingramcontent.com/pod-product-compliance
Lightning Source LLC
Chambersburg PA
CBHW030225180626
46810CB00008B/2970